ECLIPSED HEART

TWISTED FATE TRILOGY
BOOK 2

JEN L. GREY

CHAPTER ONE

SNARLS, whimpers, the stench of blood, and darkness surrounded me while agony swirled within. The pain was blinding as my wolf magic sparked, making the sensations overwhelming.

This must be what it felt like to be swallowed whole.

Strong arms rolled me onto my back, then slipped underneath my legs and head. As Bodey lifted me from the ground, the sizzle of the fated-mate bond zapped straight to my soul.

I'd been about twenty feet from the alpha advisors and Samuel, all of us there to witness the marking of the new king. Dina, the royal priestess, had been standing ankle-deep in the Snake River in her white priestess dress, Samuel on the embankment in front of her, and the ten other witches of the royal coven knee-deep in the water behind them. Between the blue skies, the high sun, and the beautiful backdrop of Hells Canyon, the scene had been intimate, and the ceremony should have been a breathtaking ritual...with magical ink floating above Dina's head, readying to mark the next ruler of the Northwest wolves...but of course, we'd been attacked.

As Bodey nestled me against his chest, I breathed in his

cinnamon and sandalwood scent, trying to block out the smell of blood. Despite the danger, I felt safe in his arms. I didn't doubt that he would protect me, and I hated that I couldn't return the favor, but my body was frozen.

He linked, *I'm going to get you out of here. I promise.*

I wanted to tell him to not worry about me, to save himself, but the words wouldn't even form in my mind. My body thrummed with magic so strong that I would surely implode, and the burning pain in my chest and neck seemed to intensify every second. All I could do was listen to the vicious battle around us.

"We need to get her out of here," Janet said. "All four of us if that's what it takes. She has to be protected."

Pain still coursed through the bond I shared with Bodey, reminding me that he was injured as well and carrying me.

Mom, those two can't be trusted, Bodey linked, connecting me to the conversation.

Our fated-mate connection strengthened even more as my tie to Janet warmed in my chest. I focused on my tether to Bodey. The buzz from our bond and wherever we touched was somehow easing my agony and allowing my wolf magic to merge with the pain.

I understand, son. But those two care for her, even if they're misguided. We need their help, but we'll stay with her and ensure she remains safe. The warmth of her affection seeped through our pack link as she continued, *She's my daughter and family now, too.*

"I'll take point," Theo rasped in front of Bodey. "And keep an eye out for threats—unless you want me to carry her."

"You're *not* touching her," Bodey snarled, his chest vibrating against my head. "So fucking lead."

"You two, stop it," Stevie snapped. "And let's get out of here."

I expected more arguing, but Bodey took off, and three pairs of footsteps followed us.

As we moved, the cold, late February breeze of North Central Idaho blew across my skin, a contrast to the warmth sparking in my chest. The sensation was similar to the more than two hundred pack links I'd gotten last night after Bodey and I had completed our fated-mate bond and I'd become part of his pack. This warmth was also like pockets of air without discomfort, but instead of two hundred, it was growing rapidly into thousands as the pain in my neck and chest burned even sharper.

Bodey groaned, and I felt his discomfort spike as well.

My chest began to move freely again, and I managed to open my eyes.

I'd expected darkness, but my view filled with my mate's gorgeous face.

His jaw was clenched, his normally indigo eyes almost black with terror, pain, and concern, and his messy chestnut hair covered his forehead and touched the tips of his black lashes. He was clean-shaven and still dressed in his dark suit for the ceremony. I missed his scruff, but it'd grow back fast enough.

Even in danger, he took my breath away, and my heart thudded.

Fear thickening, he dropped his gaze to me, and some of the tension eased from his face.

Your eyes are open, he linked. *I thought when your heart...I thought...*

The pain is becoming manageable. I wouldn't say *better* because it wasn't. But I was able to tolerate it. If I'd thought that broken ribs hurt, they had *nothing* on what I was experiencing now. I could've sworn that my throat and chest had been ripped open.

I blinked a few times, trying to get my eyes to adjust. The

sun was bright again, and I didn't understand where the darkness had come from. *What the hell happened?*

That was a loaded question, and I wasn't sure which instance I was referring to—the darkness, the hovering magic ink, the attacking wolves, or Zeke screaming for them not to attack *me*.

Then my chest tightened. *Samuel!* We'd left the king behind.

He's fine, and the ink reached its mark just as unfamiliar wolves attacked, Bodey replied and focused forward again. He swiveled, and a fir tree passed near my head.

I craned my neck and saw Stevie pass on the other side of the tree before easing herself back toward me. Pieces of her dirty-blonde hair had fallen out of her braid, and her dark-brown eyes were locked forward. There were rips in her pink pajama shirt that hadn't been there before I fell.

My throat constricted, and my blood boiled. She might be the very person who'd gotten us into this mess. *Where's Theo? Shouldn't he be protecting her?*

He's in front of us, keeping an eye out. Bodey rolled his eyes. *I'm hoping a wolf takes him. He'd make a good sacrifice if it allowed you, Mom, Stevie, and me to get away.*

A deep laugh bubbled into my throat, which made the throbbing intensify, so I cut it short. I had to be delirious to think that was funny. Theo wasn't the best person in the world, but it was hard to be thoughtful with a dad like his. Zeke had a way of forcing his pack members to follow his instructions, even if it meant hurting a six-year-old girl to make a point to his son.

The pain began to recede, and my lungs started working better. Bodey having to carry me was slowing us down. *You can put me down now. I'm good to run.*

He shook his head, not even pausing. *You're still in pain. I feel it.*

So are you. I lifted my chin, though the action didn't contain quite as much *oomph* when I was being cradled against a damn sexy chest.

You're not slowing me down. His displeasure coursed between us as another man linked, *Ten wolves just headed toward where the advisors parked.*

A knot formed in my stomach.

You need to let me down. If more wolves were coming, then we needed to prepare to fight. "We all need to shift."

Stevie's head jerked in my direction. "You can't. You sprouted fur and then it disappeared."

Her words were like a punch to the gut.

"She was in *agony*," Bodey snapped, the skin around his eyes tightening. "Have you ever tried shifting while thinking you were dying?"

She tripped over her feet, which shouldn't have happened since the ground was mostly bare. "She thought she was *dying*? How would you know?"

"Because they're mates," Janet said from the other side of Bodey. I couldn't see her since she was near my feet.

Stevie gasped.

We didn't have time for this.

Babe, please. I hated begging, but I didn't want to fight him physically on this and delay us more. *I might not be slowing you down much, but we can move even faster if we all shift into wolf form.*

He scowled but slowed. I could sense that he didn't want to release me, but the logical side of him knew I was right. He placed my feet on the ground.

I expected the world to spin, but it didn't. If anything, I could see even better—even the individual pine needles on trees about a hundred yards away from me. The crispness was a little unnerving.

Bodey's eyes flicked to my neck and chest. I was about to ask him why, but I heard the padding paws of the ten wolves charging toward us.

"They're getting close." I hated that I was the cause of this. Thanks to my meltdown, I'd not only left Samuel open to attack but slowed us down dangerously, even if Bodey didn't want to admit it.

Theo spun around, his brows furrowing. He'd plastered his caramel-brown hair to his head with gel, probably trying to look sophisticated to match the black suit he wore. But he'd been tugging at it all day, and it was now a pale and sweaty mess. His topaz eyes narrowed. "I don't hear anything. What wolves are you talking about?"

"Someone from Lucas's pack informed us that ten wolves just headed this way." Bodey nodded in the opposite direction. "If Callie says she hears them, then she does. You should know better than to question her."

I smiled. Questioning and ignoring me were two things that my childhood pack had always done, but Bodey had never done either.

Then his words sank in, causing my lungs to seize. How had *I* heard Lucas's pack member?

"Her chest." Janet placed a hand over her mouth as her indigo eyes bulged. The sun cast a halo around her strawberry-blonde hair, and she looked like an angel. The skirt of her royal-blue halter dress had been ripped on one side.

"Which is why we're going to shift and run like hell." Bodey removed his jacket and tossed it onto the ground.

I wasn't sure what my chest had to do with running, but I'd deal with that later. Too much was coming at me all at once, and my wolf howled in urgency. "But we won't be able to communicate like that."

"We'll be fine. We'll be able to plan our counterattack,"

Bodey reassured me, a stony expression crossing his face as he glanced at me. *I promise.*

I believed him, so my wolf surged forward, my skin tingling as she blended with my mind. It felt different from the first time, which had seemed more like we were coexisting. This time, our minds became one. I glanced down, taking in my borrowed dress one last time. The black strapless top and fuchsia skirt were gorgeous, a vision that would soon be ruined, but I didn't have time to strip it off. The wolves were getting closer.

"I hear them now too." Stevie's bottom lip quivered. "We need to get *her* out of here."

Why was everyone focused on me? We needed to worry about Samuel.

Well, we'd get Stevie and Janet to safety; then Bodey and I could circle back for him.

Stevie's concern pissed me off. She'd helped the queen of the Southwest and begged me not to come to the ceremony today. Instead of telling me the truth, she'd followed me here in case an attack happened.

I was on all fours in seconds. There'd been no pain or discomfort other than a tugging in my chest and neck where I'd been hurting in human form.

The other four followed suit, and I wasn't surprised when Stevie was the last to complete the shift; she was the weakest of the bunch, even though it included me.

The wolves would intercept us in seconds. We needed to get as close to the cars as possible and ensure that Stella and everyone else got to their vehicles safely.

I took off, knowing that I'd be one of the slowest. But after a hundred yards, Bodey was the only wolf beside me.

Why are they hanging back? The incoming wolves split up, causing a shiver to run down my spine. I could hear five running on either side of us.

He glanced at me, panting. *They aren't. You're just stronger now.*

I slowed for them. I understood what being slower felt like. I refused to leave them undefended.

They're here, I linked, a shiver running down my spine. Five of the wolves ran in front of Bodey and me, while five ran behind Janet and Stevie. Of course, Theo was in the middle of our group instead of in the back, trying to protect the others.

The ten of them formed a circle around us. They were boxing us in, and I snarled and hunkered down. Though I'd never fought in wolf form before, I was going to trust my instincts. Fighting had to be ingrained in each of us.

We should form a circle too, I linked, backing toward the other three. We needed to protect our backs... quite literally.

Callie? Stevie's voice popped into my head.

For a second, I faltered, my legs giving out. That shouldn't be possible.

The black wolf in front of me tilted its head. Its ebony eyes examined me, studying my chest before its head tilted back.

Listen to Callie, Bodey commanded, following me step by step.

Theo replied, *We are.*

I shook my head, my fur swaying. This had to be a dream... or a nightmare. The attack on the ceremony, the pain, shifting, and now, talking to two people I'd never been able to link to before had rendered me speechless.

What do we do? Janet asked the moment our five rumps touched.

That was a loaded question.

Don't get hurt. Bodey bared his teeth. *I'll protect you and Callie.*

As I scanned our adversaries, I noted that the two in front of me, one black and one light gray, seemed locked on Bodey, but before I could say anything, they sprang into an attack.

I charged at them. There was no way in hell I was going to allow him to be ganged up on.

I swiped at the black wolf, my claws sinking into its shoulder as I rammed my body into the light-gray wolf.

The light-gray wolf stumbled back with a loud yelp as if I'd surprised it, but the black doubled down. Drool dripped from its teeth as it inched toward me.

Good. *Bring it, asshole.* Anything to keep its focus off Bodey.

When the black wolf lunged, the light-gray one slammed into the black one's side. I swallowed, trying to understand what the hell just happened. The light-gray one had *protected* me, but that made no sense.

Taking a moment, I scanned the area and saw Bodey fighting three wolves at once.

If my two had attacked him, it would've been six on one. Why were they targeting him?

It had to be because he was one of Samuel's guardians.

Theo, protect Stevie and Janet, I linked, ready to end this *now*.

An auburn wolf edged up on the three wolves attacking Bodey. My mate had just risen onto his back legs, fighting the three with his front paws, when the auburn wolf went under its friends. She was going to attack him from underneath.

No.

I threw myself underneath him, surging forward. The wolf swiped, aiming for my mate's belly, and hit my neck. I barreled into her, knocking her into two of the other wolves attacking Bodey. They fell back as the auburn wolf and I tumbled over each other.

Callie! Bodey linked before the sound of rending skin filled the air.

I braced to feel Bodey's pain as I managed to roll on top of the auburn wolf and sink my teeth into her neck.

Another wolf steamrolled me, finishing off the auburn wolf by forcing me to rip her throat out. I landed on my side hard, dirt billowing around me. My eyes burned as the slate wolf bit into my right upper foreleg.

With my left paw, I struck at his face, my claws digging into his eyes and snout.

Baby. Bodey sounded broken as his fear clenched my chest.

The wolf whined, and his jaws released me. He took a few steps back, his blood pouring to the ground.

Bodey needed to focus on his own fight. I linked, *I'm fine. It's just a bite.*

It's not just a bite, he spat.

I hurt him worse than he hurt me. That had to count for something...at least, I wanted to pretend it did.

Ignoring the sharp pain, I jumped to my feet and pounced on the injured side of the new wolf's body, where he couldn't see me as well.

I bit into his neck, mauling the skin, not wanting to kill him. We needed to take at least one alive so we could question him. I'd try to knock this one out or injure him to the point of not fighting back.

The wolf whimpered as black fur flashed on my right side.

The black wolf must have gotten away from the light-gray one.

She tried to sneak up on me, but it was too late. When she was in striking distance, I dropped away, and the black wolf's teeth tore into the slate one's neck in almost the same spot I'd bitten.

I rolled onto my back and sank my teeth into the black

wolf's belly. I bit deep and hard, and she yelped. When I released her, a gaping hole showed some of her intestines.

Acid burned my throat, but a flash of pain shot through me from Bodey.

When I jerked my head in his direction, my entire world narrowed. There were three wolves on Bodey's back and one tan wolf in front of my mate, ready to strike his throat.

CHAPTER TWO

I JUMPED the ten feet to the tan wolf, Bodey's pain and terror spinning inside me.

As the wolf struck, I bit into its tail and dug my claws into its backside, pushing it to the ground. Its jaw clamped just millimeters from my mate's neck before it crumpled.

The Southwest wolves had managed to break our circle apart, leaving Bodey open to attack on all sides. Hot anger boiled through me. I was partly to blame for leaving him vulnerable.

I yanked at every sizable connection in my chest, linking to any- and everyone I could. *The wolves here are focusing on Bodey. Both Samuel and Bodey need protecting.*

Bodey? Jack linked in shock. *Not you?*

Not me. Something odd was going on, but now wasn't the time to attempt to figure it out.

The tan wolf kicked its back legs into mine, knocking my paws from underneath me. I clenched my jaws and bit into its tail even harder, blood pouring down my throat and chest.

Protect Samuel and Callie, Bodey interjected as pain sliced through our fated-mate connection. *I'll be fine.*

They aren't attacking me or anyone else here. Just Bodey. I wasn't going to let him be a martyr. I needed him more than anything in the world.

Stella linked, *I got the moms into the car and left the keys with them. I'm shifting now, and I'll be there to help soon.*

I clawed up the tan wolf's back, using its skin as leverage. It whined in agony.

No, stay in the car, Miles bit out. *I'll get to them.*

They disconnected, most likely talking between themselves. I didn't have to hear it to guess how that conversation was going.

The tan wolf rolled onto its back, pinning me between it and the ground.

Callie is right, Janet linked, *Bodey is clearly the target.* Out of the corner of my eye, I watched her jump on a marble-gray wolf and try to knock it off Bodey's back.

The weight of the tan wolf crushed me, and I couldn't breathe. I pushed up with all four legs as hard as I could, not expecting anything to happen.

The tan wolf flew away from me and smashed into a fir tree. When the wolf's head hit, I heard a sickening *crack* and then a *thud* when its body hit the ground.

For a moment, I couldn't move. I'd never been able to do anything like that before. But then my mate flashed into my head.

I turned toward Bodey, who was now fighting two wolves. My heart hit my stomach when I saw the state he was in. His dark fur had even darker trails of wetness spreading down his sides and back.

These assholes were going to die.

As I rushed toward him, a pewter wolf tried to sneak into the fight from behind Bodey, his eyes locked onto my mate's hindquarters.

I hoped my newfound strength wouldn't disappear now. I

crouched then sprang, my injured leg screaming, and hurled myself over Bodey's body. The air ruffled my fur as I dropped.

For once, Fate was on my side, and I landed behind him, facing the pewter wolf. Its dark eyes widened, and I sank my teeth into its throat. Blood filled my mouth, and I allowed my wolf to take over, jerking my head to the side and killing yet another adversary.

The wolf attacking Theo and Stevie was slapping at them as if trying to keep them distracted. It wasn't being aggressive but seemed to be using Stevie to prevent Theo from striking, keeping her between them. The wolf was playing with them.

The sound of more wolves racing toward us had a lump forming in my throat. They were coming from the same direction as these ten, which meant they were more than likely enemy wolves. I had to help my mate *now*.

Janet ripped out the throat of the wolf she'd been fighting.

Help Theo, I commanded as I moved to intercept the blow from the ash wolf attacking my mate's side.

Callie! Bodey yelped as the ash wolf's claws sank into my chest.

Fight the other one, I linked to Bodey and stumbled into him, who groaned on impact.

Samuel popped into the links. *We're on our way.*

The ash wolf snarled and yanked its claws away then lunged at me. I dropped to the ground and rolled over, and she tried to stop her jump short. I lifted all four paws and sliced into her belly as she stumbled over me. Blood cascaded onto me, soaking my light fur.

A strangled yelp emanated from her as she crashed into a heap, her intestines hanging out.

When I sat up, I saw Stella's dark wolf pummeling Bodey's other attacker. With three moves, she had the wolf's throat ripped out.

My mate slumped to the ground.

No. Not him. He couldn't be dead.

I raced over to him and nuzzled his neck. *Babe?*

I'll be fine, he replied, returning the affection. *You need to stay ready to fight.*

A shiver ran down my spine as I turned toward the new wolves closing in on us. I didn't know how, but I knew they weren't some of our territory's wolves coming to aid us. These were foes, and there were only six of us, with Bodey badly injured.

I had to get him out of here and eliminate any threat that tried to follow us.

Head to the car, I linked as I crouched, ready to protect him.

Not without you, he answered.

And our roles had reversed. Talk about karma. *I'm going with you. Trust me.*

The sage wolf that had been play attacking Theo and Stevie backed up, waiting for his allies to arrive.

Coward.

Twenty wolves barreled toward us. I could tell they were stronger than the first ten, and we were even more outnumbered.

Bodey took off toward the vehicles, moving much more slowly than normal. I stayed beside him while glancing over my shoulder to find all twenty new arrivals focused on us and gaining ground.

I wanted to fall back, but I knew Bodey would stop if I did. He wouldn't leave me—like I refused to leave him. For better or worse, we were in this together.

Stella, Janet, and Theo moved to the back of the group and began to fight three wolves, but the other eighteen, which included the cowardly sage-furred wolf, raced past them in our direction.

With each step we took, they took two.

My blood turned to ice. I focused on all the most sizable connections in my chest, hoping that their prominence meant that those wolves were the ones closest to us. *If anyone can help us, please come. We're outnumbered, and Bodey's hurt.*

The fur on the nape of my neck rose as I prepared myself for a slaughter. I could hold my own just fine against a few wolves, but not eighteen.

A smoky wolf led the charge, and I knew, without a doubt, this would be the hardest fight I'd had yet. I could feel the strength of his wolf rolling off him.

Each time Bodey touched the ground, pain shot through his back and sides, making my own breath catch.

When the smoky wolf reached Stevie, my time was up. I had to make a move before he reached Bodey.

I took a hard right and noticed Samuel and the other advisors racing up behind us.

The smoky wolf's eyes bulged just before I crashed into him. He didn't have time to correct course as I slammed into his side, driving him into the wolves on his right while I rolled over and knocked the feet out from under the wolves on his left. The first three wolves hadn't expected me to sacrifice myself, and their paws tripped over my outstretched body. I kept twisting, trying to take down every single one of them while I could.

Callie! Bodey somehow yelled through the new chaos of the pack links, and I could tell he was slowing down because the jarring sensation coming through our bond wasn't quite as intense. *I'm coming.*

Bodey, keep going! Jack linked. *They really are targeting you, and your mate is trying to save your ass. Lucas, Zeke, and I are almost to her. Just keep moving.*

The rival wolves I'd knocked into were now piled on top of

me, and I grew dizzy from lack of oxygen until they got back on their feet and took off.

I'd slowed them down, but not for long. And the smoky wolf had already charged ahead.

I jumped up and raced after them. Janet, Theo, and Stella were ahead of me by a few feet, and two advisors closed in on either side of the other pack.

The smoky wolf had almost reached Bodey, and I pushed myself harder than ever before. My paws pelted the ground, the sharp sting of my injuries burning through my body in a near-constant state.

I darted ahead of the other wolves, who barely acknowledged me, and reached the smoky wolf just as he was about to strike.

Shit. I wouldn't stop him in time. *Move sideways!*

The wolf lunged, and Bodey sprinted left, causing the wolf to be able to only claw at his side. Thrown off balance, the smoky wolf hit the ground.

Another wolf reached the smoky wolf as he got back to his feet, and I sprang. I landed between them, legs outstretched, clawing their sides and jamming us all together. For a moment, they moved without resistance, and I backed away and pulled them close, then bit into the smoky wolf's neck. When he bucked, I released him and bit into the other wolf's neck.

With both flailing, I flipped over and landed on my back with a huge *thwap*.

Ten wolves just peeled off and headed toward Samuel, Miles linked. *They've split up.*

Though that wasn't good news, at least not all twenty-one were focused on Bodey. *We need to get Samuel and Bodey out of here. They don't seem interested in hurting anyone else.*

I agree with that, the man from earlier linked. *They aren't trying to hurt us either. We're heading your way.*

Samuel, Jack, and I will distract your ten while you run to the front, Lucas linked. *Miles, Zeke, and Theo, run ahead and distract them from Bodey so Callie can get him and Stella and her sister into the car and they can get out of here.*

We'll be there in seconds, Michael linked. *We hear the fight now.*

The two wolves I'd attacked were moving slower, so I focused on the next biggest threat. Weakening them might be a better strategy than killing them. Killing took too long.

I tried to bolt again and grimaced. My right leg wanted to lag, but dammit, that wasn't happening. Not when my mate's life was on the line. Miles's dark wolf, Theo's chestnut brown, and Zeke's brown wolf blurred past me as I picked up speed.

The three of them attacked three of the wolves, leaving five still racing after Bodey. Two were on my mate's heels, and Bodey was flagging.

My chest squeezed. Pain and blood loss were catching up to him; I sensed it through the bond. I bounded around the wolves and cut between Bodey and his closest attackers.

I hunkered down, blocking them from getting to him. They startled, giving me time to strike. I stood on my back legs and slashed their faces with my front paws. My nails cut from their eyes to their snouts, making them whine like pups.

Snarling, I prepared to continue the fight, but the advisors and Stella attacked our opponents' flanks as several of our wolves galloped toward us.

Tears burned my eyes as more people came to fight alongside us.

Samuel's warm-brown wolf passed by me, and he linked, *I'm here.*

At least he'd managed to catch up. Now, we had to focus on getting Bodey and Samuel out of there. I linked with Stella, Janet, and Stevie, knowing that the three of them couldn't link between themselves. *Head to the car. Samuel and Bodey are nearly there.*

Thank gods, Stevie whimpered.

When Samuel reached Bodey, he slowed down to run at the same speed as my mate. Bodey was limping and obviously in distress.

Janet and Stevie sped up to fall in behind them, and I noticed Stella hanging back with Miles.

I wouldn't interfere. She didn't want to leave her fated mate.

Taking up the spot behind Janet and Stevie, I kept an ear out. We weren't out of danger, and more foreign wolves could come at any second.

Bodey glanced over his shoulder, his eyes connecting with mine, making sure I was there. His eyes were dark from the misery I sensed him enduring.

A sickening cry echoed around us, and I spun around to find Theo crumpled in a heap. The smoky wolf had sunk his teeth into Theo's flank.

I slowed to help my friend, but Zeke snarled and ran up beside his son, then bit into Smoky's neck.

Michael and the other advisors' parents joined him, and the tightness in my chest loosened.

Theo was already back on his feet, lurching after another wolf that tried to race by. Unfortunately, all of us had some sort of injury.

I concentrated on getting Samuel and Bodey to safety.

Though it was probably only minutes, it felt like hours until we finally reached the vehicles. I hurried to the row where Bodey had parked his Mercedes SUV.

Lucas's mom, Taylor, popped out of a black BMW parked next to Bodey's SUV, where all the other mates of the royal advisors waited, and unlocked our car.

I can't shift back yet, Bodey linked with just me. *My injuries need to heal some first.*

If wounds were deep enough, shifting from one form to the other could exacerbate them. At least his magic was at its strongest in wolf form, and he'd heal quicker that way.

Don't worry, I replied, my wolf already receding. *I'll drive... if that's okay?*

Of course, it's your car too, he replied simply. *We're mates.*

My heart expanded as my body changed from wolf to human form. Once I was back on two feet, I felt self-conscious. Most shifters didn't have a problem with nudity, but this was new to me. I wanted to cover my body with my hands even though modesty seemed frivolous right now.

I hurried to the car and took the keys from Taylor. "Thanks."

Her eyes widened as she glanced at my chest. Unease shivered down my spine.

"Of course. It's my honor, Your Majesty." She bowed her head before getting back into her own car.

I froze. Had she just called me *Your Majesty*? I spun toward the Mercedes, caught my faint reflection in the window...and my heart stopped.

CHAPTER THREE

I BLINKED AND QUIT BREATHING. But every time I opened my eyes, there it was, staring back at me.

A tattoo was etched onto my neck and chest, the area that had burned while the darkness swirled around me.

Even with the claw marks, I could make out the clear shape of a paw. Four toe marks lay over the crook of my neck and the indent of my collarbone. The design was intricate despite its simplicity, colored all black with wisps of silver rolling over it like clouds across a full moon right before my eyes.

It was a fucking *moving tattoo*. I wasn't sure if I was in awe or freaked out.

This shouldn't be possible...and yet, there was no denying what I saw.

Babe, Bodey linked, pulling me into the present. *Are you okay?*

Despite the agony he was feeling—I could tell that he could barely stand—he was worried about me.

Just— I forced myself to look away from the window and open the back door. *I'm marked.*

I know, he replied. *We need to get you to safety.* He ran up beside me and scratched at the door.

Right. Back door. Moving. Threat. I was wasting precious time and potentially causing others to be harmed.

I opened the back door, and Bodey jumped into the SUV as Janet, Samuel, and Stevie hurried toward us in their naked human forms.

My wolf *hmph*ed in my head, thankful that Bodey had already gotten in the car before Stevie ran up in her birthday suit. When I saw Samuel, I cast my gaze downward quickly.

"I'm going to stay with them while you take Bodey and Samuel home." Janet jogged to her BMW, forcing a grim smile.

She wanted to wait for Michael. I couldn't blame her. "Just be safe. If you need to leave—"

"We will." She patted my arm and then slid into the back seat of their car.

"You be safe—" Stevie started.

"You get in the car with us *now.*" I shut the back door. "I'll get someone to drive your car back to you." I wasn't going to let her out of our sight. We needed answers first.

When I opened the front door, Samuel opened the back passenger door, getting ready to join Bodey and leaving my sister to sit up front with me.

Stevie bit her lip. "But Mom and Dad—"

"You heard her." Samuel's baby-blue eyes flared. He towered over her by at least half a foot. Despite being naked, he got in my sister's face and continued, "Going against the queen is treason. We don't have time for this."

Her bottom lip quivered, and I kept my gaze firmly on her and not naked Samuel.

Get yourself a blanket from the trunk, Bodey snarled to Samuel, his displeasure weaving through me. *And get my mate one, and her sister as well. You all need to be covered* now.

At least I wasn't the only one who was uncomfortable, but it surprised me that Bodey was.

Samuel stepped to the side, trapping Stevie between his body and the car door. She had to either fight him or get into the vehicle.

Her face reddened as she huffed but then got into the car.

Bodey's pain and annoyance blended together, making my chest tighten.

I started the car, looking toward the woods as Samuel went to the trunk for the blankets.

I didn't know what I expected, but there were no more wolves chasing us, and I was both relieved and scared. If they weren't here for us, that meant they were attacking other pack members.

I linked with all the pack nearby, tugging at the bonds that were the strongest. *Do you need more fighters?* Before we pulled out of here, I needed to make sure no one was in imminent danger. Worst case, Samuel could drive Stevie and Bodey home.

As I tugged, I sensed the overwhelming emotions churning from everyone. It was a mixture of so many things that the impact was damn near incapacitating. The most common feelings were fear, concern, hope, and suspicion.

Michael replied, *They're retreating. We're running after them, trying to catch some. Most of us have minor injuries, so we're slow. You all should head out in case a few swing around and try to attack you again.*

We're leaving now. Since they weren't being attacked, any reservations I had about leaving were gone.

Samuel slid into the back, and an olive-green blanket was dumped over the seat and into my lap while a black one landed on Stevie. I quickly wrapped mine around my body and stuffed it under my armpits so it wouldn't fall down then shifted the car into drive.

Bodey huffed. *It's about damn time.*

I mashed my lips together but didn't say anything. Instead, I pressed on the gas, leaving this place behind. For all that Hells Canyon was so beautiful, I now had a lot of horrible memories associated with it.

Are you taking your sister with you? Jack asked, trepidation pulsing through his link.

I am. I can't trust her right now. Saying it gutted me. Stevie had been my lifeline growing up. The one person I always trusted, even more than Theo. Wrapping my head around her helping Queen Kel and telling her gods knew what had my stomach in knots.

We won't be far behind you, Dan replied. *Just get the three of you home and secure your sister.*

Secure my sister? I dreaded how that would look. *I need someone to drive my sister's car to Bodey's house. Can anyone do that? She always leaves the keys in the ignition. It's a point of contention between her and my parents.*

Stella and I can, Miles offered.

Thank you.

As I pulled onto the main road, another thought pushed to the forefront. Though I couldn't see my mark, I touched my neck, feeling both the scratches and the area where my new tattoo had appeared. How had I even gotten it? If I were the young princess who'd supposedly died in the fire, no witch could *ever* make me forget it.

Babe, what's wrong? Bodey asked, his pain melding into my body. My arms, shoulders, and back ached, mirroring what he was experiencing.

I'm worried about you—and how this mark got onto me. I didn't want to brush him off. *But we can figure it out later. I need you to focus on healing.*

I glanced over my shoulder into the back seat and saw that

Bodey was looking out the window while Samuel was watching me.

Swallowing, I forced myself to focus on the road. "Are you okay, Samuel?" I hadn't even considered how he might be feeling right now. For his entire life, he'd thought he would be the one with this tattoo.

"Well, given the circumstances, yes." He leaned toward me.

Bodey growled.

"Man, she's got a blanket over her." Samuel lifted both hands as if in surrender. "I'm not trying to look at anything but her tattoo."

Huffing, Bodey lowered his head, causing an ache to shoot through him and me. *You could still wait until she's dressed.*

The scent of iron hung heavy in the vehicle, reminding me that my mate was still bleeding. In less than twenty-four hours, both of Bodey's cars had been coated in blood.

"How are *you,* Queen?" Stevie sighed and shook her head.

"I'm betting we all want to know that answer." It had to be a mistake.

Licking her lips, Stevie rubbed her hand over the black fleece blanket. "We need to go home. Mom and Dad are going to be worried about us."

"That's not an option." I tightened my hands on the wheel. "You can link with them, or *I* will."

"Dammit, Callie." Stevie's body tensed. "You're my sister. Whatever *this* is doesn't change that everything I did was to help *you.* I shouldn't be punished for trying to protect you!"

I laughed, the sound more hysterical than I'd intended, but damn. My fated mate was hurt, I now had some blasted tattoo that shouldn't be there, and we'd been attacked twice in less than twenty-four hours. If that wasn't hysteria-inducing, I didn't know what else this emotion whirling within me could be. "So you thought everyone else's lives were worth less than mine?"

"No one was supposed to get hurt." She leaned her head back against the headrest. "And so what if someone else got hurt? No one has ever protected us before."

"Every single alpha advisor except Zeke protected me from Charles's attack with Pearl and the other three goons that night." It was like she'd forgotten that part, so I was more than willing to remind her. "So you *know* that's not true."

She flinched, and my throat tightened.

No. This had to be some sort of sick joke. "Please tell me you weren't working with Queen Kel before that?"

Stevie turned toward the window, hiding her face, which told me everything.

"How long?" I forced out. The words were like razors slicing my throat.

"What was I supposed to do?" Stevie turned back toward me, lifting her hands and causing the blanket to drop below her breasts. "They wouldn't let you out of the pack to work, and seventy-five percent of the money I brought home Zeke demanded to cover pack expenses! We were never going to be able to leave, and yes, you took the brunt of the mistreatment, but the rest of us weren't far behind...except for Pearl."

Yes, Pearl. The sister who hated me. I was certain she'd told Charles and the others when and where I was going so they could harass me.

"But by teaming up with the queen, you were allowing others to be treated the same way as us." That was the part I didn't understand. She was trying to help us by doing the same thing to other people. "That's hypocritical."

Stevie pulled the blanket up over her boobs and glared out the passenger window again. She didn't say another word, and I wasn't sure whether she was absorbing what I'd just said or ignoring it.

Silence hung thick in the vehicle as I continued the drive

home. My head was spinning. But everything came back to the tattoo on my chest and why the ink had marked my skin. Did the spell get messed up due to the wolf attack and latch on to me because the spell that had trapped my wolf was wearing off? That was the only thing that made sense.

I focused on pushing my magic through the fated-mate connection to Bodey to hopefully give his magic a boost and heal him faster.

You don't have to worry about me, Bodey linked. *I'll be fine, and we're going to figure out this whole tattoo thing together. I promise.*

I wasn't hiding my thoughts and emotions well. He'd read me like an open book. *My priority is making sure you heal. Then we can determine how this mistake happened.*

No matter what, I'll be beside you, he replied, his warmth settling deep within me.

Somehow, he knew exactly what I needed to hear. In just a little over two weeks, he already knew me better than I did myself.

As WE PULLED up to Bodey's—er, *our*—two-story modern colonial home, I couldn't believe that the sun was still out. Though it was only late afternoon, my eyelids were so damn heavy. It felt like a week's worth of drama had happened during the past day.

"Is this your new neighborhood?" Stevie asked a little bitterly as I pulled into the garage. "Since you're *mated* and all."

That was like a punch in the gut. I hadn't told her about Bodey and me, but I was just as shocked by her revelation as she was mine. "Yes, it is, and that's why I planned to come to the house after the coronation—so that Bodey and I could tell you all."

She blew out a breath. "And that's why you were so determined to be there?"

"Exactly." I turned off the car and climbed out, wrapping the blanket more snugly around myself and opening the back door for Bodey.

Once we were all out, I moved to the door of the house and hit the garage control to close it. We all entered the large mudroom, passing by the white bench built into the wall where we'd normally put our shoes.

Bodey moved slowly beside me as we went into the kitchen, his nails tapping against the dark mahogany floor.

Right on my heels, Stevie surveyed everything, taking in the spotless black stove and matching microwave to one side and the sizable black refrigerator surrounded by gray cabinets and a matching island that was centered about eight feet from the stove. The dark granite countertops seemed to sparkle under the chandelier centered above the island.

We went into the den with its tan leather L-shaped couch, dark wooden coffee table, and beige-tiled fireplace with a large flat-screen TV hung over it. A gigantic covered patio with a rectangular table and six chairs stood outside the den's glass doors, and directly past the den was the large dining room furnished with a light mahogany table and sixteen matching chairs.

Stevie's gaze swung to the family portrait that hung in the den. It showed Bodey, his younger sister Jasmine, and Janet and Michael. Seeing Bodey and Michael side by side, I noticed how similar their features were. The main differences were their ages and their eyes; Michael's were jade, while Bodey's were the blue of Janet's. Jasmine was the opposite, her strawberry-blonde hair and heart-shaped face matching their mother's, but her jade eyes coming from their father.

"I saw three of those people at the coronation today." Stevie pointed to Bodey's sister. "Who's she?"

My sister, Bodey linked, his discomfort flooding me. His injuries were throbbing, and his muscles had stiffened up during the two-hour car ride home.

She tilted her head. "Why wasn't she there?"

I opened my mouth to tell her that Jasmine was at college but then closed it. That was more information Stevie could feed the queen.

"Jasmine's *away*," Samuel interjected from behind us. His eyes narrowed on her, full of suspicion.

Her jaw clenched, not missing the fact that we were being vague. She was smart; she knew Samuel had done that on purpose, and I hadn't interjected to fill in the holes.

Bodey limped his way to the spot on the floor in front of the fireplace. Though his wounds weren't bleeding anymore, his fur was matted with blood. He flopped down a little harder than normal, like his legs weren't cooperating.

I still can't shift back to human form. The injuries are too fresh, he linked.

I hated to leave him alone, but I didn't trust Stevie enough to leave her with him. I said, "Stevie, let's go grab some clothes in my room."

Please do, Bodey linked. *I want everyone to be wearing clothes now.*

I pressed my lips together and took Stevie's hand, leading her toward the stairs. Samuel was right on our heels.

I'll change fast and help you keep an eye on her since Bodey's hurt, Samuel said as we walked up the stairs.

His paranoia about her had me moving even faster. At the

top of the stairs, I took a right as he went straight toward his room.

Within seconds, I'd walked past the spare room I used to sleep in and into Bodey's and my room. The walls were the same color as the rest of the house, but up above the bed was a huge drawing of an acoustic guitar. I looked around, trying to judge the room through Stevie's eyes. Bodey had decorated with black nightstands and a matching dresser, and he'd hung his maroon sports jersey, printed with *Valor* and the number sixteen, on the wall without windows. I smiled at the bed's cream comforter—Bodey had taken that off what had been my bed in the guest room. He'd slept with it during my absence.

Shaking my head, I strolled to the dresser and fished out two shirts and two pairs of boxers. "This is all we've got until we get some clothes."

Stevie hugged herself. "Like I said, we should go home. That way, I can be somewhere that people won't glare at me, and you can have your own things."

"Good try, but not happening." I shut the door and quickly dressed, thankful to wear something other than a blanket.

Scowling, Stevie put on my mate's clothes too, and my wolf growled. She didn't like my sister wearing his clothes, but it was better than the alternative.

A knock sounded on the bedroom door, and I startled. It had to be Samuel.

When I opened the door, his gaze immediately swung to my sister. His nostrils flared as he walked in, rubbing his hands on his jeans, the collar of his burnt-orange polo shirt standing on end and his hair in disarray. He'd rushed to get here.

Stevie stepped back, keeping her arms wrapped around herself.

What's wrong? I linked to Samuel, a lump forming in my throat.

You need to lock her in the basement. Samuel lifted his chin. *She can't be trusted, and everything she sees and hears could get back to the queen. In fact, we should block her pack link so if she has someone helping her, they can't get the messages to the queen.*

My heart free-fell into my stomach.

He was right. I loved my sister, but these were my people, and not just because I was marked. I was now an alpha advisor's mate who couldn't allow division, even across states.

Samuel, Bodey snarled, and I realized he'd linked to us both. *That's her sister. You know how much she means to Callie. If you want to imprison her,* you *do it. Don't make her.*

And there was my mate, on my side like always.

She bears the mark, not me. It's her call, not mine. Samuel's jaw clenched.

The walls seemed to close in on me. I hadn't considered how upset Samuel must be about all this, but why wouldn't he be? He should be king. He should be the one with the mark.

But he was right. For now, the decision was on me.

"Callie?" Stevie's voice quivered. "What's going on?"

Before I could question my decision, I forced the words from my mouth, hoping I wasn't making a mistake.

CHAPTER FOUR

MY CHEST SQUEEZED as if a vise had closed around it, turning my breathing ragged. I wasn't sure what the right answer was—lock Stevie up or not—but I couldn't ignore everything that had happened.

"Callie?" Stevie's voice broke. "Are you going to answer me?" She hugged her waist even tighter.

Straightening my shoulders, I prepared for the reaction that would follow. "With everything that's happened, I have to make a decision about something awful that I don't want to."

She took a step back, her body tensing. "Like?"

Bodey linked, *We don't have to do that if you don't want to, babe. We can keep an eye on her here.* The guilt curled through me.

That was so *damn* tempting. I didn't want to lock up my sister. I winced even thinking about it, but Samuel was right. The longer she was out here with us, hearing everything we said or did and getting more familiar with the advisors, the more information she would have to tell the queen. "We're going to have to put you somewhere so you can't leave."

Her brows furrowed. "What do you mean? You're going to throw me in a basement like that scout?"

I shrugged. "Stevie, you betrayed *us*. You betrayed *me*." I gestured to the new tattoo that moved across my skin. "There's no other choice. We can't trust you."

She dropped her arms and marched up to me. "I didn't betray you! I was trying to *protect* you the *only* way I knew how." She took my hand, grasping it hard, and continued, "I would never betray you, Callie. With you as the queen, there's no reason for me to continue feeding Queen Kel anything."

"That doesn't fix the problem." I squeezed her hand back. "You should've never gone to Queen Kel to begin with, or at least come clean when..." My voice trailed off. "Wait. The scouts that attacked me. Were you behind that?" After spending time at Bodey's and with Samuel, I'd been attacked seemingly at random in the woods behind the office of my new job. Stevie had taken my injury hard. At the time, I'd thought it was because she didn't like seeing me hurt, but now...

The pack connection I had with her grew heavy and icky...*guilt.*

"That wasn't supposed to happen." She dropped her hand and took a few steps back, finding the wood floor very interesting. "I told the queen about Charles and their attack on you at Hells Canyon and the rift between Zeke and the other advisors. I didn't expect her to send scouts after you. She wanted to question you, and since the advisors seemed to like you, she said she wanted to capture you to force their hand."

"And you still told me *nothing*?" A knife in the back would've been less painful than this.

What's going on? Bodey linked. *You're upset. I told you—*

Stevie informing on me to the queen was the reason for my attack by those scouts.

She ran her fingers through her hair. "Zeke was still being a prick, and Bodey hurt you! I thought we might still need her protection, and I didn't want to involve you."

Samuel took the spot beside me, his nose wrinkling. "You not only put Callie at risk but every family living in the territory."

Huffing, Stevie lifted her head. "I'm sorry. I didn't mean for anyone to get hurt."

"When you pick a side in war, there are always casualties." The words fell from my tongue, and somehow, they sounded familiar. "Either way, you betrayed everyone, and I can't risk you funneling Queen Kel more information. Intention doesn't matter. We need to keep you somewhere and block you from communicating information to someone else who could get it back to the queen." The problem was, I had no clue where. I'd walked around this pack neighborhood all of once—with Samuel.

He caught my sister's arm and said, "I'll take her to Michael and Janet's basement. It can be locked, and you'll be close enough to check on her."

"What? No." Stevie tried pulling away from him. "Callie, don't do this. You know me."

My heart fractured. "I thought I did, but I never expected you to work with the Southwest queen. We have to take safety precautions. What if she tries to use someone against you to keep information coming?"

"Are you serious?" Her bottom lip quivered. "I did all this for you...for us. Now that you're mated to an advisor and have been marked queen, everything has changed." There was no stench of a lie. "Don't you believe me?"

"None of that matters." I blew out a breath as my eyes burned. I tried to keep the tears at bay because letting them spill wouldn't solve anything. "What you did wasn't right, and until the advisors get here and we can discuss the situation, you need to be detained. I'm sorry, but this is how it has to be. We need everybody to feel as safe as possible. And they're not going to feel that with you around. At least, not right now."

"Then take me home," she begged. "I don't want to get our parents involved."

I scowled. She acted as if we were abusing her when that wasn't the case. "How can you not realize going home would involve them? Do you truly think you'll be treated as well back at the pack as you will here? You think Zeke isn't going to want to make an example of you? You should know better than anyone that I'm the one person who understands what being on his shit list is like." That was the main reason I wanted her here—I could protect her. But now she'd brought up my parents, which made me nervous. What if Pearl was involved, too, and the two of them were communicating?

I exhaled. "Is Pearl working with you? I need to know if she is." She'd do anything for status, even hurt a person in the family.

Stevie blanched. "She's not." She lifted her chin. "I would never include her. She would turn on you if given the chance, and I was trying to protect *all* of us."

Some of my worry eased.

"Let's go. I'll reach out to Dina to get one of her coven members to meet us there to put the block on." Samuel tugged on Stevie's arm and led her to the door. He frowned as our eyes met. "I'll be back in a few minutes." Concern lined his forehead.

He seemed to care that I was struggling with my sister. Someone who resented me for being marked queen wouldn't be trying to help me.

"Callie." Stevie's voice trembled as she fought against his hold.

I faced the wall, unable to watch him drag her away. My

heart was shredded. This felt so wrong, but I didn't have a better option. She'd forced my hand.

Warmth pushed into my chest from my mate. Bodey linked, *I'm sorry you had to go through with that.* The concern pouring through our bond urged me to go downstairs to be with him.

Still, I waited. Samuel and Stevie were also heading downstairs, and I didn't want to see her face again. Maybe I was being a coward, but having her taken away like a hardened criminal had acid inching up my throat.

Whether I want to admit it or not, Samuel was right. She needs to be kept somewhere until we determine she's not a risk to us. I clenched my hands, focusing on the sting of my nails cutting into my skin. *We don't know what she's already told the queen. What we've learned might not be everything.*

Silence was my answer, which told me he agreed but wanted to protect me from making such a call about my family.

From below, Stevie cried out, "Callie! Please."

My heart twisted, and a salty tear ran into my mouth. I glanced down and found wet spots on my maroon shirt.

I was crying.

"Don't do that to her," Samuel's voice chastised. "You're making it harder on both of you. You can't expect to aid an enemy and not be punished. Life doesn't work like that."

The front door opened, and I could hear my sister crying quietly as the two of them walked outside. When the door shut, I wiped the moisture from under my eyes and dealt with the last thing I needed to do.

Informing Zeke.

I linked with him, giving him an update.

She needs to be brought to my pack, Zeke demanded. Even without being able to sense him like the others, his frustration was palpable. *I'm her alpha and should deal with the discipline.*

Absolutely not. I had to be firm; otherwise, he'd keep trying to force the issue. *I'm the queen, and every territory was attacked as a result of her choice. I'm the one to handle it, and that's not up for debate.*

As you wish, he snarled, despite being in my head.

I closed the link, not wanting to hear more, and headed downstairs to check on my injured mate.

How I wished it was nighttime. I was ready to crawl into bed and cuddle with Bodey. After fearing I was going to lose him, I needed alone time with him more than air.

In the den, he lay in the same spot in front of the fireplace. I hurried over to him, and his eyes opened. His agony washed over me, but it wasn't quite as bad. He was healing.

You've been crying, he linked as his irises darkened.

There was no point in lying. I sat beside him, running my hands through the dark fur on his back near his tail. *Do you want something to eat? I can make you something.* He'd taken care of me when I was injured, and I wanted to return the favor.

He shook his head, causing his body to cringe. *Thanks, but I don't think I can handle anything right now.*

You need the calories to heal. However, I wasn't going to pressure him. I didn't like it when others did that to me, so I lay down beside him, careful not to touch any part of him that was injured.

Dina and the others are almost here. I linked with Lucas while you were talking to Stevie, and they were nearing the neighborhood.

As if he'd summoned them, I heard two vehicles pulling into our driveway.

I shot to my feet and hurried to open the door for the new arrivals. Lucas and Jack were in front, with Stella and Miles in the center. Michael, Janet, and Dina brought up the rear.

"Whoa!" Jack's mouth dropped open as he pushed his wavy

blond hair out of his face. His cobalt eyes locked on my tattoo. "That's freaking *badass*."

Lucas's dark-brown eyes stared at the same spot. The corners of his eyes crinkled as he rubbed his faint, dark goatee. His skin looked a touch paler than its normal tan. "And it moves."

"What?" Stella pushed between the two guys. She was the complete opposite of me in every way, with long, wavy, dark-brown hair and violet eyes that reminded me of a flower. Her bronze complexion seemed to glow in the twilight. "I didn't realize it would move."

"I don't think that's normal." Miles's brow furrowed, emphasizing his dark complexion. He ran a hand through his short ebony hair, and his dark-green eyes filled with confusion.

"Maybe I'm not supposed to be queen?" I moved out of the doorway, letting them in, and headed back to Bodey. I needed Dina to use her healing magic on my mate. "Where's Zeke?" I was surprised he wasn't here.

"He and Theo raced back to their pack home," Michael answered. "Apparently, there was an attack there while they were gone."

I froze and spun around. "What do you mean an attack?" My mind flashed to my parents, and I sorted through the pack links, trying to determine which of them were connections to Mom, Dad, and Theo. I still didn't know how this all had happened. "Is anyone hurt?"

"From what he said, only his mate was attacked. The queen had someone in place to rescue the scout he had in his basement." Lucas shrugged. "That was it. No one else was hurt, but they wanted to get back and check on everything. Besides, Theo got injured in the attack in Hells Canyon."

Theo.

"Is he okay?" Then I flinched and glanced at Dina. "And

the witches? How are they?" The witches were just as much part of our pack as the wolves.

Dina removed the tie from her hair, and the auburn strands spilled across her shoulders. Her dress had bloodstains all over it. Her charcoal eyes narrowed, and goose bumps spread across her pale skin. "He was fine, just a tad dramatic." She rolled her eyes then sobered. "One of our witches lost her life today—the one who set the perimeter. They killed her to take it down."

I rubbed my chest, trying to ease the pain. "How many did we lose?"

"That's what's odd." Miles bit his bottom lip and he strolled past me, heading into the den. "The witch died, Theo was injured, and Bodey would've died, too, if we hadn't gotten him out of there."

That had my blood running cold. "He and Samuel were their targets even after I got this." I gestured to my neck and chest. The entire tattoo was visible because Bodey's shirt was too big on me. "You'd think that I'd be the target, so why wasn't I?" I hurried into the den too, needing to be close to Bodey. Things didn't seem quite as dire when I was near him.

I took my spot next to him. He lifted his head but didn't move beyond that.

"Maybe they thought your tattoo was an illusion from a spell." Dina tilted her head as she examined it.

I hated the way everyone was looking at me...at *it*. I wanted to hide my neck and chest, but that would be futile.

I swallowed. "Dina, I hate to ask, but is there any way you can help him?" I gestured at my mate. I wasn't above begging.

Dina walked around the couch, her face stern. "I can help a little, but not all the way. Between the magic we used at Hells Canyon and losing a member of our coven, my magic is tired and grieving. But I can ease most of the pain."

"Whatever you can do would be appreciated." I didn't want

to pressure her, but I would really like to sleep with my mate in human form tonight.

She nodded, taking a spot on the other side of Bodey. Michael, Janet, and Stella sat on the couch and the three advisors moved behind them. Miles placed his hands on his mate's shoulders as he watched Dina work.

"It'll take a minute." Dina moved slowly, the corners of her mouth tipped downward. I didn't have to pack link with her to know the grief she was carrying. She kneeled beside my mate, placing her hands on the area with the deepest gashes.

Pain shot through Bodey's and my connection, and he whimpered.

"In a second, you'll begin feeling better," she murmured.

I could feel her magic through our bond. The comforting, warm feeling was an echo of what I'd felt the day she'd used her magic on me.

The front door opened, and Samuel's musky scent wafted into the den as the door shut behind him.

As soon as he entered the room, Samuel sighed. "She's in the basement for now."

"Is she safe there?" Jack clenched his jaw. "Maybe she should stay in the bachelor house with the rest of us."

Lucas's and Miles's brows rose as they glanced at Jack, who stood between them.

"I'm not happy about it either." I hung my head, wishing that anyone but Stevie had been the informant. "But we have to make sure that she isn't still feeding information to the queen."

"You know her better than any of us," Jack said, pointing at me. "Would she do that now?"

I huffed as my limbs quivered. "I wouldn't have thought she would do what she already did, so I'm not the best person to ask."

His head jerked back, but then he nodded. "That's fair, I guess."

The warmth of Dina's magic receded from Bodey, and soon the witch lifted her head. "I've done all I can for him."

Tugging at our connection, I could feel the substantial difference in my mate. He wasn't aching anymore, and when he stood on all fours, there was only a twinge of discomfort. He linked with his parents, the advisors, Samuel, and me, *I'll be right back. I'm going to shift.* He trotted off, moving damn near close to his normal speed. Some of the weight lifted from my shoulders.

Now that I wasn't as worried about Bodey, my mind went back to the mark. "How did this happen?" I brushed my fingers over my neck.

Dina stood again and paced between the wall and the couch. "I'm as clueless as you are."

"Do you think the magic made a mistake?" That was the only thing I could fathom.

"Maybe. Or it could be due to an illusion spell that one of their witches used to distract us." She cleared her throat and paused, regarding me. "If you want, I can read you to see if there's magic on you. Before, all I could sense was the blood magic that suppressed your wolf. This is faint, so I'd need to search within you to even attempt to find the answers."

My pulse quickened. "Do you have enough strength?" I didn't want her putting her magic or health at risk. "Or should we wait until tomorrow?"

"I held enough back in case you wanted me to check." She licked her lips. "May I?" Dina lifted her hands as she moved toward me, asking permission to touch my arm. "It'll feel odd, and I need you to not access your magic while I search within you."

I nodded and offered her my arm.

This time, when her magic entered me, it wasn't comforting like it had been when she'd healed us. It was hotter and more jarring, and the magic prodded things within me. I could feel each nudge and stab as her power moved through the magic of my body.

What's going on? Bodey linked, but I couldn't answer. She'd told me not to access my magic. I should've given him a warning, but I hadn't thought of it.

When I didn't answer, the dresser in the bedroom upstairs slammed.

"Don't worry, I'll tell him what's going on." Janet smiled.

Every person in the room watched as Dina searched for answers inside me. The prodding got stronger, and I groaned.

Just as Bodey strode into the room, Dina lowered her hands. Her face was lined with even more confusion.

"What did you find?" my mate asked, coming toward me.

I glanced up at him, smiling. I was so relieved to see him back in human form and moving without too many issues.

My eyes drank in every place where he'd been injured, and his muscles were damn distracting. His messy chestnut hair covered his forehead, and his olive skin was just a tad paler than normal, but he looked delicious.

He crouched next to me and took my hand.

"That's the thing." Dina's jaw twitched. "I didn't find anything, which can mean only one thing." She paused, her face strained.

That wasn't a good expression, and I wasn't following along.

Samuel, however, must have understood. He gasped.

CHAPTER FIVE

BODEY'S HAND froze inches from mine, making my pulse gallop. Whatever Samuel had realized, Bodey must've too.

Taking a few steps toward me, Samuel scanned my face as if searching for something.

"Are you saying it's possible that she's—" Michael's jaw dropped, and he blinked several times.

My body tingled. I had no clue what they were thinking, and I wanted to curl into a ball. Anything to get away from the prying eyes that were locked on me. Somehow, this was worse than when they'd all stared at my brand-new tattoo.

Bodey took my hand, his surprise morphing into calm. He squeezed my hand and took the spot next to me, our legs brushing.

"Are you saying that she's my sister?" Samuel murmured. His voice was thick with feeling.

Dina nodded, and my body went numb.

I wasn't sure what I was actually feeling. Terror and hope bloomed, mixing together, negating each extreme. "Sister?" I said the word slowly, despite it being a common word in my vocabulary, struggling with the new meaning in relation to Samuel. "But that's not possible."

Tilting her head, Janet stared at me. "Now that I look at her, I can see King Richard's features in her. The eyes and hair color. It's uncanny."

I shook my head, and a tremor rolled through my body. "I would remember. Being a princess is a huge-ass deal. Something *has* to be off. Maybe the witch hid the spell from others." You'd think a princess wouldn't be able to have her memory wiped. There had to be a mistake. I couldn't be the girl the king and the queen had hoped would unite shifters across the US.

"A witch can't hide a spell from another witch, especially one with my power." Dina moved about five feet away from me and continued, "In regard to your memory, even the strongest supernatural can have their memories blocked or altered if a witch is strong enough. Though it's faint, I feel enough magic to know something in you is still being suppressed, and it's not your wolf."

"There has to be a way to get my memories back. I've heard stories." I furrowed my brows.

"There are two possible ways." She lifted a finger. "One, a witch removes the spell. Two, if a vampire was the one who altered the person's memories, they'll usually come back—the loss won't be permanent if a person has a strong, intelligent mind. I doubt you were wiped by a vampire."

I blinked, trying to absorb this new information. Every time I thought I was catching up, Fate bitch-slapped me again.

Stella placed a hand on top of one of Miles's on her shoulder. "Then remove her spell."

"Easier said than done." Dina blew out a breath. "The only witches who can do that is the person who cast the spell or one of their direct descendants."

My eyes burned. That was just my luck.

"Then tell us who cast it so we can find the witch and unblock her." Jack leaned forward, bracing his arms on the couch.

Bodey laughed bitterly. "Let me guess; you can't tell who cast the spell."

His resentment flowed through our bond into me, making my lungs struggle to fill.

"No. It's not an energy I've felt before." Dina pursed her lips. "However, that doesn't mean I can't find them."

At least all wasn't lost. "None of this makes sense." I rubbed my free hand on my thigh. "How can someone like *me* be queen? A wolf shifter who's been treated like crap and couldn't shift for most of her life?"

Everyone cringed, and Bodey snarled. The calm that had been flowing from Bodey switched to boiling anger.

That was when realization dropped on my shoulders.

Zeke would know.

"No," Janet said, placing a hand over her heart. She continued, "Zeke wouldn't do that. Surely."

"He must have." Michael pinched the bridge of his nose. "There is no way he didn't recognize Callie. He visited the queen and king several times a month, even when there wasn't anything pressing going on. He was with them for every celebration, including birthdays."

A shiver ran down my spine. If that was the case, Zeke had known me as a baby. He knew exactly who I was, and he still treated me like trash. "What about Theo?" My heart ached. Had everyone I'd trusted betrayed me? Stevie was like a gut punch, but if Theo had too...

Michael shook his head. "Theo never went with Zeke to visit them. He stayed home with Tina, so he wouldn't have known who you were unless Zeke told him."

At least that was something, but had he eventually figured out who I was? So many questions rushed through my head.

"Think about it." Bodey wrapped his arm around me, pulling me into his side. "So many things that didn't add up finally do. He didn't want you to attend school with other wolf shifters and humans." He wrinkled his nose. "He didn't want you in town. He wanted you to stay on your pack lands. He was trying to hide you."

Stella tapped her finger against her chin. "But there could be reasons for all of that...couldn't there?"

"Maybe." Samuel leaned against the wall beside the fireplace. "For all we know, he could be the person who locked up her magic and blocked her memories."

There were still so many pieces missing. "So Zeke somehow kidnapped me, blocked my magic, hid me, and treated me like crap. *Why*?"

Lucas cleared his throat. "Theo was trying to get you to agree to mate with him."

My stomach churned as Bodey's anger turned into white-hot rage.

That had been Zeke's plan—Theo and I mating. But still, nothing made much sense. I would've thought that if he'd found me, Zeke would have been enthusiastic and informed everyone that he was a hero.

The room stayed silent as the magnitude of the situation swarmed over us.

Bodey released me and stood. "I'm going to kick his ass." His jaw clenched as his irises turned nearly black.

That sounded like an excellent idea, so I jumped to my feet.

"Fuck yeah." Jack pumped his fist. "Let's teach the old man a few lessons."

"Slow down." Michael lifted a hand, stood, and moved to the end of the couch so he could address all of us. "We don't know the story, so we can't be reactive. We need to be smart about how we handle this, or we could give Zeke an edge. One we don't know how he'll use."

Bodey's neck corded. "Be *smart* about it? We need to go and confront his sorry ass!"

"Son, I know. We do." Michael steepled his fingers. "But not tonight."

Bodey stared at his dad, his anger so palpable that I struggled to breathe. He clenched his hands, his nostrils flaring. "If he did this to her—"

"We don't know that he did," Miles interjected. "Your dad's right. We can assume, and we're probably right, but we can't be rash. Reacting too quickly could back him into a corner that he's already strategized for."

I hated that he was right. My wolf howled in my head, eager for blood, and every cell in my body sizzled. I wanted to torture the prick like he'd done to me my entire life.

"In other words, if we run over there with our pitchforks, he might run away or make things worse for us." Lucas wrinkled his nose.

"Exactly." Michael lowered his hands. "There could be a rational reason for his actions. If we confront him with unproven accusations, the tension will weaken us and help the Southwest queen to act against us."

Bodey laughed bitterly. "You really think there's a rational reason?"

"There could be something we don't know." Michael shrugged. "We can't just assume. You are king of our territory now, Bodey, which is a bigger responsibility than I ever prepared you for."

My mate's head jerked back, and a jolt of shock ran through our bond.

Yeah, I understood that feeling. He hadn't considered what

my new role meant for him. If this situation weren't so dire, his reaction would have been comical.

I huffed and placed my hand on Bodey's back. His muscles relaxed marginally under my touch.

"Whether we like to admit it or not, Zeke is smart." In fact, saying those words hurt my throat. "We're tired from the two battles last night and today, and Bodey was injured very badly. We need to take the night off and rest. We can head out first thing in the morning."

"Boo." Jack gave me a thumbs-down with a smirk. "That's no fun," he finished.

Lucas smacked him on the back of the head. "Shut up, man."

Annoyance flared through Bodey. "My mate is right. We'll do just that, but I'm going to send five wolves over to Zeke's pack to keep an eye on things. If something does happen, we'll know about it immediately."

Good suggestion. Most of Bodey's pack hadn't gone out there today. I straightened my shoulders. "They can search the area and see if they notice anything suspicious. Bodey can get some rest while I talk to my sister and try to get more answers. Then we can head over first thing in the morning to talk to Zeke."

"Look, I was kidding about booing, but seriously... If he's a traitor, will he still be there in the morning?" Jack arched a brow.

If the queen hadn't thwarted the coronation, we could've been addressing all of this with Zeke *tonight*. "It won't make a difference now. If he was going to run, he'd already be gone. If he's there when our five people show up, they can alert us and follow him if he runs."

Even though Bodey's rage was barely contained, he spoke calmly. "I don't like this either, Jack, but we do need rest. He's had seventeen years to plan whatever he's doing, so he'll have every contingency in place. Dad's right. We need to go in rested and prepared for a fight."

However, questions circled my brain. Was Zeke the person who'd had me spelled? Was he behind everything? Or was he just a small player in the grand scheme of things?

"Fine." Jack crossed his arms. "But Bodey and Callie need the most rest since they were the most injured during the past twenty-four hours, which means I should be the one to question Stevie. She might be more willing to talk to me than the sister who had her locked up anyway."

I recoiled. I couldn't help it. Guilt crashed over me like a tidal wave.

"Don't be a jackass," Bodey growled, feeling my emotions.

"What?" Jack's brow furrowed.

Lucas shook his head. "I'll go with you." He grabbed Jack's arm and pulled him toward the back deck.

"I can question her on my own." Jack scowled. "I know how to talk to women."

"You just proved otherwise," Lucas replied, opening the door and leading Jack outside.

When the door shut, Janet sighed. "He didn't mean it like that, Callie."

But he did; he just hadn't meant to hurt my feelings. He was stating facts, and I couldn't be upset with him for doing that. "He's fine." I wanted to say I was fine, but that would be a lie. The whole day had been shit.

Miles squeezed Stella's shoulders and forced a smile. "I'm going to take my mate to get some rest too. I'll admit, the two of us are exhausted." He removed his hands and took a few steps back.

Yawning, Stella stood. "I'm ready to take you up on that."

"And we should follow their lead." Michael climbed to his feet and helped Janet up.

"Well, then, I guess it's good night." Janet came over and hugged the two of us while Dina stood by watching.

Soon, everyone walked out the front door, leaving Samuel, Dina, Bodey, and me in the living room.

Dina tapped her fingers on her leg, nervous energy surrounding her.

I smiled. "Thank you for everything."

Her forehead creased, and then she bowed slightly. "Of course, My Queen. Anything for the royal family."

My heart warmed. "Let us know if you and your coven need anything."

Wrapping an arm around my shoulder, Bodey nodded. "Please, go grieve, and know that you all are in our thoughts."

Dina's eyes shimmered, and she mashed her lips together. "Thank you. I'll be in touch soon." She turned and left like the others.

When I glanced at Samuel, he was staring at me.

A twinge of discomfort pulsed in my chest.

Bodey cleared his throat awkwardly. "I'm gonna take a shower." *Feel free to join me if you two finish talking in time.*

My body warmed for a moment, but then I focused on my breathing. Samuel obviously wanted to speak with me. "I'll be up to our room soon."

He kissed my cheek and took off up the stairs.

Samuel didn't move his gaze from me, and I swallowed. He studied my entire face as if he was taking in every blemish.

When Bodey's and my bedroom door opened and then shut, Samuel grinned. "So we're family? Blood family." Hope sparked in his eyes.

My body almost sagged from the weight lifting off me. "Yup, we are." I beamed, returning his joy. My parents and Stevie were family, but this was different. I'd felt a bond with both Samuel and Bodey when I got here. The easy connection I had with Bodey made sense. He was my fated mate, and we were born to complement each other. Even though we hadn't been able to feel our magic at first, our souls had recognized one another. That had to be why we'd fallen in love so effortlessly and quickly. Now I understood why I clicked with Samuel as well—we had a true familial bond. The blood and magic that ran through our veins had been created by the same parents.

More oddly, we were raised similarly, even though I'd been treated as a lowly, weak wolf and he as a future king. Neither of us had been able to leave our pack and attend school like our peers, and we'd missed out on a lot of things other shifters were able to do, like work.

"If you ever get your memories back..." He took my hand. "Will you tell me anything that you remember about our parents?"

My heart ached. Neither of us remembered them, only the stories that others had shared. "I will. I promise."

He hugged me, crushing me against his chest with the warmth of his affection swirling between us. He linked, *I couldn't ask for a better sister.*

My eyes burned. "I couldn't ask for a better brother."

He blew out a breath and stepped back. "I really want to spend time with you and get to know you even more, but you and Bodey need each other after the fight." He glanced at the wooden floor and shrugged. "Maybe in between all the chaos, we can find some time to hang out together?"

"Most definitely." I placed a hand on his chest and said, "Besides, you're living here with us. We can start with breakfast in the morning before we head over to Zeke's."

His head jerked up. "You want me to come along?"

"Well, yeah. I don't only need Bodey to help me figure out

how to read Zeke, but you too because, clearly, I haven't been doing it well. Otherwise, I would've pieced everything together."

"You were brought there as a young child. You didn't know any different." He patted his chest. "I'm honored that you want me there, but I don't want you to feel undercut because everyone thought that I was the future king until today."

"And I don't want you to be upset with me for that same reason." I rubbed my hands together. "I know that's hard for alphas."

He laughed. "You don't remember me telling you that I didn't want to be king? Honestly, I'm relieved."

The fact that there was no sign of a lie had relief floating through me, my knees growing weak. "So you don't want to be an alpha?"

"Oh, yeah." He nodded. "I do, but not the ultimate alpha. I'm good with being second place." He winked.

I exhaled. No matter what, Bodey, Samuel, and I would be okay.

The shower turned on, and my wolf whimpered. She wanted to see Bodey and inspect him for injuries...and other delicious, hard things.

"See you at breakfast." Samuel rolled his eyes, but the corners of his mouth tilted upward. "Good night."

He was giving me the pass to leave. "Night. See you." I scurried away and jogged up the stairs. When I reached our room, I shut and locked our door then stripped. Getting wet and clean with Bodey sounded like a better ending to a shitty day.

When I stepped into the bathroom, my gaze went to the gray-tiled shower on the right. Bodey stood there, soaked and completely naked, though the fog prevented me from seeing his delicious body in detail.

He linked, *I was hoping you'd get here in time. I got a towel for you.*

I strolled over the cool gray tile past the sink in the Jack and Jill bathroom with its dark-gray granite countertop. The walls were a light gray, which made the room appear large and homey.

I grabbed the bronze handle and yanked open the shower door.

His front side was under the stream of water. *How are you doing? I know locking up Stevie wasn't an easy decision.*

I flinched. Even with him naked, that question changed my mood. *I'll be fine. I just wish there was something else we could've done, but Samuel is right. She can't be trusted.*

He turned toward me, and my desire returned twofold.

Are things okay with Samuel?

Great, but I don't want to think about him right now. Need clenched in my stomach.

Oh really? he teased and winked. *What do you want to think about instead?*

I stepped to him and took in every inch of his face then let my gaze work its way down.

When I got to the wounds on his chest, I froze, thinking I must be seeing things.

CHAPTER SIX

I BLINKED, and despite the scabs on Bodey's chest, I could easily make out the mark. Water poured down his skin, his usual scent mixed with soap.

What's wrong? he linked, concern washing through him.

My hand shook as I traced the outline of his mark, being careful whenever it ran over the scab near one of the edges. His tattoo wasn't as intricate as mine, consisting of just the paw print. It was a third of the size, coming in around three inches, and underneath the center of his collarbone. *You have a mark too.*

Eyes widening, he glanced downward. His breath caught. "That's where I was hurting when the ink wrapped around you."

I remembered the pain I'd sensed from him. "I thought you were hurt." My finger kept tracing the mark, and I could feel my faint touch against my own chest like I was stroking mine as well.

Odd.

"Not then," he sighed, goose bumps sprouting across his

skin despite the water's warmth. "I thought I was feeling your pain."

Considering how much agony I'd been in, I could see why he'd thought that, especially since our tattoos were in similar places. "You probably did, but some of it must have been your own."

He smiled. "I love that we have almost identical tattoos." He waggled his brow. "Kind of like we're both branded now."

His joy eased some of the tension in my body. Feeling a little more like myself, I teased, "We're branded as king and queen."

"Because we're *mates*," he countered. His eyes darkened, and he wrapped his arms around my waist, pulling me against him. The water now doused both of us, and I loved every moment.

Need flared within me, so I kissed his lips, wanting to taste him.

He responded with vigor, his tongue slipping into my mouth. His minty taste filled my senses, and his scent made my head spin.

All too soon, he leaned away from me, and I frowned.

Chuckling, he turned me around so I was directly in the spray then tilted my head back so the water soaked my hair.

"Let me wash you," he murmured and pumped some coconut-scented shampoo into his hand.

I wanted him to take care of me in a different way. My body was ready for him, and I desperately needed the connection after seeing him so hurt.

When I pouted, he smirked and turned me so I faced away from him. Then his strong fingers tangled into my hair, sudsing the heavy strands. After getting the shampoo worked through, those fingers kneaded my head gently until I moaned.

Somehow, this was more erotic than foreplay.

He nuzzled my neck as his fingers continued to work, and I turned into putty, my legs wanting to give out underneath me.

As my body sagged against his chest, he took a few steps back, getting me out of the direct spray, and then grabbed a bar of coconut soap. He slowly washed my body, paying extra attention to my nipples, and then he had me lean against the side of the shower to clean my legs. Finally, he stood and linked, *Let's rinse you off.*

He turned me and dipped me back in the water, and as I rinsed off, he kissed me again. His tongue slipped into my mouth, and my arms wrapped around his neck, needing to touch him and also have him support my weight.

He stepped forward, pushing me so my back was against the tile as he moved into the water.

My eyelids were heavy with desire as I ogled him. "What are you doing? I need to clean you now."

"Nope. I did that before you got up here, and I forgot one part of your body," he rasped, one of his hands brushing my nipple while he soaped up the other hand then slid it between my legs.

His mouth went to my breast, and his tongue licked the nipple while his fingers rubbed between my folds.

I moaned, unable to stop myself. I clenched in need so hard that I nearly combusted, but all that accomplished was his fingers circling faster as he sucked my nipple into his mouth. My hips ground against his hand, and he slipped two fingers inside me.

Before I completely lost it, I linked, *You're not fully healed. We should head to bed.* But damn, those words were so hard to say because my body was on fire.

I'm fine. And if I don't get to taste, touch, and fill you tonight, I won't get a wink of sleep. His teeth gently grazed my sensitive flesh, making me groan.

Thank gods he needed me as much as I needed him.

My muscles tensed as he moved both his fingers and tongue faster.

I desperately reached down to stroke him, our bodies slick with water and desire. His breathing turned ragged as his hips jerked in time with my hand. Both of us worked each other's bodies into a frenzy.

And then an orgasm consumed me. My muscles tensed, and pleasure rolled through me, my body spasming around his fingers, urging him faster.

As soon as the ecstasy eased, I tried to pull away, hypersensitive to his touch now, but he held me firm.

"Again," he growled, his words igniting something wild inside me.

And just like that, my body was ready for his torment again. "Not your fingers. I need *you*." After seeing him so beaten and broken, I couldn't wait any longer.

"Fuck, yeah." He nodded, stepping between my legs and lifting me against the wall. He pressed against my opening and then pushed himself inside, filling me. My head thumped against the cold tile, a slight discomfort that ebbed afterward.

He paused and placed one hand behind my head, keeping me from hitting the wall again, then pressed his mouth to mine.

With him inside me, I wrapped my legs around his waist, pulling him closer so his body pressed to mine, and he sank deeper.

Then he thrust and ground against me. Each time he completed me, our connection opened a little more. Our emotions and sensations mingled together as our souls became one.

Soon, that knot of desire tightened again, with release imminent. Our kisses became messy and urgent as our pace quickened. He pushed hard inside me and stilled, and I writhed against him as ecstasy filled our bond.

He growled as his body quivered with his own release, and I dug my nails into the small of his back where he hadn't been injured. Our pleasure melded, and the world hazed around us.

I wasn't sure how long our orgasm lasted, but it wasn't enough. Being with him like this, with our souls fully connected...I needed the pleasure more than oxygen.

Damn. He peppered kisses over my face as he pulled away and stepped back into the water. I followed him, not ready to give up touching him. I pressed my lips to his, and our tongues tangled again.

I love you, Callie, he linked. *I don't know what I'd ever do without you now that we've found each other.*

His love filled my chest, reaching the spots that had been vacant and dark and infusing them with warmth and light.

"I love you, too," I whispered. I cupped his face with my hand. "But we need to get our rest so we're both physically and mentally prepared for tomorrow." I hated bringing it up, especially with the time we'd just shared together, but we had to face reality. *Even if I'd rather make love to you again.*

His eyes warmed to a cobalt hue. *As long as I can hold and smell you, that's all I need.*

Gods, I was so damn lucky to have him.

The two of us rinsed off again, and soon we'd thrown on some clothes—me wearing one of his shirts and his boxers—and then crawled into bed.

Tonight, I needed to be in my mate's arms.

A loud buzzing woke me, and I lifted my hand, shooting my alarm the middle finger. Despite my reaction, the alarm continued to buzz on the end table so loudly that my ears throbbed.

Beside me, Bodey groaned, pulling me so that my back was

pressed even more into his chest. His warmth surrounded me, and I could have easily fallen back asleep if the phone would just be quiet.

"Pretend it never went off," he murmured, nuzzling my neck and taking a deep breath.

I laughed. "That sounds more than perfect, but we know it's not possible." We were the king and the queen after all, even if that notion still seemed like a dream—completely surreal.

Forcing myself from Bodey's embrace, I leaned over and snatched my phone from the end table, swiping the alarm off. I quickly kissed him, and he reached toward me again. I giggled as I rolled off the bed before he could grab me, and his eyes peeled open as he scowled.

"That's just not nice." He pouted.

I rolled my eyes just as the scent of eggs, sausage, biscuits, and pancakes enveloped me. My stomach growled, ready to devour breakfast. "Your mom must be here."

He laughed. "I'd rather have your body for breakfast."

My blood warmed at that damn tempting offer, but if Janet was here, that meant Michael was too and that Miles, Lucas, Jack, and Stella would be here shortly. "You know we can't." I tugged on his black shirt, wishing I had some actual clothes to wear. "But one day, that better damn well be possible."

His eyes sparkled. "Oh, it will be."

I scurried into his bathroom, searching for something to use to tame my wild blonde hair. All I could find was a comb at the edge of the sink, so I used it as best I could.

As I ran the comb through my knots, I glanced at myself in the mirror. My Caribbean-blue eyes were brighter than normal and my light-olive complexion glowed. Despite the battles and not enough rest, I still appeared to be a healthy version of my prior self, most likely due to the magic now able to run through my body.

The comb was doing a shit job, but I continued to attack one tangle at a time. I needed to bring my stuff here. At least, that would be one benefit of talking to Zeke this morning—I could run by my house and grab some items, though questions about Stevie were sure to come.

Bodey strolled in and stopped, watching me with a huge smile on his face.

I paused and turned toward him, raising a brow. "What?"

"You have no clue how it feels to find you in our bathroom, using my stuff." He beamed. "It's a dream come true. I've waited for you most of my life."

My face flamed as butterflies soared in my stomach. Ever since he was a kid, he'd been waiting for me even though he hadn't known my name or face. He'd just somehow known that I was out there—his fated mate. The fact that he'd chosen me over an unknown fated mate before we'd realized we *were* fated made our relationship that much stronger. Learning we were fated was the icing on the cake.

He and I truly were meant to be together. Not only had Fate chosen us, but we'd chosen each other too.

Maybe Fate wasn't a complete bitch after all.

"There's no place in the world I'd rather be." I kissed him, and at that moment, my stomach chose to grumble *again*.

I winced. "Sorry. We didn't eat dinner last night."

He laughed. "Believe me. I'm hungry too."

Giving up, I dropped the comb on the sink. My hair was tame enough to not look like it belonged on a scarecrow. "Let's eat."

"Go on." He kissed me and linked, *I'll be down after I change.*

"Don't be long." I winked as I strolled out of the bathroom and headed into the kitchen.

When I entered, Janet was at the stove, with Samuel sitting

on a barstool at the island across from her. Michael was perched on another stool at the edge of the island near me. The other advisors hadn't arrived yet, so I had time to drink some coffee to prepare for Jack and all his snarkiness.

"Good morning, dear." Janet scrambled the eggs, her hair pulled into a bun. "I hope you don't mind that I came and cooked breakfast." She glanced at me, biting her bottom lip as if she was nervous.

"You always do." I brushed past her, heading to the Keurig.

She nodded. "True, but now you and Bodey are mated."

I put a pod in the coffee machine and grabbed a mug. "Yeah."

Michael shook his head. "Janet was worried that she'd upset you by coming into your house and cooking for your mate, even though Bodey is her son."

"Oh, Michael." She grabbed a towel and tossed it at him. "I can speak for myself." The towel hit him in the chest and dropped onto the island.

He smashed his lips together, trying to hide his smile as she went back to scrambling the eggs.

Samuel shook his head and took a sip from his mug.

Right, coffee. I pressed brew and poured two tablespoons of sugar and a dash of cream into my mug as it filled. "I promise, Bodey would much rather eat your cooking than mine." I managed to burn eggs every time I tried to make them, which perplexed me.

Her shoulders sagged, and she nodded behind her toward the couch. "I have a surprise for you."

My gaze darted in that direction, and I saw a pair of jeans, a burnt-orange sweater, and a bra on the back of the couch.

She took the frying pan off the burner. "These clothes might not fit you perfectly, but I thought you might want to wear something of Jasmine's rather than Bodey's clothes to question Zeke."

Tears burned my eyes. Not many people were considerate of me, but this family always had been, even when they didn't have to be. "Thank you."

"Of course, dear." She patted my cheek. "Why don't you change before the others get here?"

I nodded, placing my freshly brewed coffee to one side. "I'll do that right now." I started a cup of coffee for Bodey then snatched the clothes from the couch and headed upstairs.

Back in Bodey's room, I put on the bra and shirt and then slid on the jeans. As I zipped them up, Bodey sauntered out of the bathroom.

The jeans were a tad short on me, hitting my ankles, and a size too small, but they'd work for this morning and looked way better than a shirt and boxers.

Bodey tilted his head, taking in the outfit. The spicy scent of arousal wafted around him. "I didn't think about that, but my sister's clothes work for you."

I stuck out my tongue. "You just wanted me to be wearing your clothes when we saw Theo."

His eyes darkened as he smirked. "I mean, it sure wouldn't bother me."

With every ounce of control I had, I managed to school my expression, but I knew he could feel my joy through our bond, and he grinned. I loved that he wanted everyone to know I was his. "Well, your mother thought about it, and she's downstairs with the food ready."

The front door opened, and the sounds of Jack's and Lucas's footsteps stomped through the house.

I ran for the stairs. If I didn't get down there in time, Jack would steal my coffee. He'd done it before.

Bodey strolled in behind me. *I'm assuming you made yourself a cup of coffee.* He wouldn't be so smug in a second.

And one for you, I replied as I hit the bottom of the stairs and trotted down the hallway just as Jack strolled into the kitchen.

Jack's eyes lit up when his gaze landed on the two unclaimed coffee mugs. As he reached for mine, I snarled, "Don't even *think* about stealing my coffee!"

"What?" Jack groaned. "But it's there, fixed just the way I like it."

I darted between him and my cup, knocking him back a few steps. "Then make yourself one."

Lucas laughed. "Is that why you were rushing down here?"

"Hell yeah." I took a sip, the warmth heating my insides like the sun on a summer day. "This is mine." I then took the mug that was in the Keurig. "And this is Bodey's."

"Whatever." Jack snatched a biscuit off the pan.

"Hey," Janet chastised as she smacked his hand. "You can wait with everyone else."

Jack lifted his palms. "Why is everyone being so mean this morning?"

"We aren't being mean." Bodey entered the kitchen, squeezed between Jack and Janet, and stopped at my side. He took his mug from me as he continued, "We just know how you are."

Leaning against the island, Jack sulked.

Now that he and Lucas were here, there was no point in prolonging the inevitable. "Did Stevie tell you anything? How's she doing?"

"Nothing more than what she'd already told you." Lucas shrugged.

Jack crossed his arms. "And I believe her." He reached over

and snagged a plate that was on the counter. "In fact, I'm gonna take her some food this morning."

"That's a wonderful idea." Janet loaded the plate with eggs, sausage, and pancakes. "She's Callie's sister, and until we know whether or not she plans on working against us, we shouldn't make her feel like a complete prisoner."

"Then I should eat with her too." Jack took another plate and held it out to Janet.

She filled his plate up too, and then he called over his shoulder, "I'll be back in a minute."

He hurried out the back, damn near racing next door.

There's something weird going on with him. Bodey took a sip of his coffee.

I turned toward him, placing my hand on his chest. *When is there not?*

True. He tilted his head and then kissed me on my nose. *And even though you look beautiful, you look even better in my clothes.*

My heart fluttered as I nuzzled his neck. *I like being in your clothes too. Don't worry. I'll sleep in some tonight.*

Nope. He nipped at my ear. *My goal is to make sure you're naked.*

I laughed but cut it short when I noticed Lucas staring at us from a few feet away, his brows furrowed. "I never thought I'd see Bodey like this."

"Me neither." Janet beamed. "But I'm so happy. Now Jasmine needs to find her mate." She pointed at the food. "Eat before things get cold."

The five of us were filling our plates when Miles and Stella joined us. We took seats at the table, me between Samuel and Bodey, and everyone focused on eating.

Miles looked at Bodey. "Have any of your wolves notified you of anything strange going on at Zeke's?"

Bodey swallowed his mouthful of eggs. "Nothing worrisome, and Zeke is there, so there's that."

Silence descended again, and just as we were finishing up, Jack strolled back in with two empty plates. Janet and Stella stood, clearing the table.

"I guess we better go," Bodey sighed. "We need answers sooner rather than later."

"Let me help Janet and Stella—" I started.

Janet lifted a hand. "The two of us aren't going. Our place is here, keeping an eye on the pack while you're gone, so we'll clean up."

My body stilled. I shouldn't have been surprised; Janet and Stella had never gone to the advisor meetings during the planning for the coronation, but I was used to being with them. Yet my role had changed, not theirs.

I nodded. "Thank you."

"Just... All of you be safe," Janet said and then kissed Michael.

"We will, dear," he murmured.

Then Stella and Miles kissed too.

With goodbyes over, the seven of us headed to the garage. Samuel and Michael climbed into the back seat of Bodey's Mercedes-Benz to ride with us since the Jeep still wasn't repaired from when the windshield had been cracked at the coronation dinner. Miles and Lucas strode to Jack's Navigator, which was parked in the driveway.

Way too quickly, we were pulling out of the neighborhood. I picked at my cuticles with each minute that we drew closer.

Heading back to the pack like this was hard. My nerves were frayed and my chest tightened. At the end of the day, we were heading to the pack that had abused me.

They can't hurt you anymore, Bodey linked, reaching over the center console and taking my hand. *You won't allow them to.*

He was a smart man. Most would've said that they wouldn't allow their mate to be hurt, but he recognized that I could take care of myself.

I love you, I linked and turned on the radio. I flipped through the stations until I found "Fight Song" by Rachel Platten and focused on the words, getting ready to do just that.

THOUGH THE DRIVE TOOK HOURS, it felt like only minutes had passed when we rolled into the pack neighborhood. The yards were empty, even more so than normal, especially for a Sunday. It was as if everyone had been told to stay inside. I could see people in the windows, watching us pass by.

I ignored all the stares as I gave Bodey directions to Zeke's house. I'd rather see my parents first, but I didn't want Zeke to claim that we were nosing around *his* pack's land even though I was the queen and part of them. However, I did want to tread carefully, at least at first, with him.

As soon as we pulled up to his one-story brick house, Zeke marched out the front door.

All of us climbed out of the vehicles as Zeke's emerald eyes focused on me. He lifted his chin and balled his hands at his sides. His short salt-and-pepper hair was messy, and his olive complexion was a shade paler than normal as if he was stressed but trying to hide it. The skin around his eyes was taut. "I wondered how long it would take you to come here."

I marched forward, refusing to cower. If I were to truly be queen, I had to act like it, even in front of the man who'd tried to break me. "We figured you'd have answers."

"Did you now?" He smirked.

Bodey moved beside me, and the two of us stared him down. A lump formed in my throat, and I had to force out my next words around it. "Why did you hide me, knowing who I was?"

His irises darkened, filling with the hate that he always showed when looking at me. He remained silent, and I wasn't sure he was going to answer.

I straightened my shoulders, ready to fight. Then he lifted a hand and sneered at me.

CHAPTER SEVEN

MY BODY RECOILED, but I managed to hold my ground. I had no idea why this man hated me so much, but he'd never hidden the fact, except during the few days after I'd first come back from Bodey's house.

Bodey's jaw clenched as he took my hand. Despite the animosity emanating from him, his thumb rubbed the inside of my wrist, reminding me that he was there. He snarled, "Answer her, or I'll make you."

Crossing his arms, Zeke glared, and I couldn't help but wonder if he was pushing our buttons. We couldn't risk a rift with him right now. There was enough chaos without the alpha in charge of all the Oregon packs trying to split off and causing a civil war.

There was one strategy I knew would work best. *We need to goad him*, I linked with Bodey, Jack, Lucas, Miles, and Michael. I wasn't sure if Zeke's reticence was because he had something to hide or because he didn't want to answer *me*. Either way, discounting his importance would make him start talking faster. And none of us had time for the pissing match Zeke so clearly wanted.

"Just like I suspected, Zeke doesn't know shit." Jack chuckled as he strolled to my right side. "I bet he and Queen Mila weren't even really friends since he clearly didn't know what you looked like. Maybe their *friendship* was merely a ruse to help her family pack elevate their status."

I bit the inside of my cheek, trying to keep a smile from forming. I should've known he'd be the first to jump in.

Zeke's eyes hardened. "Of course I knew who Callie was." His nostrils flared. "Michael, tell them. The queen and I were *best* friends."

A hint of something flashed through Zeke's eyes, and my breath caught. But as soon as it came, it vanished, making me wonder if my imagination was getting the best of me. Not only that but there was no hint of a lie.

I was having a hard time reconciling the woman whom so many spoke highly of with her alleged friendship with Zeke. He was a horrible person, so how could someone said to have been kind and gracious have been friends with him, let alone given him control of this territory?

"He was. She often talked about Zeke when he wasn't around. She loved him dearly." Michael sighed and moved to the other side of Jack. "Why did you keep Callie hidden? Why wouldn't you tell *us*? The advisors deserved to know."

"I did what was best for her. I was the only person who knew she was alive, and I made her part of my pack. No one—including Queen Kel—knew. By keeping her hidden, I saved her life," he spat, then he lifted his chin. "Mila would've wanted me to watch over both of them, but you took in Samuel as one of your own."

A clear line divided Zeke from us. Though it wasn't visible, it was palpable. He held deep hate and resentment.

"You knowingly kept my sister and me apart," Samuel

gasped, his voice thick as he stood behind me. His heartbreak coursed through our pack link, settling hard against my chest.

"I did what had to be done." Zeke thrust out his chest. "Nothing more, nothing less."

Bodey's anger soared through me, making my own blood warm. He growled, "King Richard wanted his ancestral pack to protect his children—it was in his will, and the queen agreed. You should've known that."

"What?" Zeke's jaw dropped. "No. She wouldn't do that. She trusted *me* to protect them. No one else."

"*Protect* us?" A bitter laugh escaped, and my whole body shuddered. "Is that what you think you did? Forcing me to live like a fucking servant at the bottom of the pack? You let people —including yourself—mistreat me. If anything, I needed protection from *you*." I wanted to punch him, and my wolf snarled within, but I held myself back.

Bodey wasn't nearly as controlled. He stepped toward Zeke and shoved the older advisor back into the white garage door.

Zeke's eyes never left mine. They glowed as he stared at me. "I protected you by making sure no one knew who you were. No one could've fathomed you were the future queen."

"Is that your fucked-up way of trying to make everything you did to her okay?" Bodey snarled, his spit droplets landing on Zeke's face.

Michael linked, *Son, until we know more, I need you to calm down.*

I'm going to make the bastard pay, Bodey vowed.

Oh, he will, I replied. I needed him to know that I was definitely on the same page, but Michael was right. We needed to remain somewhat calm right now. *But we need answers. Don't think for a second that I'm okay with how he treated me and kept me away from my brother.*

I touched Bodey's arm, and our fated-mate connection buzzed, helping him relax marginally.

"Is that why you hid my magic?" I watched Zeke closely. I didn't want to miss the stench of sulfur and let him get away with something.

"*I* didn't hide your magic." He shook his head. "I found you that way."

I narrowed my gaze, waiting for something to flicker across his face, but there was never a hint of a lie. And yet, I *knew* he was hiding something.

"Where did you find her?" Michael asked, scratching the back of his head.

"When the fire started, I was there. I was about to leave, but then there was some sort of explosion from the study." His brows furrowed. "Callie had been blasted back against the wall, so I grabbed her and left."

Miles and Lucas came to stand on the other side of me, all of us forming a line except for Bodey, who released Zeke but still didn't step away. I kept my hand on his arm.

"You were there?" Miles tilted his head. "Why didn't we know that?"

"Because it was none of your business," Zeke said as he yanked down his shirt and moved so that Bodey wasn't directly in front of him. "If I hadn't taken Callie and run, there was no telling what would've happened."

My heart thundered. "You were there and kept it from everyone?"

"I rushed you to the car, desperate to get you help," Zeke huffed. "By the time I got you settled, Michael had pulled up on the other side of the palace. I saw him running in. I knew he'd save Samuel, and I needed to get you out of there."

Rubbing my temples, I tried to make sense of all of it. "So my memories were already gone?"

He shook his head. "No. I took you to a witch near the palace so she could heal you. I had to leave to get some herbs she needed. I tried to get the supplies from our pack's coven, but they refused, so my beta, Julian, got involved. He was my dearest friend besides your mother. He got the supplies for me and met me back at the witch's place. By then, she'd cast a spell to suppress your memories and killed my beta to lock down your magic. She told me to take you away before she decided to do something even more drastic... That's when I took you and ran back here."

Never trust witches. Zeke had chanted that mantra for all these years. Now I at least understood his resentment. A witch had killed his best friend—his beta—because of me. Even though that didn't make his treatment of me right, at least there was a reason he disliked me so much.

"Wait." Lucas scratched the back of his neck. "You're telling us a witch killed your beta to hide Callie's magic? But why?"

He shook his head. "I never try to understand the mind of a witch. I brought her here and found her a family and a home."

"Where she was mistreated and beaten," Bodey grated. "I'm not sure you did her any favors."

Zeke rolled his eyes. "Stop being so pussy-whipped." He gestured to me. "She is strong. She survived."

My heart ripped in two. I couldn't believe how nonchalant he was about the seventeen years I'd been trapped here. "You made me work with broken ribs! You allowed Charles and his gang of idiots to attack me on numerous occasions, each time worse than the last, and you took their side each time!" My anger was getting the best of me. I marched toward Zeke.

"I made you *strong*." He scoffed and pounded on his chest. "Something none of these other idiots could do. It should've *broken* you, and yet, here you stand." I could've sworn his face twisted into regret, but I wasn't sure for what—not treating me better or that I *hadn't* wound up broken?

I pushed a finger into Zeke's chest, and his breathing quickened. "You isolated me, made me utterly alone. I couldn't attend school with the rest of the pack, get a job in Halfway, or even breathe too far from my house. You even prevented Theo from being able to help me, making things worse for me when he did. You made me feel weak and pathetic...like I didn't matter."

"You're taking this too personally." Zeke smirked. "You always were quite the drama queen."

"You sick son of a bitch." Jack's face twisted in disgust. "You think what you did is right?"

"I did what was necessary," Zeke retorted, removing my finger from his chest.

His touch made me want to gag, the sensation like a slug crawling across my skin.

"Do *not* touch her," Bodey roared as he slammed Zeke into the garage door. "You didn't do what was necessary; you caged her inside the pack."

Zeke wrinkled his nose. "You kept Samuel prisoner too. You kept him in your pack—he didn't get to leave or do much of anything either. So don't act like what you did was better. We both kept them safe. Until now."

Son, he's goading you now. He wants us to threaten him so he can use this against us and divide our packs. Michael stood as still as a statue. I would have thought that he was hanging out with friends. His face remained relaxed as if we weren't interrogating a narcissist. In other words, I needed to learn from him because my parents weren't around to teach me how to interact with potential threats.

Trying to model his behavior, I rolled my shoulders to release some tension. "You're right. The past is irrelevant right now." We'd pushed him hard enough for today. If we kept on, he would feel even more threatened. Besides, I doubted he'd share more than he had.

Zeke visibly relaxed while Bodey's shoulders heaved.

Babe, please, I linked, touching his arm. *Your dad is right. He's going to tell people that we came to his pack land and threatened him.*

Good, Bodey countered, but I could already see him loosening his grip on Zeke.

I pushed calm toward him though it was damn hard. I was so angry with Zeke myself that I really wanted to treat him the way he'd allowed me to be treated my entire life. *It's hard, and it sucks, but we're king and queen now. We can't be the same people we were two days ago.*

This is for you, *not him.* Bodey let go then and stepped to my side once more.

Zeke huffed, yanking his shirt down. "If this is how you two are going to rule—by being bullies—"

"You're right. We won't resort to *your* tactics," I interjected, not wanting to hear a lecture from him about this.

Snorting, Jack shot me a wink and said, "She's got you there."

Zeke scowled, clearly not finding our commentary funny.

Even Miles struggled to keep the corners of his mouth from lifting.

"The real question is: How did the queen's scouts learn the location of the coronation?" Michael steepled his hands. "Do you have any idea how that happened?"

"Are you serious?" Zeke lifted his brows, taking a moment to scan each of us as we reformed a line. "You have Stevie in custody. She admitted to aiding the queen."

Samuel nodded. "True. Someone you put Callie in the same home with and who is part of your pack. And we're wondering how Stevie knew the location to tell the queen."

It all led back to Zeke, and he was a fool if he didn't realize we were all aware of that.

Straightening his shoulders, Zeke's face hardened. "I don't like what you're insinuating."

I smiled sweetly. "We aren't insinuating anything, just stating facts." I stopped myself from asking if that was guilt I heard. "You did leave the group to get some air before the coronation."

"Excuse me if I was upset that a pack member of mine went and got mated without informing me." Zeke scoffed. "And Queen Kel's wolves were already in the area due to the coronation dinner." Zeke huffed. "It's not a stretch to assume they realized the site would be close by."

He did have a point, but that didn't mean they'd know exactly where we were holding the ceremony. There were too many coincidences, so I tried to word my next observation carefully. "True, but they arrived just as the spell started…when it couldn't be stopped. Their timing was perfect."

"Well, didn't someone say the witch who cast the perimeter spell was killed?" Zeke rocked back on his heels. "So there's no telling how long they were there."

"Our wolves were running patrols." Bodey shook his head. "They would've seen them."

"Weren't our wolves farther out?" Zeke shrugged. "Maybe they pulled into the park somehow and came close by. Our wolves weren't manning the area around the park because of the perimeter spell. Hell, they could've had their own witch on hand, searching for magic and hiding them."

I clenched my hands, allowing my fingernails to cut into the skin on my palms. I relished the sting because I was going to lose my mind otherwise. My vision began to darken at the edges. All we were getting was this *what-if* shit when I'd hoped we'd be able to figure out all the answers. I should've known better. After all, Zeke was involved.

I rubbed my temples. "Stevie got there just as the coronation began."

Miles bit his bottom lip. "As much as I'd like to pin this on someone aiding the queen, I'm not sure if Stevie is the person who did it. If it was her, she learned of it last minute, and Queen Kel's wolves wouldn't have had time to take out the witch and then attack like that."

"Unless Stevie was there before..." Zeke lifted both hands.

"Then that's what we need to find out." Samuel placed his hands into his pockets. "Ask her more specific questions to see if she did aid them."

"Maybe you should bring her home to her pack." Zeke gestured to his house. "We have a basement we can keep her in. I can force her to talk to me."

I laughed. He had balls. I'd give him that. The problem was that I could force Stevie to talk to me as well, being her alpha's alpha, but doing that would only further damage our relationship.

Bodey shook his head. "After you just lost an informant? Not happening."

A deep snarl rumbled from Zeke. "I wasn't here when that happened."

Jack cackled. "That makes it worse. You left your pack unprepared."

"That's what I was thinking," Lucas said.

"They attacked my mate," Zeke snarled. "Do you really think that's something I wanted to happen?"

Shrugging, Bodey frowned. "You didn't make sure the prisoner you had was adequately guarded. I'm not sure if that was intentional or if you were just careless. Either way, you're not getting Stevie. She's safer with us."

Zeke's face reddened, and his neck corded. "I made one mistake—"

"A costly one," I interrupted. I didn't want the advisors to be the only ones to address him like this. As his former pack member, my instinct should have been to submit to him, but I didn't have to anymore, and my wolf wouldn't even let me appease him now that she was out and free. "One that we can't repeat, especially when my sister is involved."

Even if I was mad at Stevie, I'd never want anything bad to happen to her. I did believe her as to why she'd aided the queen, even if I didn't agree with her logic. She'd done it to protect me, and maybe if she'd been the one being treated like shit, I'd have done the same for her. I'd like to think I wouldn't, but fear and trauma had a way of distorting our realities and helping us rationalize things that we wouldn't normally do.

"Listen here—" Zeke started, and his tone had me snapping.

Before I even realized what I was doing, my wolf surged forward. Power rolled off me and into him. The time had arrived for Zeke to learn a very important lesson.

CHAPTER EIGHT

POWER FLOODED MY BODY, but there was no tingling to indicate fur was about to sprout like there was during a shift. My blood thrummed as Zeke's eyes widened and his bottom lip trembled.

I could feel my wolf surging and knew that the blue of my eyes had to be nearly white from the power she sent through me.

Bodey's shock struck me, but I pushed the distraction away. Putting Zeke in his place was my focus.

A faint hint of spice emanated from Bodey, indicating that he'd become aroused. His voice popped into my head. *Damn, babe. You're sexy as hell like this.*

Sweet-talk me later. Though my wolf was thrilled that we'd affected him. *Down, girl.* I didn't need those types of thoughts when staring this asshole down.

Taking a menacing step forward, I crowded Zeke, his overly musky cologne nearly choking me. "My sister will remain with Bodey and me where we know she'll be protected." My voice sounded deeper, raspy, with a hint of my alpha will laced in. "I get that you don't like it, but you're outvoted."

"Just as the law states that the majority vote of the advisors is final, if the royal by blood wants something done, unless it risks the safety of others, the advisors don't have to vote." Samuel stood tall, calmly stating facts he'd grown up learning due to everyone believing he would be king. "So Callie isn't required to ask the advisors. If you were best friends with our *mother* and a knowledgeable advisor, surely you know that."

Even as Samuel spoke, I glared Zeke down, not wanting to break the stare-off the two of us were having. If I broke first, he'd view me as weaker.

"Please. That was when a king was the true leader." Zeke's nose wrinkled as sweat beaded his forehead. "A woman deemed the true leader? That's laughable."

I inhaled sharply, a low growl vibrating from my throat. Maybe that was the real reason he'd hidden me. He hadn't wanted *me* to be the one in charge. Bastard.

"Well, the *king* agrees with his mate," Bodey spat.

Zeke grimaced, and his eyes lowered to the ground, *finally*. I hadn't struggled at all, other than having to look at his face the entire time. But it wasn't over.

"You, a king?" Zeke sneered. "Of course, out of everyone here, *you'd* find a way to mate with her." He took a step back and smacked into the garage door.

Fire scorched my veins. "Is that why Theo was so desperate to mate with me? He wanted to be king?" Had Theo also known and left me in the dark?

"Theo had no clue you were the heir to the throne." Zeke rolled his eyes. "Don't worry."

No wonder he hadn't tried to dissuade Theo from mating with me. I'd found it strange that he hadn't been upset over the thought.

"I'm still lost." Lucas pursed his lips. "Why didn't you tell anyone that Samuel wasn't the rightful heir since we were having the coronation? What if Callie hadn't been there to receive the mark?"

My breath caught. I hadn't even considered that, but if the spell could be performed only once, what *would* have happened if I hadn't been there? Would Samuel have been marked, or would the magic have been able to sense me and thus done nothing? The Southwest queen might have been able to take over this territory even more easily.

"Her wolf was weak and her magic repressed." Zeke gestured toward me and continued, "I didn't know she'd mated and somehow freed her magic. I wasn't sure if she even could be marked."

He had some solid reasoning, but he couldn't have *known.* We were all lucky that everything worked out. The what-ifs were futile now. It was over, and I had the mark, though I couldn't help thinking Samuel was still far better suited for this.

Moving backward to gain more distance from Zeke, I ran a hand down my face. "It doesn't matter. Right now, we need to determine how Stevie was conversing with the queen and whether she was working with anyone else." I didn't want Zeke to control the conversation and keep us from getting anywhere.

"Good point." Zeke smirked. "Hopefully you can get those answers before something else happens. At least, next time, it'll be on you, not me."

Bodey's jaw cracked from how hard he clenched his teeth. "Are you threatening us?"

Someone growled menacingly...and then my chest vibrated, making me realize it was me.

Laughing a little too loudly, Zeke lifted both hands. "You two need to calm down, especially if you expect to rule over our territory. We don't need a couple of hotheads throwing their weight around whenever someone doesn't agree with them."

Michael gasped. "Is that the story you want to create? I'd

reconsider whatever you're planning. They aren't being irrational—they're new and worried about their people and an advisor who is clearly out of line."

"Because I don't conform to their way of thinking?" Zeke scoffed. "Please, I was respected by King Richard and Queen Mila; otherwise, I wouldn't be standing here."

"If I remember well, you and she had an argument earlier that day." Michael's jaw clenched. "I was waiting for you to bring that up."

Zeke's eyes flashed with anger. "That is irrelevant and *none* of your concern."

"Maybe it is." I leveled my gaze at him and sneered. "Especially since she died shortly afterward, and I conveniently don't have any memories." I *had* to get them back. I suspected if I did, I'd get a lot of answers Zeke didn't want me to have.

"And there you go again, accusing me of things because you want a scapegoat." Zeke's face twisted. "I shouldn't expect more from the likes of all of you."

We need to be careful, Michael linked. *For him to spew things like that, he's got an angle, and he could easily influence other packs, especially those in his state.*

Bodey froze, and I could feel his revulsion and anger swirling between us. Surprisingly, he held more intense negative feelings toward Zeke than I did, and I'd grown up in Zeke's pack. We'd come here to prod Zeke into revealing answers, yet he was using the same strategy to gain ammunition against us. We had to stop playing into his hands.

"We aren't trying to blame anyone." I spoke slowly, trying to keep my voice calm. "And if we came across that way, my sincerest apologies."

Don't apologize to this douchebag, Bodey linked, his loathing choking our bond. *He doesn't deserve to breathe the same air as you.*

I love you. I pushed warmth toward him, wanting to offset his hatred. We had to get through this without creating a permanent enemy who would actively seek war against us. We were already divided enough, and Queen Kel wasn't going to stop her attacks. She'd put pressure on us while our people were struggling to accept me as the queen when everyone had been prepared for Samuel to rule. *And I agree that it's hard to work with him, but right now, we can't handle more of a rift between our people.*

Bodey blew out a breath.

"Well, I guess that counts for something." Zeke buffed his nails on his shirt.

My stomach clenched. Yeah, now I wished I hadn't said those words either, but I already did, so I needed to lean on it. "It's just that when you said it would be our fault if something happened to Stevie, it did sound threatening." I tried to smile kindly. "So, can you tell us what you meant by that?"

"What I meant was that the Southwest queen is unpredictable, and she surely has something planned." Zeke rubbed his hands together like he had all the answers. "If Stevie knows things, Kel will want her captured or dead. So maybe you should spend your time interrogating her instead of me."

Yeah, he was playing a game, and I hated how smart Zeke was. All the men were tense; I could feel it through my pack links. I gritted my teeth, wanting to lash out again.

He continued. "After all, I'd hate for you to be wasting time here while Stevie's injured, or worse, due to your negligence. That would be so unfortunate."

"Ah, yes." Jack tilted his head. "Because you care *so much* about your pack members. Like when the four of us found Callie being attacked by five of your wolves, and you punished Callie for it instead of them. I understand that you're such a *caring* alpha."

Yeah, there was no way we could accept those accusations after my olive branch and Zeke snapping it in half. He'd always held resentment toward this group, and now that I'd become one of them, I could very likely be the thing that ruined Zeke's control completely.

Even though Zeke had treated me like shit, could I really complain? At the end of the day, had Bodey, Lucas, Jack, and Miles not run into me during that original attack at Hells Canyon, I might not be standing here with them right now.

"She's fine now, isn't she?" Zeke said, motioning toward me as if we didn't know who he was talking about.

"Because we interfered," Bodey raged, his chest heaving. *Before this is over, I'm going to kill him and relish every drop as the blood flows from his body.*

I wasn't sure how much longer Bodey would be able to not punch him. Michael's warning that Zeke was trying to make us look bad was the only thing holding him back.

Maybe there was one saving grace. "Where is Theo? Shouldn't he be present for this conversation? He's taking over the pack now that the coronation is over."

All smugness vanished from Zeke's face. "Under the circumstances, that won't be happening." He tugged at the collar of his shirt. "Theo is badly injured, and Queen Kel just initiated a war. Handing Oregon over to him right now wouldn't be smart."

"That's not what we agreed to." Miles crossed his arms, causing his muscles to bulge.

"I'm well aware, but things have changed. Between the attack on our pack and the turmoil the Southwest queen is creating, it's better if I stay in charge for now, considering all my years of successful leadership."

Michael scoffed. "You act as if the other advisors and I, who served alongside you, don't have any influence over the current royal advisors' decisions. We do; they listen to us, which Theo would as well. The only difference is they get the final say, but they respect and hear our opinions."

"Are you worried that Theo won't listen to you?" Samuel arched a brow.

"My son knows his place." Zeke slashed the air.

My throat constricted as realization weighed on me. Zeke had always dominated and controlled Theo as he did me, but instead of the hard labor Zeke had always assigned me, he'd controlled his son through words and by threatening others. Having an overbearing father like Zeke couldn't be easy, so maybe Theo's strength had been in trying to make Zeke happy and keep the peace so others wouldn't be hurt.

I swallowed, knowing that Bodey wouldn't like my next words, but Theo was destined to be an advisor and work with us. "Where is Theo? I'd like to see him, especially if he's that bad off." Theo had helped me when I'd been injured and heartbroken; the least I could do was stop in and check on him. Besides, I had a few questions I wanted to ask him.

"He was adamant about recuperating in his own house." Zeke gestured toward the pale-blue one-story next door. "Tina goes over there five times a day, making sure he's taking his medicine, eating, and drinking so he can heal, but his injuries were severe. It's gonna take a couple of days for him to rebound."

"Why don't you have a witch heal him?" Miles placed his hands behind his back.

Zeke scowled. "Need I remind you that a witch messed with Callie's mind and killed my beta?" His jaw twitched. "We just went over what witches are capable of."

I think my presence is making him even more ornery. I'm

going to visit Theo and give you all a few minutes to see if you can get any more information from him since he isn't thrilled with me being queen. I also wanted a chance to speak to Theo alone, but I kept that part to myself.

Displeasure wafted through Bodey, but he nodded. *I'd like to go with you.*

He might not say as much if you're there. I frowned, not wanting to tell my mate no, but also not wanting to just say yes to make him happy.

Babe, he might not, but that prick was trying desperately to get you to agree to form a mate bond with him. Though I trust you and know nothing will happen, the thought of you being alone with him in his house does not sit well with my human or *wolf sides.*

When he put it that way, I saw his point. If I were in his shoes, I'd feel the same way.

I wasn't thinking. Of course, come with me, please. I had no right to make him feel insecure, and the peace that filtered between us after my agreement showed me I'd made the right call.

"So it's okay if Bodey and I check on him?" I asked out loud while taking Bodey's hand. I could've linked with Zeke, but the thought sent a shudder through me. I didn't want to share any intimate link with him even if it would feel the same as linking to everyone else. Besides, it would probably help if I didn't. Doing it would serve as yet another reminder that I was his queen.

Zeke frowned. "He's probably sleeping and shouldn't be disturbed."

"We can be quiet." Bodey smiled a little too widely, revealing his teeth.

"Fine." Zeke's nostrils flared. "Just don't bother him if he's resting."

Bodey and I took off as Lucas asked, "Do you mind if we look at where the prisoner was held?"

"I went over everything," Zeke huffed.

"I'm sure you did," Michael agreed calmly. "I'm sure we won't find anything, but we'd still like to take a look. Five heads are better than one."

For my entire life, Zeke had been difficult about everything. I'd hoped that the imminent threat would change his tune. Clearly not.

"Fine, but you won't find anything." When I glanced back, Zeke was stalking toward the back of his house, followed by our group.

Bodey and I continued to Theo's door. As soon as I pushed the light-brown door open, Theo croaked out, "Mom?"

My pulse pounded. Thank gods he wasn't asleep. "No, it's Callie."

"Callie?" He coughed and then groaned. "Yer 'ere?" he slurred.

Tina must be giving him that pain medicine she'd tried to give me.

As with the other houses in the neighborhood, the front door opened into the living room. Bodey followed me through it toward the kitchen, passing the small hallway on the right that led to a bathroom and two guest bedrooms. A few steps before the kitchen, I turned left down the other hall that led to two more bedrooms on the left and the garage door in front of us. Through the second door, I entered the master bedroom, where Theo lay in his bed.

Should I be concerned that you know exactly where his room is? Bodey linked, his jealousy slamming through our bond.

I froze. *What? No! All the houses here have the same floor plan. This is where the master bedroom is in each one. I've never been inside his house before.* He was an unmated pack member, and I'd refused to visit him here to prevent us from becoming the focus of rumors. I'd believed his dad would've punished him for "dating" me, but now I wasn't so sure.

Scanning the room, I took in the warm browns and earth tones. On his chestnut wood nightstand, there was a picture of Theo and me taken when we were around twelve, and there were personal things, such as Theo's guns, lining the walls.

When I reached the foot of the bed, Theo's topaz eyes focused on me. His normally caramel-brown hair was dark and matted to his face, which showed deep scratches that were starkly pronounced since his olive skin was a shade lighter than usual and looked unhealthy.

He gave me a faint smile. "You came to see me. I knew you would."

However, when Bodey stepped in beside me, Theo's smile faltered.

"Why is *he* here?" Theo's nose wrinkled.

Lovely, another pack reunion that was going super well.

Bodey snarled, "Because I'm her *mate*. That's why."

"The two of us wanted to check on you." I cut my eyes to Bodey, glaring as I linked, *Please, don't. We need him to be willing to talk to me. That's why I initially said no to you coming.*

He started it, Bodey sighed, his guilt flowing into me.

Not bothering to reply to him, I sat on the edge of the bed and smiled sadly at Theo. His neck had claw marks on the sides, and blood from a gash in his shoulder had stained the sheet draped around his chest. He must have gotten slashed a few more times after Bodey and I escaped the area.

"I've had better days," he said stiffly as if it hurt to talk. He scanned my face, and when he reached my neck, he stiffened. "Holy shit, you really are marked! I thought I saw it on your wolf form, but I wasn't certain. How is that even possible?" he gasped.

I lifted a brow. "You didn't know?"

"Of course not. Why would you ask that?" Theo tried to sit up but couldn't rise more than an inch before groaning and giving up. There was no hint of him lying.

"Because your dad knew from the moment he brought me here when I was five."

His jaw dropped. "He *did*? He never told me, but that makes sense. He spent so much time with the royal family." His face twisted. "So why was your wolf hidden, and why didn't he tell anyone?"

Some of the worry I'd had about him betraying me flitted away. "He said he didn't tell anyone because he was protecting me, especially since my magic had been blocked by the witch who killed his beta."

Bodey cleared his throat as if reminding us he was still in the room. "How did you not recognize her? Didn't you spend time with her as a kid like the other advisors and I did? We hung out with you, too, sometimes."

My head snapped to Bodey, and I linked, *We hung out as children?*

He nodded. *We were close, you and I. When I met you as an adult, you actually reminded me of yourself as a child, but I didn't realize you were the same person.*

"Dad never took Mom or me to meet the royal family." Theo bit his bottom lip. "Entire weeks would go by when we wouldn't see him. He said being around them was too much of a risk and that the two of us needed to stay home."

There had to be more to this story. It didn't feel complete, but Theo's eyes were closing.

We were running out of time to question him. "Do you have

any idea how the queen's wolves knew where and when to attack us?"

His eyes shut, and I reached over and nudged his hands gently. "Theo, did you hear me?"

He shook his head. "I wish I did. I want to kill the bastards," he murmured.

I blew out a breath. He was fading, and he needed rest to heal. We wouldn't get answers with him in this state. I'd link with him later and try to get them.

"Okay, we'll leave so you can rest." When I'd been seriously injured, I hadn't liked having people around. "Do you need anything before we leave?"

He shook his head and then snored faintly.

Slowly, I stood and tiptoed across the room into the hallway, Bodey right behind me.

When we walked out the front door, the guys were missing from Zeke's yard. Bodey linked, *Any luck?*

We're checking out the area now, Samuel replied. *It'll take a few minutes.*

A part of me wanted to scan the area with them, but I knew that wouldn't be wise with Zeke around. And I was putting off the inevitable. *While you do that, I'm going to see my parents and talk to them about Stevie.*

Sounds good, Lucas replied. *We'll meet you there.*

Bodey got into the driver's seat as I climbed into the passenger side, and we drove to my parents' place.

My stomach dropped when I saw Charles, Trevor, Pearl, and my parents standing in our yard, talking.

When the car stopped and I climbed out, Pearl laughed bitterly, her blue eyes flat. "Look who finally decided to show up." Her light-blonde hair lifted in the cool breeze.

I blew out a breath, expecting no less from her as Bodey walked over to me.

Charles's dark gaze landed on my neck, and he grimaced. This was already going so well.

But when Mom turned around, the look on her face almost drove me to my knees.

CHAPTER NINE

MOM'S normally aqua eyes darkened as she stared me down.

I hadn't known what to expect from her, but it was definitely not *this*. The possibilities that had floated through my head were anger, hurt, or some variation of the two. Not the look of pure disgust etched on her face.

Jaw clenched, she pushed back her shoulder-length, ashy-blonde hair. For a moment, I almost didn't recognize her. Stevie was blood family, but Mom had always cared about me, even if it hadn't been as deeply as she had her biological daughters.

Now, there was no concern for my well-being anywhere on her face.

Chest aching, I kept my head held high. I hadn't done anything wrong.

Bodey stepped beside me, taking my hand. He linked, *I'm right here. You aren't alone.*

The warmth of his love helped dull the pain. Those words were exactly what I needed to hear. I'd felt so alone for so long, but I wasn't anymore. I had my fated mate.

Forcing my gaze from Mom, I looked at Dad. He seemed more like himself—indifferent, his usual emotion when it came to me. He was never cruel, but neither was he affectionate. We just existed with one another. His russet-brown eyes homed in on Bodey's and my joined hands as the cool early March breeze ruffled his short, dirty-blond hair.

Mom pointed at me, her lavender sweater inching up to show a sliver of light-tan skin. "All this time, you never mentioned to any of us that you were our queen."

My head tilted back and my breath caught. "Are you being serious right now? I didn't even know I was the heir until I received this mark." I pulled down my shirt a little more to reveal most of the tattoo.

"And instead of trying to elevate the family that protected you, you thanked us by not only throwing Stevie in jail but allowing Zeke to be the one to tell us," she spat, her hand shaking. "Now I wish we never took you in."

A punch to the gut would hurt less than the agony ripping through me. My lungs seized, and Bodey's anger pulsed between us. He released my hand and wrapped his arm around me, our connection springing to life and alleviating some of the heartbreak.

"Stevie was working with the Southwest queen, which resulted in Callie being attacked by those scouts, and you say that to my *mate*?" Bodey asked, his voice between a growl and a rasp. "The person who's the most innocent of *all* of us?"

Charles's dark eyes narrowed as he sneered. "At least we have answers as to why he was so protective of her and decided to mate with her. He must have known and wanted to be king." He waved a hand dismissively. "If I'd known, I would've treated her differently too."

Bodey snarled, and Pearl snapped her head in his direction. Her eyes bulged, which made her light-blue irises seem small.

Dropping his arm, Bodey marched over to Charles. Mom took a few steps closer to Dad while Pearl remained on the other side of Charles, not interfering, which spoke volumes—she didn't like what Charles had said either. But she shouldn't have been surprised. Charles was an entitled jerk who thought the world should bow down to him.

All I could see was Bodey's back, but his muscles were so tense that they bunched underneath his shirt. Maybe I should interfere, but Charles deserved to have his ass beaten, especially considering how he'd treated me.

"Say something like that again, and I won't hold back. This is your one warning. You won't get another one...*ever*," Bodey vowed. "Callie is my *fated mate*, and I'll be damned if I let a pompous, little-dicked wannabe alpha insult our relationship or insinuate you want her. She's *mine* and your queen, so you best fucking get in line."

My body heated, and my wolf brushed my mind, telling me she felt the same way. Not only was our mate hot, but damn, he was even more scorching when he was claiming me.

Eyebrows raised, Dad glanced at me and then Bodey. This hadn't been how I wanted to inform my parents that I'd gotten mated, but nothing in my life ever went according to plan.

I focused back on my parents, not wanting to spend any more of my attention on Charles. "Holding Stevie is the last thing I wanted. But as queen, what else could I do?" I released my shirt and placed a hand over the top of my chest, where the tattoo was now partially hidden once again. This time, I felt the shadows of the moon whisper under my palm. "She aided another territory, and our wolves were hurt. I'm the queen *no one* expected, but I refuse to be a pushover."

Pearl scoffed, crossing her arms. "There's no way you didn't know you were queen. You might not smell of a lie, but I'm not buying it."

Bodey pivoted to Pearl.

I didn't want him to threaten her...at least not in front of Mom and Dad. *It's a legitimate concern.*

Not the way she said it.

Under Bodey's gaze, Pearl flinched, once again proving that she wasn't an idiot.

"Tell me how I was supposed to know." I lifted both hands. "I couldn't shift, which resulted in *him,*" I said, pointing at Charles, "giving me hell at every opportunity. When you all attacked me that night, if I could've shifted, don't you think I would have instead of trying to fight in human form?"

For once, Pearl seemed speechless. Her mouth opened and closed, reminding me of a fish out of water. At this point, I wouldn't be surprised if she started flopping around on the ground.

"Believe me. I wish I had known instead of Zeke being the only person who knew who I was and that I was alive." Bitterness stung like razors against my throat. "Even now that my wolf is free, I still can't remember my life prior to coming here. Apparently, some witch spelled me." I gritted my teeth, trying to not let my pain and anger slip out more than it already had. I didn't want them to know how much this affected me, certain it would get back to Zeke. I needed him to think I was taking this all in stride so he wouldn't think he had power over me.

"But still. Your sister? She wouldn't do anything to h...hurt our pack." Mom's voice broke as she placed a shaky hand on her stomach. "Zeke said you blocked the pack link, so she can't communicate with us."

I inhaled sharply. Good ol' Zeke was already working on turning everyone against me. I should've known.

Bodey ran a hand through his hair and glanced at me. His brown hair settled back into his eyes, just the way I liked it.

Zeke's a fucking prick, Bodey linked with me.

Oh, I'm well aware. I smoothed my expression. "She was

feeding information to Queen Kel, Mom. I didn't want to believe it either, but she admitted to us that she had, and there was no stench of a lie. I was attacked outside the real estate office because she informed the queen that I'd been with the advisors. I blocked her from pack linking in case she wasn't working alone and could communicate information back to the queen. It wasn't so that she couldn't talk with you."

Both Mom and Dad sniffed the air, clearly hoping to catch me in a lie. They'd rather I be the awful adopted daughter than have their youngest natural child turn out to be a traitor.

The biggest problem for us with Zeke's strategy was that if we weren't careful, it would be extremely effective. Most of the pack was indifferent to me, and a handful of them strongly disliked me. Even with the mark of a royal on my chest, this entire pack had disregarded me for nearly my whole life, and that would take time to change. It would be even harder with Zeke actively working against me.

"If you think I'm trying to cover up something, please ask more questions." I dropped my hands to my sides. "I have no reason to lie to you. Get close enough so you can smell me right away."

Bodey shook his head. "They're not getting anywhere near you with the way they're acting. I won't allow it."

"Oh, so you're the alpha in the relationship, despite her being the heir." Charles snorted. "Thank gods. For a second—"

Heat blasting through our bond, Bodey spun and punched Charles in the jaw. Charles's head snapped back as Mom and Pearl gasped.

Groaning, Charles lifted his head, eyes narrowed as he stared down my mate. Pearl scrambled to his side, trying to touch his jaw, but he pushed her away and snarled, "I'm fine."

"Yeah, because I held back." Bodey clenched and

unclenched his fist. "Run your mouth again, and it'll be worse. I'll make sure I leave you worse off than you did Callie."

My mate was dangerously close to losing it. I moved, so I stood behind him and placed my hands on his back. His muscles relaxed marginally, but the anger still roiled steadily inside him.

He cracked his neck, his attention never leaving Charles. "Let me be clear. I may be king, but Callie is the queen by birthright. She is stronger than any wolf I've ever encountered, and unlike you, I'm not threatened by it. Even when her wolf was trapped, there was strength in her, which is why your threatened ass always targeted her...always wanted to break her. That won't be happening anymore."

"Why is he even here?" I gestured to Charles, looking at my parents. "He's not part of the family."

"Because he's my *boyfriend*." Pearl wrinkled her nose. "Who your mate assaulted!"

I wanted to hang my head and cry. No matter what I did, even if I begged for their forgiveness, becoming the weak wolf they'd always desired, Pearl and Charles would still despise me. They would back whatever story Zeke concocted as long as I got harmed in the end. "Bodey punched him for talking ill of your queen. Shouldn't you be happy about that?" I held my head higher, wanting her to know that the urge to cower wasn't part of me.

"You aren't my queen." Pearl sneered as her body quivered. "And I don't believe you. Stevie would *never* do something like that."

"Pearl," Dad warned as his eyes glowed, indicating that he was talking to her through their pack link.

Pearl's hatred of me had been bottled up for so long; it was time for it to explode. I'd give her this one chance to let it out. I understood how resentment brewed because I felt similar things toward her.

"No." I shook my head. "Stevie wouldn't normally, but all the advisors, Samuel, the advisors' parents, *Theo, Zeke*, and I heard her words. Didn't you think it was odd the morning of the coronation when she ran off with the car? You can ask any of us who were there what happened."

"Yeah, since you've made it so I can't link to her and hear it myself." Pearl's hands quivered.

I strolled over to my *beloved* sister and stared her in the eyes. I asked, "Do you want to know why she did what she did?" I wanted to be close so that she'd know every word I spoke was the truth.

"I do," Mom said from the other side of Charles.

"She said it was to protect our family due to how this pack treated Mom, Dad, her, and *me*." I watched Pearl's face as I continued, taking in every twitch. "Especially *me*, due to what Charles, *you*, and your friends did to me. The queen promised her a safe and respected place for the *four* of us in the Southwest Territory if Stevie helped her."

Pearl's expression sagged, the tang of regret hitting my nose.

"Gods," Mom murmured. "My baby girl."

"And despite her trying to protect you, you imprisoned her?" Dad's chest heaved.

I lifted my hands. "I had to. I'm queen now, and she put everyone in this territory at risk. Even good intentions don't make a wrong thing right." I loathed hurting them, but my hands were tied.

Bodey moved back beside me, the two of us shoulder to shoulder. "The advisors agreed, as did Samuel. That decision was hard for Callie, believe me. I felt it."

My parents leaned against one another, taking that in.

I could offer them something of a compromise. After all, they were the only thing close to parents I had now. "When I get back home, I'll let her call you. That way, you can hear everything she has to say and talk to her for a little while."

"And we're supposed to trust what she says?" Pearl crossed her arms. "For all we know, you could force her to confirm what you just told us, and we wouldn't know any better."

There Pearl was, trying to sow more doubt between my parents and me. I hated that it was so easy for her to do that—to paint me as the villain.

When Bodey casually placed an arm around my shoulders, I froze. I'd expected him to be angry at Pearl, but instead, it was like he'd banked the fire inside himself.

He cleared his throat. "Good point. I'm thinking Mr. and Mrs. Beck should either ride back with us or drive themselves up so they can talk to their daughter face to face."

"Why am I not invited to see my *sister*?" Pearl thrust out her chest. "You'd think I'd be given that courtesy too."

"If you hadn't taken part in routinely being cruel to your sister—the queen and my mate—you'd be welcome." Bodey didn't bother to hide his contempt. "Not only that, but you insulted her today, knowing that she is now your leader. Disrespectful people are not invited into our home."

Charles snarled. "We've been there before. Why does it matter now? She has a right—"

"Theo brought you, and it wasn't his place." Bodey stared Charles down, his wolf surging forward. His eyes took on a glow. "And if you keep trying to argue with us or spread rumors about us, then you'll only prove that you're as dumb as I thought and will make an enemy of us."

"Are you threatening me?" Charles averted his gaze despite his eyes twitching as if he was trying not to look away.

Bodey beamed. "Oh, I'm not threatening you. I'm merely informing you of the consequences if your ass doesn't get in line."

I leaned into my mate's shoulder, enjoying having him at my side. I linked, *Just remember that there's no telling what Zeke told them. Dad and Mom didn't know what really happened, so it made sense that they were upset with me.*

Yeah, your parents are less angry now, but I think Charles and Pearl have gotten worse, he replied, leaning down and kissing the top of my head in front of everyone.

Couldn't disagree there. That resentment had festered for years. They'd wanted to break me, but instead, I was stronger than them now. Accepting that had to be bitter for wolves like Pearl's and Charles's...not that it gave them a pass.

"If your offer is sincere, I'd like to come and see Stevie." Mom bit her bottom lip.

Dad nodded. "And it's best if we go today since we work tomorrow. We can drive ourselves."

That was what I'd figured they'd say. Zeke wouldn't like them staying with us; he liked to have all his pack members in one place. "Sounds good to me." I gestured toward the house. "Do you mind if I grab some of my stuff?" Though Jasmine's clothes worked, they were too tight and short for true comfort.

"Of course." Mom waved me toward the front door. "I'll grab some bags so you can pack."

Dad, Bodey, and I entered the house while Charles and Pearl headed toward his home, most likely to tell the rest of their crew what had just gone on and make me look bad. Moments like these used to scare me, but not anymore. I had Bodey, and I wasn't stuck here. Though they might be a threat, we'd suss them out the same as we would Zeke.

Bodey and I went into Stevie's and my room, his eyes scanning everything. He chuckled. "I love that fuchsia is your favorite color. It fits you."

The room was small with Stevie's full bed on the left, covered by her navy-blue comforter, and my full bed covered by my fuchsia comforter on the right. Between the beds was our shared white nightstand.

I shrugged. "I don't know why, but the color just always spoke to me."

I went to the closet across from Stevie's bed and began pulling out my clothes. As soon as Dad brought in a few pieces of luggage, Bodey packed the bags while I sorted through everything. I even grabbed a few outfits for Stevie so she could wear her own clothes since I didn't know how long she'd be there.

Soon, Bodey and I went back into the kitchen, Mom and Dad waiting patiently. Dad had the keys in his hand.

Everyone was ready.

Bodey lifted the bags. "Thanks for this. We'll need to pick up my dad and Samuel at Zeke's before taking off."

Dad nodded. "Sounds good; we'll follow you from here."

We walked out the front door, and I heard the lock turn. By the time Bodey and I had tossed the bags into the trunk of his Mercedes, the garage behind us opened, and then Dad and Mom drove out.

As we climbed into the SUV, Bodey linked with the others, *Are you ready to leave?*

We're finishing up now, Michael replied.

Nothing alarming wafted from them, so I asked, *Did you find anything?*

Nothing substantial, Samuel replied, his frustration leaking through. *Something isn't right though. Since only Zeke's mate was home when the captive escaped, it makes sense that there wasn't a struggle. She has a bump on her head from where they knocked her out, but something's off. The prisoner's chains didn't have as much scent on them as I expected.*

My heart sank. Could Stevie have taken them off? That wasn't outside the realm of possibility. *We'll need to ask Stevie about it.*

Bodey frowned as he turned down the road to Zeke's. *I agree but don't say anything to Zeke. We can't trust him with this information...not yet.*

Oh, don't worry, Michael laughed. *We definitely didn't say anything to him.*

When Zeke's house came into view, Jack, Lucas, and Miles were climbing into the Navigator while Samuel and Michael stood at the foot of the driveway, waiting on us. Zeke and Tina were standing in their front doorway.

A shiver ran down my spine, seeing the darkness in Zeke's eyes. When he glanced behind me at my parents, he scowled and stalked down his front walk as Michael and Samuel climbed into the SUV.

"What's going on here?" He gestured at my parents' car.

I rolled down my window. "They're coming to visit Stevie. That's all. They'll be back tonight."

Zeke frowned. "And why wasn't I asked about that?"

"Bodey and I invited them." I gestured to my mark, forcing him to acknowledge who I was.

He huffed and crossed his arms. "It still would've been nice to have a conversation. That's how a true partnership works."

My face burned. I hated that he was right. Even if I didn't trust him, he was still the territory advisor—unless we wanted to cause even more turmoil right now by replacing him, and I couldn't risk it. "You're right. I'm sorry."

Bodey growled lightly. *Don't apologize to him. He doesn't deserve it.*

But he's right, and I don't want to be like him. I want to admit when I'm wrong.

Zeke smirked, my apology no doubt exactly what he'd wanted. "You're still new at this, but don't let it happen again." He nodded and went back to Tina then turned to watch us.

My hand clenched on the door handle. His gloating made me wish I hadn't apologized.

Jack backed out, and soon we were pulling out of the neighborhood. And I couldn't stop myself from praying that I'd never have to come back here again.

ABOUT THIRTY MINUTES from our pack neighborhood, my tension from being around Zeke was gone. We still had questions that needed answers, but at least we weren't around *him.*

"Perfect" by Ed Sheeran came on the radio, and Bodey smiled and squeezed my hand. Our mate bond thrummed with love and affection, no doubt because both of us were thinking about the last time we'd heard that song.

The song he'd played and sung to me just before we'd completed our mate bond. Before my wolf was freed and we'd discovered we were fated.

So when we were young, did you suspect I was your fated mate?

You know, thinking about it now, I should have. He chuckled. *I felt a strange sensation right around the time you were born, but I was too young to put it together. I'm only four years older than you. But I remember thinking you were cute and kind, and no matter what, after you started walking, you'd always follow me around.*

I turned toward him, taking in his strong jawline and full lips. *It's a fact I'd be drawn to you at any age.*

He winked. *Oh, I know. I can feel what you're thinking as you look at me now.*

My face flamed, but not enough to make me force my gaze from his.

But I will say, every day, I thought about you. Bodey's blue eyes lightened. *For the past seventeen years, I could see your face and hear your voice. I assumed it was because we lost an amazing future queen. I never imagined it was because you were alive and my fated mate.*

Heart aching, I blew out a breath. *I hate that I can't remember you or the night of the fire.* I was positive those memories had answers that I couldn't access.

Bodey nodded. *We'll talk to Dina when we get home. We'll search for the witch who repressed your memories and your wolf.* His thumb caressed my wrist, and the jolt between us intensified.

But as we were pulling onto the road that led us home, someone from our pack linked, *We smell unfamiliar wolves.*

CHAPTER TEN

MY JAW POPPED from the pressure of my teeth clamping together. Three attacks in three days was excessive...unless the queen was making it clear that she meant war.

Bodey replied, *What do you mean, "smell"? Is our perimeter not being watched?*

There are twenty of us out here, but our land is over five hundred acres, so it's hard to be everywhere at once.

My stomach dropped, and guilt pulsed from Bodey.

You're right. Bodey gripped the steering wheel tight, making his knuckles blanch as he stomped on the gas. *How many are there?*

The scents are jumbled. I don't even know how to explain it, but a few feet farther toward our land, there are five distinct scents.

Jumbled? That *was* odd. Normally, each scent could be distinguished. Even in groups, wolf scents don't get mixed, so this made no sense. Something else had to be going on.

I focused on what we knew; their numbers were small. I linked to everyone in the vehicle, *Why would they have such small numbers?*

Because of Stevie, Michael replied, his fear leaking through our connection, constricting my throat. *They aren't here to attack...they're here to get her out of our custody.*

The Mercedes roared into the pack neighborhood, Bodey slamming on the brakes and stopping between our white house and his parents' next door. The four of us jumped out of the car, not bothering to shut our doors as we raced toward my sister.

Jack's Navigator and my parents' cars rolled to a stop behind us as Jack's voice popped into Bodey's and my heads. *What the fuck is going on?*

The queen is going after Stevie, I replied, not bothering to glance behind me.

I broke away from the other three, running a little faster, and cut to the right as we reached the back of Janet and Michael's house. When I reached the corner, I turned and clomped down the white cement stairs, only to find the dark-brown basement door wide open.

Five scents hit me, just as our pack member had said. Dammit, I didn't even know his name, and he was my pack, but that was an issue I'd deal with later. Right then, I had to check on my sister.

As I got closer to the bottom of the stairs, the stench of copper filled my nose, confirming my worst fear.

Blood.

"Stevie!" Mom screamed, cold tendrils of fear shooting into me from one of the pack links, making me aware it was my connection with her. "Did something happen to my daughter?" Her voice cracked.

When I reached the bottom of the stairs, I forced myself to look inside, though my body wanted to freeze. Whatever I found, I didn't doubt it would haunt my sleep.

Stevie lay on the floor with a knife in her chest. Her shirt was stained crimson, and blood puddled underneath her.

Do you see them? Samuel asked.

Luckily, Bodey was now racing down the stairs to me.

A sob strangled me as I dropped to my knees beside Stevie. Her eyes were open, and they turned toward me as a stream of blood oozed from one corner of her mouth. Her heartbeat was steady but weaker than normal, her breathing shallow.

"Fuck," Bodey growled and dropped beside me. He scanned my sister, taking in everything.

Even that word wasn't accurate enough to describe what I was feeling. Yanking on every warm bond, I linked to anyone and everyone nearby. *I need someone to bring Dina here* now. *My sister is injured and dying.*

Three pairs of frantic feet pounded down to the basement, and I wasn't surprised to see my parents barrel in and drop down on the other side of Stevie.

What? Janet linked. *Stevie's hurt? How the hell is that possible? I'm in the house and didn't hear a thing.*

Right now, that didn't matter. Kel had managed to not only figure out a way past our wolves on patrol but also to get here without anyone knowing.

Bodey snarled, *We all thought our patrol would pick up on any intruders.*

This was a clusterfuck.

Miles and I are following Michael and Samuel, Lucas linked, informing us of their plans as Jack ran into the room and kneeled next to Stevie's head.

Stevie tried to speak, but her mouth couldn't seem to form words.

Heart fracturing, I sobbed, tears traveling down my face. Taking away her ability to pack link had been cruel, especially right now. But I couldn't reverse it. There was no witch here to do it.

Her head tilted toward her parents and then back toward Jack.

"Stay with us," Jack grated out. "Dina's on her way. She'll heal you. We just need you to hang on."

Bodey placed an arm around my shoulders as he linked with the pack, *Has anyone located the wolves? They couldn't have just vanished.*

Not yet, the male from earlier replied. *But we're closing in.*

I think Samuel and I are catching up, Michael linked.

A lump formed in my throat. If Michael and Samuel caught up to them first, they'd be outnumbered. I couldn't handle anyone else getting hurt.

Bodey's arm tensed, and I could feel his conflicting emotions. He didn't want to leave me but also didn't like the idea of his dad and Samuel stumbling upon them before more pack members could catch up.

Go, I linked and turned my head toward him. *I'll be there as soon as I can.*

His brows furrowed. *Are you sure? You're—*

I am, but if someone else gets hurt, I'll be even worse off. I wanted to go with him but didn't want to leave my parents alone with Stevie. What if the wolves who'd attacked her circled back? Someone needed to be here to protect them.

I won't be long, Bodey vowed as he stood and headed toward the door. "Jack, come on." My mate ran out the door, and I could feel the slight tingle shoot through our connection as he began his shift.

However, Jack didn't move from his spot. Instead, his cobalt eyes glistened as he cradled my sister's head.

My heart dropped to my stomach. "Jack, you need to go with Bodey. What if something happens and they corner him? They were targeting him in the last attack." Bodey couldn't be out there alone.

"I...I can't." His voice broke as he ran his fingers through Stevie's hair. "I left earlier, and look what happened to her."

I inhaled sharply as I understood what I was seeing. He was refusing to leave her side, just like a fated mate would. The time he'd volunteered to bring her food and question her added up.

If my gut was right, there was no way he'd leave her side in this condition. And now, my own fated mate was out there on his own, trying to desperately catch up.

"Jack, if you're staying here, I have to go." I squeezed Stevie's hand and stood. "You'll protect them if it comes to that, right? My parents included?"

"With my life." He flicked his eyes toward me, emotion shining through.

That was all I needed. "I'll be back." I spun around my parents and headed for the door. "Do not remove that knife until the witch says it's okay."

As I sprinted up the stairs, I let my wolf surge forward. My skin tingled as my shift began. When I reached the top of the stairs, I almost ran into Dina. Fur sprouted across my body as my bones broke.

"Hurry," I half rasped and half growled, continuing my dash outside. My clothes ripped from my body, and my spine shifted, forcing me onto all fours.

"I'll take care of her," Dina answered as my paws dug into the ground.

Trusting her, I focused forward, pushing my legs, my paws hitting the soft grass as I soared into the fir trees. *Where is everyone?* My focus was on reaching my mate, but luckily, that would be on my way toward the others.

We see the wolves, Samuel linked, but then his link cooled with unease. *There are twenty of them and a witch. Not five.*

No wonder the scents were jumbled, Bodey replied, and

luckily, he wasn't far away. I could hear his breath quicken. *She must have been hiding them.*

As the trees blurred and I raced toward the others, I tried to even out my own breathing, so I didn't tucker out. *Hiding them with magic? But then, why would we eventually smell the five?*

Because she wouldn't want to use magic too close to the neighborhood. Our witches would be alerted if they sensed it, Bodey answered, and through the tree branches, I could see his dark fur.

That only urged me to go faster. For once, I wasn't the slowest person around.

A wolf howled, sending a shiver down my spine.

We're on them, the guy from earlier linked. *We're attacking now.*

We'll attack from this side, Samuel replied.

Shit. I wanted to get there before this all happened. *How many wolves are with you?*

Ten and ten more are close. A few should be here in minutes, the man replied.

Snarls erupted, and I heard a woman's voice command, "Force them down and out of our path."

Wolves whimpered as if they were in some sort of pain.

We're with Samuel and Michael, Miles linked. *Let's attack the two closest to us in the circle they've formed.*

A circle. They were protecting their backs like I'd tried to do that day in the woods after the coronation. Given they had a witch with them, their formation would probably be more effective.

I reached Bodey's side, his head turning my way.

Why are you here and not Jack? His eyes narrowed.

I laughed, which sounded more like choking in my wolf form. *Because he refused to leave my sister, and I needed to be here with your ass.*

You need to go back, he linked, focusing forward again. *You're the queen. They'll target you.*

Not happening. My blood heated. *My pack is out here fighting, and I'll be damned if I stay back in safety. If I'm not willing to fight, then I shouldn't ask them to do it either.*

Bodey huffed. *Damn that logic.*

Pain blasted through my link with Samuel. He'd been heavily injured. *Samuel!*

I pushed some of my magic toward Bodey through our mate connection, and he picked up his speed alongside me. Together, we barreled toward our family and friends.

Protect Samuel, Lucas commanded.

Bodey and I ran between two large firs, and then we could see the fight. There were twenty gray wolves of varying shades in a circle, which I'd expected, but they weren't protecting each other. They were protecting the witch in the center.

Her dark hair levitated around her, and her skin appeared unnaturally pale. She held her hands up as her light-blue eyes focused on the ten wolves she was using her magic to keep away.

The enemy moved in a jog as one, completely in tune with one another. They were retreating farther away from our neighborhood, and they weren't harming anyone...except Samuel.

I focused on my brother.

Five of the wolves pulled away from the main circle, and six others filled in their spaces. Two of them attacked Samuel, while the other three kept Lucas, Miles, and Michael preoccupied.

One wolf jumped on Samuel's back, and as my brother tried to buck him off, a light-gray wolf clawed him all the way down his snout.

He jerked back, keening as the wolf on his back dug his nails into Samuel's sides.

This ended *now.*

I kicked up bits of the ground as I pushed myself toward my brother.

My brother tried to throw the prick off his back just as the lighter gray one struck at his face again.

The light-gray one's gaze darted toward me, and she raised her leg to swipe at my brother once more. I leapt and sank my teeth into her paw.

She yelped, jerking her paw back, tearing her skin as my teeth sliced through it.

From the corner of my eye, I noticed the witch jerk her head in our direction. I expected her to focus on me, but instead, she homed in on my mate.

Knowing I had to end the gray wolf's attack on my brother, I diverted my attention to the immediate threat.

A cry behind me wasn't from Samuel, which told me Bodey was handling the dark-gray wolf on Samuel's back.

The light-gray wolf tried to put pressure on her foot, but it gave out under her weight, which gave *me* the opportunity I needed. I stood on my hind legs and shoved her shoulders, causing her to stumble into a fir tree and crack her head.

Pivoting, the witch said, "Stop his heart." Then lifted her hand toward my mate.

My wolf raged like never before, and my body moved of its own accord. With every ounce of strength I could muster, I lunged.

Callie! Bodey linked, his fear palpable. *No!*

The witch's eyes widened as my body soared in front of her hands. She gasped and quickly lowered them, and a charcoal-gray wolf standing right in front of her whined as it dropped to its knees.

The rival wolves froze at the death of their own but then jumped into action as ten of our wolves arrived and attacked the other side of the circle.

Chaos descended, and the witch remained stock-still, staring at the dead charcoal wolf that had been protecting her.

Finally, we were gaining an advantage, their circle broken. We were no longer the ones outnumbered.

The witch shook her head, tearing her gaze from the wolf and taking in the battle.

This was my chance. I had to reach her.

Turning around, I saw Bodey rip out the darker gray wolf's throat. Immediately, his gaze met mine, but I looked away, determined to end this now that I knew both he and Samuel were okay.

As I ran toward the witch, she raised her hands. "Immobilize—"

I jumped over the dead wolf right at her. My teeth sank into her shoulder, and she gasped. She turned with my momentum and flung me away, and my back hit the ground with a *thud*. My bite marks marred her body, and her eyes were ice.

"You're going to pay for that," she vowed.

Rolling onto all fours, I leapt up to finish her off. If we took her out, the wolves would be easier to detain.

Bodey flashed past me, going for the witch.

Bodey! I yelled, fear taking hold. My adrenaline pumped so hard that the pain in my back ebbed and I could move freely once more.

The witch held out her hands toward my mate and smiled sinisterly. "Make him—"

I lunged and sank my teeth into her arm, but Bodey crumpled, agony twining through our bond.

My heart thudded, thinking he was going to die, so I thrashed harder, making her hand move away from my mate.

"Get off me," the witch shrieked, but I locked my jaws tighter. I wasn't going to let this bitch survive after everything she'd done.

When I swiped my claws at her, she cried, “Stop. Please, help!”

But none of them could. They were engaged in their own battles.

The witch must have noticed because her eyes widened. With a ragged breath, she used her free hand to yank off her necklace then tossed it to the ground.

Everything went gray.

CHAPTER ELEVEN

NO MATTER how many times I blinked, smoky gray surrounded me. I spun around, desperate to find Bodey, but I was off balance.

I couldn't see, and I smelled only lavender. Two of my main senses had just...vanished.

I could still hear and feel, especially the connections in my chest. The fur on my nape rose, and a shiver ran down my spine.

Whimpers echoed in my ears as Bodey's agony crashed through me, intensifying. Not only that, but frantic, faint ebbs pulsed from the pack links of my twenty pack members and Michael, Lucas, and Miles, and I could sense the essence of the pain Samuel was feeling, though it was nothing like Bodey's.

The only comparison I had to this sensation was when the ink from the tattoo had swirled around me, but even then, I'd been able to smell things nearby.

This was different.

And though I wasn't the one in agony, this was so much worse because I didn't know how to protect any of them... including my mate.

I can't see. Lucas's voice popped into my head. *And all I can smell is lavender.*

Snarls sounded, and then someone cried out as they tried to fight.

Shit. Was everyone having this issue and not just me? *Can anyone see?* My throat tightened.

No, was the response I received from everyone, until Samuel replied, *Yes. You're all covered in smoke.*

Another growl came from my left, and I froze. For all we knew, we could be fighting our own people. *Everyone bark so we know where our friends are.* I didn't know what else to do since seeing and smelling weren't options.

A strangled whimper slipped out, followed by a *woof.* Soon, everyone was making the faint noise, and I noticed that at least three wolves were very close to me.

Back out of the smoke, toward Samuel, and take it slow. If someone attacks and they aren't barking, then it'll be our opponents. A part of me wanted us to move forward, but that could be what the witch wanted. The last thing I wanted was to lead my people into a trap.

We'd suffered enough.

The agony surging through Bodey's connection almost debilitated me, but I didn't have the luxury of shutting down. I had to find him. He was somewhere in the gray.

I spun in a circle, trying to get my bearings. He had to be close by. I linked, *Bodey? I need help finding you.*

A faint noise sounded about five feet to my right, and I inched forward, not wanting to trip over him.

Please keep making that noise, I linked to him—and then to the rest of the pack, *Be careful not to trip over Bodey. He's injured and on the ground in this mess.* I didn't know what else to call it.

His cries grew louder as I got closer, but even after ten steps, the gray still hung thickly around me. I wanted to go after the witch, but I couldn't risk endangering all of us further, or worse, something happening to Bodey in the fog.

My foot hit something solid, and I linked, *Is that you?* I hated to keep bothering him, but I needed to make sure it was him and not someone else.

Yeah. He groaned at my feet.

I had to move him, but I wasn't sure how in animal form, which meant there was only one option.

I had to shift.

My wolf whined loudly in my head. She brushed against my mind, her frustration compounding mine. We were cut off from almost every sense that made being in animal form stronger, and she wanted to protect her mate but couldn't.

She retreated, eager for us to help him, and soon, my body transitioned to its human form. My *woof* alerting the others to me became hoarse, and soon, I was back on two legs.

I kept woofing, despite it sounding silly in this form, as I bent and wrapped my arms around Bodey's body then gently picked him up. The jolt of our bond, even when we were in opposite forms, was just as strong, taking me by surprise.

His fur caressed my skin, hiding the front side of my nakedness—not that it mattered. His safety was way more important than my modesty.

A soft bark came at my side, and I kept making my own ridiculous human version of the noise.

Muscles straining, I kept my arms tight around Bodey. He squirmed, making him hard to hold, but there was no way I'd drop him.

With the *woofs*, we were able to walk through the smoke and not collide with each other, and so far, there'd been no attacks by the other pack.

With each second, Bodey's torment increased. I linked with

Jack, *How are things there?* Sweat beaded on my forehead, dropping into my eyes.

Dina's finishing up healing Stevie, he replied, his relief flaring through our connection. *She's going to be all right.*

That was music to my ears for more than one reason. *Thank gods. We need Dina's help desperately out here. Samuel's injured, and Bodey's in immense pain.*

You got it, Jack replied. *We're heading that way.*

Breathing rapidly, I did my best to ignore the negative sensations and focus on the present. We still weren't out of this damn smoke.

I'm out, Miles linked. *It's like a huge fucking gray cloud hovering ten feet high.*

At least someone was with Samuel. But why hadn't he been attacked? *Do you see the enemy?*

After a few seconds, Miles replied, *No. They aren't anywhere that I can see.*

My legs grew weak from the strain of carrying Bodey, but I gritted my teeth, determined to get him out of the miasma. Though the other wolves seemed to have vanished, that didn't mean Bodey couldn't get hurt by our pack trying to get free.

Five more wolves alerted us that they'd made it out. We had to be approaching clear air.

A wolf howled about a mile and a half away, in the opposite direction of the houses.

That's near where our property ends, the guy who'd alerted us to the Southwest wolves on our land linked. *They must have used this as a diversion to escape.*

As if to confirm his words, multiple engines revved.

We're going to follow their trail to the best of our abilities and see if we can find anything, the guy added.

I wasn't sure that was wise. *Fine, but if anything seems off, I want you to run back here. Enough of us are hurt as it is.*

My arms ached, and my right leg buckled for a second, succumbing to the weight of my mate. I stumbled and moved forward, and in one large step, the gray gave way to light.

For a second, I was blinded by the abrupt change, but then my eyes adjusted. I staggered a few more steps, making sure Bodey was far enough out of the gray mist that no one rushing out would harm him. And then my legs gave out. I held him tight to my body as my butt hit the ground, jarring my back.

Tailbone throbbing, I clutched my mate. He whined as his voice whispered in my mind, *Okay?*

Even in debilitating pain, he was worried about me. *I'm fine. Just concentrate on you.*

Samuel's brown fur caught my eye, and I winced. He'd taken more of a beating than I'd realized. Blood dripped from the gashes in his sides and oozed from his snout.

Kel had to be stopped. She was causing way too much pain and chaos.

Unable to be patient, I connected with Jack, *Do you know when you'll be here?*

I can hear you guys barking. We're close. Any second now.

Our bond buzzed between us, but it wasn't helping Bodey's pain. He yelped as the agony intensified inside him.

My eyes burned as I held him. I was afraid to move him and cause any additional suffering.

He'd been spelled and was enduring all this hell because he was mated to me. Maybe I'd had it right to begin with—I wasn't meant to be part of a pack, and I should have run off and been solo. Had Samuel received the ink, maybe none of this would've happened. Now they were stuck with me.

Someone who didn't know how to be queen.

But I was the one marked, and that couldn't be undone, no matter how much I wanted it to be. All I could do now was protect the ones I loved.

Which was going swimmingly.

At the end of the day, I felt helpless. The void that had haunted me all my life wasn't there anymore, but the ghost of it somehow weighed more. People needed me now, and hell...for twenty-two years, I hadn't been able to help myself.

I had to snap out of this. I had packs to lead, and even if I failed, I'd go down trying.

When I raised my head, two wolves were staring at me while the other seventeen kept scanning for a new threat.

I should've pulled my act together sooner. Despite being naked on the ground, my mate sprawled over me; I lifted my chin and nodded to the wolf I'd knocked out not that long ago. "Make sure that wolf doesn't get away." She lay outside of the fog. "She could wake anytime, and we can't lose her. We need answers."

The two wolves nodded, trotting over to the still-unconscious wolf. At least, that got their eyes off me for the moment.

Michael and Lucas appeared from the gray fog. Michael looked at me and then Bodey. He hurried over, stopping several feet away.

What happened to him? Michael's eyes widened.

The witch spelled him. And I hadn't been quick enough to stop her. That was something that I'd have to live with, especially if we couldn't figure out how to stop the pain.

Miles's dark wolf hovered in front of Samuel, facing the direction the enemy wolves had gone, while Lucas's brown wolf positioned himself behind Samuel, the two of them guarding him.

All of a sudden, there was a drastic dip in Bodey's pain. His labored breathing smoothed out.

I gasped.

What's wrong? Michael moved closer, staring at his son.

The pain he's in...it's easing. Hope expanded in my chest, and I braced myself, knowing it could get worse again. For all we knew, the witch was messing with us.

Are you seriously sitting out here naked? Bodey linked, his eyes opening slightly.

I snickered. I couldn't help it. Out of everything he could have said, that was the first thing he wanted to address? *Well, I had to get you out of the mist somehow, and I couldn't in wolf form without hurting you worse.* Warm tears streaked down my face, and only then did I realize that I was crying.

Well, it's a damn good thing I'm in your lap, but Dad needs to move away. Bodey growled faintly, but it didn't hold much anger. The noise was still weak.

Why are you crying? Michael's panic picked up a notch, and he moved so close that he almost touched me, staring into his son's eyes.

Bodey's pain was still receding as his protectiveness flared. I said, "He wants you to get away from me because I'm naked." I laughed. "In other words, he's getting better."

Dina, Jack, and Chelsea, a witch who'd helped at the coronation, came into view through the fir trees.

Her gaze landed on me before her head jerked in Samuel's direction. Dina pointed to Samuel and ordered, "Chelsea, go heal him."

Chelsea nodded, her aquamarine-blue eyes narrowing in determination as she beelined over to Samuel.

Taking several steps back, Michael moved so Dina could take his place. When the witch squatted beside me and touched Bodey's head, I snarled.

I did *not* like her touching him.

"Do you want me to help him or not?" Dina arched a brow.

"Yeah." I sighed, realizing that I had to tamp down my possessiveness...for now. "I thought you'd be healing Samuel."

She slid her hands into Bodey's fur again, and I swallowed hard.

Even Bodey shook his head, trying to get her hands off him.

"My priority is the king and queen," Dina said then grumbled as she tried to hold Bodey's head still. "However, Chelsea is the coven's next in line and almost as strong as me. Samuel is in good hands. Bodey, do you want me to see what's going on or not?"

Jack cackled, sounding more like himself than he had in the past day. "Mates don't like the opposite sex touching them or their mate. You're dealing with an angry queen and an annoyed Bodey right now. I can't wait to see which one winds up biting you."

Of course, *now* smart-ass Jack appeared. Honestly, it relieved me to see him. Somehow, the situation seemed less dire when he was acting like that.

Babe, it's okay, I linked, trying to soothe my mate.

Bodey growled, his eyes opening wide. The pain was more like a sore arm or muscle now than anything. *Tell her I'm fine.* He stood but then dropped back into my lap.

"The pain is almost gone." I furrowed my brows. "How is that possible?"

Dina dropped her hands. "It must have been a spell. The witch must be out of proximity, so it's fading now."

I arched a brow. "Isn't that something you can tell?"

She rolled her eyes. "Well, I'm drained after healing your sister. It took everything out of me to heal her wound. Had I been just a few seconds later..." She shivered. "And then Bodey wouldn't stay still, so between that and my weak magic, I can't get a good feel for it. But I still would if it were a permanent spell, so that's what makes the most sense."

My body sagged. "So...it won't come back?"

Dina shook her head. "Unless she spells him again, but then

it would work only while she's close by. The only way to make a spell permanent is to sacrifice something of great importance."

I lifted a hand, causing Bodey to snarl. He linked, *You need to shift back before someone sees you naked.*

Of course, Jack placed his hands into his jeans and kicked at the ground. "What's wrong, Bodey? Don't want her to point to anything?"

I'm going to kill you and savor each moment, Bodey vowed.

Ignoring him, I nodded toward the gray mist. "What is that?"

"That's a spell only strong witches can cast. It's based on using rosemary to clean the air around the caster, and this particular witch was smart enough to use lavender to override your sense of smell as the air was cleansed of anyone's scent, and the mist obscured your vision. She used it to cover their getaway." Dina pursed her lips. "But it's strange...it's like she went out of her way not to hurt you."

"I'm not sure I agree." I glanced at my mate, who was busy staring daggers at the wolves near us as if daring them to look my way. "She tortured Bodey."

Dina bit her bottom lip but said nothing.

We seemed to have no answers when it came to the queen and her strategy. I wanted to scream.

"Hey, Callie." Jack waggled his brows. "Did you see that?"

I turned to look in his direction just as Bodey snarled, *Don't fucking move. He's messing with me.*

"Seriously, Jack." I stiffened and tried not to laugh. If Bodey hadn't warned me, I would've turned around and exposed one of my boobs to the world. "Samuel's hurt and we just had a fight."

"Please. We're all fine, and Samuel is being healed." Jack huffed. "And after your sister got hurt, let's just say I need to do something other than be stressed."

My heart ached in sympathy. Sometimes, after a horrible situation was over, you needed a distraction, and unfortunately, Bodey and I were on the receiving end of Jack's recovering humor.

Your Majesty, one of the wolf shifters I'd asked to watch over our prisoner linked to me. *The wolf is stirring.*

We needed to get the wolf into the basement before they woke up completely. I exhaled. "How's Samuel doing?" I glanced at my brother, who was now standing. The blood was drying on his snout and the fur around his sides.

"Healed, Your Majesty." Chelsea turned toward me, the breeze catching her long navy skirt.

Clearing my throat, I tangled my hands in Bodey's fur. "Let's head back to the house. We have a prisoner to detain before she wakes up. Stevie can recover in our house, and the girl can stay in the basement."

Stevie's attack could've been for show, Samuel linked just with Bodey and me.

My chest constricted because he was right. Though I didn't want to believe it, this could be a ploy. *We play along until we learn the truth.*

Bodey replied, *I agree. It'll be easier for us to watch her close by anyway. And she'll think we might somewhat trust her.*

Knowing that I wasn't going to walk back to the house naked, I linked to Bodey, *I'm going to shift.*

Relief flooded him, and he linked with everyone, *Turn your back so my mate can shift without people seeing her naked, including you, perv.* His indigo eyes focused on Jack.

"Don't worry." Jack rolled his eyes. "I don't want to see her like that."

Everyone turned, and Dina's brows furrowed. She could hear only one side of the conversation, but when I stood, understanding seemed to dawn on her face.

I called my wolf, and she rushed forward. Within seconds, I was back on all fours with fur all over my body. Once I settled, I linked with the three wolves who'd gone to hunt down the others, *Are you okay?*

Yeah, we're heading back, the man replied. *We didn't find anything, and they're definitely gone.*

That was both good and bad news, but I'd take it.

Jack strolled to the foreign wolf and lifted her, purposely knocking her head into the tree once again. He threw her over his shoulder.

My head tilted, and he turned toward me.

"What?" he asked. "I don't want her waking up on our way there and clawing the shit out of my back."

Good point. Bodey and I trotted toward the house, leading everyone to our home. The entire way back, Bodey's emotions were all over the place. He was tired, angry, and relieved, in that order.

Are you okay? I asked.

Birds fluttered in the distance, indicating that animals were returning to the area. That was a good sign.

Bodey replied curtly, *I've been better.*

His curt answer stung, but I tried to push the hurt aside. We had just gone through a terrible ordeal.

Before I could push the matter, we stepped back into our yard. Stevie, my parents, Stella, and Janet stood huddled together on the deck, watching us return. Janet opened the sliding glass door for us.

We bounded up the stairs to our bedroom, and once again, Bodey tossed me a shirt and a pair of his boxers since my clothes were still in the trunk of his car. That could be fixed later.

Noises came from downstairs, and I slipped the shirt over my head. Before it completely covered my waist, Bodey's arms slid around me.

The jolt of our bond eased some of the hurt I'd felt from his curtness. My heart thundered, and I turned so I could look into his eyes, expecting to find warmth.

Instead, they were narrowed, and he wore a scowl on his face. He growled, *We need to talk before we go downstairs.*

CHAPTER TWELVE

I SWALLOWED AS I FLINCHED. I'd sensed his anger, but I hadn't expected to find it directed at me. He'd never looked at me this way before.

My heart ripped in two. Whenever someone had glared at me like this back home, punishment followed. Just like all those times, my chin lifted, but this time, my wolf brushed against my mind, her hackles up. "Do I have a choice in the matter?"

His jaw twitched. "No, because you went too far back there."

The air rushed out of my lungs. "Excuse me?" I gaped. The man before me right now wasn't the one I'd fallen in love with.

"What the *fuck* was that?" he growled, his arms wrapped around me so tight that I couldn't move unless I fought him.

Nope. I'd never allowed someone to manhandle me before, and I wasn't about to start now. Even him.

I shoved at his chest and took a step back. It was enough for him to release me, and he didn't fight it.

At least he wasn't trying to be physical with me, just alpha-y, but it still wasn't okay. He was being a domineering ass.

I crossed my arms, my own blood heating. Too bad it wasn't

the good kind of heat. "What do you mean? You're going to have to be more specific because a ton of shit went down today."

"Oh, really?" His nose wrinkled. "You've got *no clue?* How about when the witch cast that spell to stop my heart? Does that ring any bells?" His anger flowed into me, adding to my own.

There was one bell I was about to ring. "Yeah, but I'm not sure what you expect me to say on that other than that bitch will die eventually." By my own hand. No one got to hurt my mate that way...other than me if he didn't get his head out of his ass.

"You jumped in front of the spell." Bodey's eyes glowed. "You were going to take the hit instead of me."

"Well, yeah." I arched a brow. "She was trying to *kill* you. Was I just supposed to stand back and watch?"

"If that's what it takes to keep you safe, then abso-fucking-lutely." His jaw clenched like it did whenever he talked to Zeke and Theo, but this time, it was all for me.

I shook my head and lowered my arms. He had some nerve, acting like this right now. My patience was worn thin, I was worried about both my brother and sister, and he wanted to argue about me trying to save his ass? "What would you have done if she'd cast that at *me*?"

"The same thing, but that's different." His breathing quickened.

"Oh, really?" I laughed bitterly, the sound vibrating deep within my chest. "How?"

His hands clenched. "Because your life means more than *mine*. It means more than *everybody else's*."

"No, it doesn't." There was no one person worth more than any other unless you viewed it from an individual's perspective.

Bodey stepped forward, his hands quivering with the rage I felt through our bond. He rasped, "Do you know what will happen if you die?"

"I'll stop breathing." At least this time, when my mouth ran,

I understood why. My wolf was agitated. Bodey might be our mate, but we weren't happy with him right now.

He winced as pain soared between us. He linked, *Not funny, Callie.*

In fairness, I understood why he was upset. I'd feel the same way if the situation were reversed. But the way he was handling it was a problem. He didn't get to be growly, angry, and demanding just because he didn't like a decision I made.

"Your life is the most important to *me*." I spread out my arms. "You're the alpha of Idaho. Your people need you."

Pounding on his chest, he bit out, "You're talking about how my people need me. You're the *queen*. Losing you would've been a huge blow to everybody."

I rolled my eyes. I couldn't help it. We both knew that wasn't the truth. I hadn't been raised to lead. "Samuel would be a great king. Hell, he should be king now, but somehow, I wound up with the tattoo. If I died, someone more prepared would be in this position of power."

Snarling, Bodey bared his teeth. "That's bullshit, and you know it. You are the true heir, and the magic recognized you as such. I remember that little girl—"

"That little girl doesn't *exist* any longer." I pointed at my head, the loss taking me by surprise. "She's trapped, hidden, and I don't remember a damn thing about my time with my parents. Anything from that time has been erased, and at least Samuel grew up being taught to rule. So, yeah, maybe Fate got things wrong *again*. I'm just a girl who grew up in a pack that hated her."

No one had ever valued me as a person...except Stevie. The one person who'd risked everything to try to save me and our family.

Realization slammed into me, stealing my breath. I'd locked

her up alone in the basement and blocked her pack link, allowing my emotions to get the best of me.

I should've had a guard down there or something in case she needed help.

"You are *her*." Bodey's anger ebbed as his forehead creased. "I see so much of that girl in you, and yes, there are some things that you can't access, but your parents still impacted you."

I scowled. He didn't get to be all growly and mean and then change his tune. That wasn't how this worked, even if he had good intentions. My strange little habit of kissing my fingers and lifting them up to the moon reemerged.

"See, that right there." Bodey pointed at my hand and continued, "That was something your dad did. He said he was asking the gods to bless a person for their good intentions even if they were misguided. They're still a part of you...even if you don't know it."

My legs nearly gave out. I'd never known how I came up with that gesture, and the one time Zeke had seen it, he'd snapped at me for no reason. Maybe it had reminded him who I really was.

"You don't get to be mean and then kind." My voice broke, my vision blurring.

He pulled me into his arms. My traitorous body melted into him as the thrill of our bond helped ease my hurt.

"I'm sorry." He breathed against the top of my head and said, "It's just...seeing you jump in front of that spell to protect me scared the shit out of me. And then when I saw you go after the witch while I was debilitated..." He pulled back and winced. "I *can't* lose you, Callie. I wouldn't survive it."

"And I can't lose you." My voice broke as I buried my face into his muscular chest. "You're the only person other than Stevie who took care of me before my wolf broke free." I lifted my head, a tear trailing down my face. "I can't live without you either."

He caressed my cheek with his palm. "You could, and you would. You're the strongest person I know. I can't think of anyone who would have suffered like you did and still wound up being so strong, empathetic, loyal, and funny."

"Maybe I could survive, but, Bodey, the truth is, I wouldn't want to." The thought of losing him sent a chill down my spine. "And I don't regret jumping in front of you. If I hadn't, we wouldn't both be here to fight about it."

His brows furrowed, but he pressed his forehead to mine. He murmured, "That's true, but that was damn risky, babe." The icy tendrils of his fear coursed through the bond and into my veins. "I thought that I was going to lose you."

"But you didn't." I leaned back and cupped his face with my hands. I linked, *And now we're going to figure out the next steps together.* I kissed him, his lips molding to fit mine perfectly.

We haven't resolved anything, Bodey linked but didn't break our kiss.

True. He didn't like that I'd protected him, but I wouldn't agree not to do it again. *It's an agree-to-disagree situation. Because if you ever jumped in front of me like that, I'd be angry with you as well.*

The corners of his mouth tipped upward, and he nipped at my lips. *Yeah, but in that case, that would be the right thing to do. Today—*

I poked my finger into his stomach and growled, "Watch it, bubba. I'm still not over how you spoke to me."

"Whoa." He inched away so he could see my face. His brows shot upward. "Did you just *bubba* me? I don't even know what that means, but I don't like it."

"So don't be a jerk again." I booped his nose and placed a hand on my hip. "Then we won't have any problems."

He bent down, lifted me up, and cradled me in his arms. "I'm sorry, but I won't apologize for not liking what you did."

I nodded. "That is acceptable, noted, and now promptly disregarded."

He tossed me on the bed, jumped on top of me, then straddled me. His irises lightened to cobalt. "Then I guess I'll get my revenge the best way possible." He tickled my sides, forcing me to laugh.

Unable to hold it in, I couldn't catch my breath until he relented.

"There. If you ever try that again, next time, it'll last longer." He waggled his eyebrows, and I could feel him harden against me.

My breath caught, and my wolf pressed to the fore, eager for the two of us to connect, especially after that fight.

But the voices downstairs grew louder as if they were arguing.

We'd already stayed up here too long. I pouted because my body was heating up in a way only Bodey could satiate. "We need to go downstairs."

He huffed but nodded. "Now I'm going to have raging blue balls."

"Until tonight." I leaned forward and pecked his nose. He thrust against me once more, making my mind foggy. I sighed. "Or we could—"

"We aren't making any decisions until Callie gets down here," Michael said loudly, pulling me back to the moment.

It was the equivalent of a cold shower, and even Bodey jumped to his feet. Taking my hand, he led the two of us down the stairs and into the den with everyone else.

Stevie, Mom, and Dad sat on the couch while Samuel leaned against the island. His face was still paler than normal, but he wasn't struggling to breathe.

Jack stood across from Stevie with Lucas, Miles, and Stella on his left, all four of them facing the kitchen. Michael, Janet, Carl, Dan, Phil, and Dina were on the side of the room, close to the sliding glass door.

"It's so nice that you two could finally join us. I figured there would be a creaking bed and loud moans before you got down here." Jack crossed his arms, narrowing his eyes at us. "Must have done it on the floor or something."

"Son," Carl warned. Somehow the gray in his hair seemed more prominent, making his blond hair look lighter than his son's.

My face flamed. I hadn't expected to get chastised by *Jack*, but if what I suspected was happening between Stevie and him was true, then it shouldn't have shocked me.

"The two of us had something to discuss in private." Bodey wrapped an arm around my waist, anchoring me to him, and continued, "So don't you dare try to make her feel bad."

"Stevie was severely injured, and you think that you two can have a quick—"

"I was worried about Stevie and *Samuel*, but I knew the witches healed them," I cut him off. "Bodey was spelled to endure torture, and that couldn't be healed the same way. It was all mental. If you disagree with our decision to take a few minutes upstairs to discuss something serious between us before coming down here so we wouldn't be distracted, then you can take that up with me...*alone*." I didn't know where that came from, but the words poured out of me.

I expected Jack to push back, but instead, he averted his gaze.

Stepping away from Bodey, I touched Samuel's arm and asked, "Is there something I can do for you?"

He shook his head. "Just need a good night's sleep is all."

"And maybe a nap now?" I hated for him to wait that long. I could see the scabs peeking out from the top of his shirt.

"Let's see how this conversation goes."

I couldn't argue with that. I went to the couch and stood by Stella. I focused on Stevie, who stared at the floor, avoiding my gaze.

My heart ached, but I deserved it. "Stevie, I'm sorry—"

She lifted a hand. "Don't, please. I'll live, which is a vast improvement over what I thought just a short while ago."

A lump formed in my throat, and I blinked as my eyes burned. I didn't want to cry...at least, not here.

Babe, I'll handle this, Bodey linked, stepping next to me. His protectiveness filled the bond, making me feel less alone.

Don't. I deserve her anger. Though I wasn't sure what the right call had been, I was certain ensuring she couldn't protect herself while not leaving someone to protect her couldn't be fixed by an apology. *She almost died, thanks to a decision I made. She has a right to be mad at me.*

"So what's our next move?" Lucas asked, his gaze on me and then the other advisors.

"I'd like to hear what our queen thinks." Dan leaned against the island. Like the first time I'd met him, his brown hair was spiked, suggesting he'd been running his hands through it. The dark circles under his eyes made them look sunken against his tan complexion.

I winced. I had no idea what to say. But they were looking to me for answers. Something that never would've happened two weeks ago, and for the first time, I missed the scant responsibilities I'd had before now.

Phil shook his head. His dark-bronze complexion seemed to glow under the kitchen lights. His eyes were locked on me, waiting for my answer.

No pressure at all.

"First things first." I rubbed my hands together, knowing there was one thing I wanted to rectify. "Dina, can you remove the pack link block on Stevie?"

Dina's jaw dropped. "Uh, are you sure that's wise? She could still be working with someone. The attack on her could be a setup."

"Maybe, but I doubt it, especially after seeing how they left her to die." If we'd been just a few minutes later, the outcome would've been extremely different. There was no way the queen could know that we would return in time to save her. "Either way, my decision left her vulnerable, and she almost died because of it. I want it removed, and I'm going to trust that my sister isn't telling me lies."

My parents' shoulders sagged with relief.

Mom placed a hand on her chest. "Thank gods. We can at least link with you now."

"Will you still keep her in the basement?" Dad asked, his eyes wide.

I shook my head. "We have another prisoner there now. Stevie will stay in the room I slept in before Bodey and I mated."

I think that's a great idea, Bodey linked, squeezing my hand.

"That's not safe enough." Samuel frowned, his eyes meeting mine. He linked with Bodey and me, *I understand she's your sister, but she worked against us with the enemy. What if she sneaks out when you two are busy and I'm in the shower or something?*

My cheeks burned, knowing exactly what he was implying when talking about Bodey and me being busy.

Bodey cleared his throat. "For added protection, maybe Dina would be willing to spell the perimeter of the house so, if she tries to leave, we're alerted immediately. Just so others know we're keeping a watchful eye on her."

I love you so much. That was a brilliant plan and would keep Stevie confined to our house and yard. Some of the weight lifted from my body.

"Yes, I can do that if the queen agrees." Dina clasped her hands, watching me.

"That would be great. That way, if she needs help, she can link with me, and she can talk to our parents at her convenience."

"I like that idea a lot." The lines on Jack's face smoothed. "Then you two having quickies won't be a problem."

This time, it was Miles who smacked him on the back of the head.

Dina moved around the couch and stood in front of Stevie. She tapped my sister's forehead and intoned, "Remove the block."

Brown eyes glowing, Stevie's wolf surged forward, and I tugged at our pack link connection, feeling a sense of ease filter back into my sister. But wisps of terror from what had happened to her trickled through to me as I homed in on the connection.

Guilt weighed me down again, and I linked with Zeke, *No one is to share the information that Stevie is alive outside of our pack.* Alpha will laced my words as I connected with him even though I hadn't meant for it to happen. However, if someone else was working with the queen, we had to ensure that her being alive didn't get out. I continued, *And alpha will everyone in the pack the same way now.* I could do it, but I didn't have the time or the energy this far away.

Fine, he growled before cutting off the link.

"The prisoner is in the basement now, and three of my best men are with her. They've roused her for questioning, which begins now," Bodey informed us, moving so that our arms touched.

The memory of Jack smacking the poor girl's head into the

tree washed over me, almost making me laugh. However, this would've been a very inappropriate time.

Dad exhaled. "You captured one." He nodded to Bodey in approval. "I'm glad someone like you is here to protect my daughter." He reached over and patted Stevie's leg.

My heart dropped. Of course. His daughter...not daughters. He'd never truly considered me one of his.

"Actually, *Roger*," Bodey emphasized, using my dad's name instead of a title of respect, "your *older daughter* was the one who knocked the shifter unconscious. I will protect *both* your daughters, especially my mate, with my life."

"*You* knocked the shifter out?" Dad stared at me. "How do you always manage to do such things? That's a man's place."

And there was the proof that he'd been raised in Zeke's pack.

"She's the strongest wolf in our region." Bodey smiled adoringly at me. "I, for one, would never want to go against her."

My stomach fluttered. This was the mate I knew and loved.

"So, we should probably wait to see if we find out anything from our prisoner. Acting would be premature." I turned to Dina. "But on the memory front, is there a way to locate the witch who performed the spell on me?"

Dina steepled her fingers. "We'll start by having some witches visit you so they can sense the magic. Essence can't be explained, only felt."

Yeah, because that made complete sense. "Would it be easier if we went to them?" I didn't want to inconvenience multiple covens.

"It's not a good idea for you to travel far distances like that," Phil interjected. "It's safer if they come here."

"And, according to tradition, the witches would come to meet the territory's new royal, so it won't be too much to ask." Michael smiled reassuringly.

Dina nodded. "Very true. It won't put them out at all. They'll be excited that they can aid you."

At least there was that.

The same male voice from earlier popped into Bodey's and my heads. *We need the witch's help. Now.*

CHAPTER THIRTEEN

THE PANIC POURING from three of the pack members closest to us set my pulse galloping.

"Dina, they need you in the basement," Bodey said flatly, his body tensing.

Her gaze landed on my mate and then me. "What's wrong?"

"I don't know." Bodey gritted his teeth. "But they need you *now*, so please. Come on."

Face blanching, she nodded, and they raced toward the door. And, of course, everybody was ready to follow her.

"I don't think everyone going is wise." Samuel straightened and looked to Stevie and my parents.

Bodey froze at the door, his frustration leaking through. *Samuel, you aren't in charge, and we don't have time to debate it.*

But Samuel was right, and after all, he'd been trained for this. I hadn't, so I wanted to hear what he had to say. *Go on with Dina*, I told Bodey. I hated to separate from Bodey, but it didn't sound like there was another attack. *Just let me know if you need us immediately. We'll be there soon.* He nodded and followed Dina.

"What the fuck does that mean?" Jack's eyes narrowed at Samuel.

"Let's see." Samuel rolled his shoulders and winced. "We have someone here who worked with Queen Kel, and she's now with her parents. Maybe someone should stay with them."

I glanced at my parents and sister, who had scowls on their faces. The three of them hadn't moved from their places on the couch, which meant they hadn't planned to join us to begin with.

"Everyone go," Stella said, placing a hand on Miles's arm. "I'll stay with them."

"That works for me." I pivoted toward the back door, wanting to catch up with Bodey and Dina. However, as I turned my head, I noticed Stevie frowning at me.

My stomach knotted, but I didn't have time to reassure her. I needed to reach my mate and make sure no one was in danger.

As I jogged onto the back porch, I saw Bodey and Dina reach the stairs that led into the basement of his parents' house. I darted across the yard as Miles, Lucas, Dan, Phil, Carl, and Michael raced out behind me.

I linked to Carl, *Where's Jack?*

He decided to stay with Janet and Stella to keep an eye on your family. Carl's surprise pulsed through our connection. *He didn't want to risk them being unprotected while we were distracted.*

Normally, Jack wanted to be with the action, and this further confirmed what I suspected. Could he and my sister truly be fated mates? That was the only thing that made sense.

As I reached the stairs, Bodey's horror sucker punched me. Chilled by the cool early March breeze, I hit the bottom of the stairs and yanked open the door.

I froze, causing Lucas to barrel into my back, shoving me forward.

Lucas said something as I caught my balance and stopped just shy of the woman on the ground, but his words bled together.

Everything went out of focus around me as the other guys entered the room.

The wolf shifter was back in human form, completely naked, and lay on the cement floor. She was staring at the ceiling, her brown eyes wide and her breathing ragged.

All my wolf could focus on was the fact that Bodey was touching her. She howled in my head, brushing against my mind, trying to take control. She wanted to rip the girl's throat out.

"She must have swallowed poison." Dina placed her hands on the woman's arm and grimaced.

The shifter who'd alerted us moved behind the girl and lifted her toward Bodey. He said, "She opened the pendant from her necklace and swallowed some sort of pill inside it."

"Fuck," Bodey snarled as he crammed his fingers down the girl's throat.

That spurred me into action, and I took the spot next to him. "What if we can't get her to vomit?" Our plans depended on extracting information from our captive. Losing her wasn't an option. I looked at Dina. "Can you heal her?"

Dina shook her head as our captive foamed at the mouth and her body convulsed. Nostrils flaring, Bodey shoved his fingers in deeper, causing her to gag. My wolf snarled in my head.

"That won't work." Dina's shoulders slumped. "It's too late. I can't heal her from this sort of poison. I'm drained, and it's fast-acting."

My gaze flicked to the thin black string around the dying shifter's neck from which a small, empty silver container hung.

Bodey removed his fingers from the girl's mouth and wrinkled his nose as he wiped them on his pants. He scooted back from the woman, and my wolf relaxed some, but she was still unsettled.

I tried to ignore my animal side as I considered the severity of the situation.

The woman's eyes became bloodshot as her body shook harder and her heart slowed.

Her death would be here in moments.

The magnitude of the loss slammed into me, and I dropped, my butt hitting the floor. This was our lead...our chance to get on more even footing with the queen and her plans.

But once again, Queen Kel was two steps ahead of us, and she'd managed to make me even more uncomfortable. She was either able to convince people to believe in her cause enough to sacrifice themselves for her mission, had leverage over them that made them obey, or even alpha willed them. Either option was equally bad.

Who the hell are we up against? I linked with Bodey. Tears burned my eyes, and I clenched my hands. I didn't understand what type of person would do this to her people. How much was the queen willing to sacrifice?

Someone sick and sadistic, Bodey replied, taking my hand.

Silence descended as we all watched the woman die. When she passed, the queen would know. Her pack link would be extinguished.

Then her heart stopped.

After a few seconds, the shifter who'd alerted us said, "I'm so sorry."

Now that our captive was dead, I turned toward him.

His face was filled with regret, making him appear older, but I guessed he was in his early thirties. He dipped his chin, the lights of the basement reflecting off his shaved head. I knew that his hair was a light brown based on his fur when we'd all been in shifter form. His gray eyes looked stormy. "I hadn't even considered that she might have poison. She shifted to human form and immediately took it. I didn't see the necklace until it was too late."

Of course, with the string being so thin, wolf fur would easily hide it.

"Gary, it's not your fault." Bodey leaned against me and sighed. "None of us considered that possibility."

Running a hand down his face, Michael stood at the woman's feet. "We're going to have to consider all the supernatural and human tactics and weapons they could employ."

"I scanned her for magic while Jack carried her here." Dina climbed to her feet and smoothed out her long gray skirt. "The witch was aware of us and our abilities, so she'd know we'd check for spells on anyone we captured. They thought of something I couldn't detect."

I glanced at the dead girl, and my heart squeezed painfully. What could be so important to her that she'd pick a horrible death like *that*?

"So...what do we do now?" Lucas hovered in a corner of the basement. His eyes held my gaze as if I had all the answers.

When I scanned the room, I found everyone else staring at the body. My skin crawled.

I had no idea what to do.

Bodey's thumb brushed my hand, and he cleared his throat. "First things first, we stop scrutinizing a dead woman and have Gary bury her." He helped me to my feet.

Thank you. I squeezed his hand. That was a very good step, and I didn't want to hang around in the basement with a naked dead woman. She deserved respect. "And we head back to the house to discuss strategy." Though it wasn't earth-shattering, at least I'd had something to add.

"I'm all for that." Miles stared at the ceiling, avoiding looking at the captive.

I smiled. I suspected that was more about Stella than having a problem with seeing a dead person.

The guys hustled out of the room, but when I headed toward the door, Dina leaned over the girl. I paused, wanting to see what had attracted her attention.

She brushed her fingers through the captive's hair and murmured, "Goddess, please protect her in death."

My heart clenched at Dina's mercy.

She's a good woman, Bodey linked as he nudged me toward the door. He kept his head forward, not glancing back.

My wolf was finally at ease, though slightly flustered by the ordeal. *Should I be jealous?* I teased, trying to make light of everything.

Never. You own my heart, body, and soul.

When the two of us headed back to our house, I expected to feel relief. But every step felt heavier. *They're expecting me to have answers, and I don't have any.*

That's fine, he reassured me. *We'll figure out the next steps together. All of us. This is new territory for everyone, not just you.*

The words fell flat. Even if this were a routine situation, they'd all know how to handle it before I did. I hadn't been brought up in this world and had no clue what was required of me on a *normal* basis, let alone *this*. Samuel should've been marked. Not me. I didn't care if I was the true heir.

"I hate to leave, but my magic is depleted, and I need to contact the other witches so they can plan their travel here." Dina gestured to me and said, "So we can figure out what happened to you."

"Of course." That was exactly what I wanted.

She waved and headed toward the street while Bodey and I continued inside.

When we entered the den, I found that my parents were gone, and Jack, Stevie, and Stella were sitting on the couch. Janet was heading down the hall from the living room to join us.

I paused. "Where are Mom and Dad?"

Janet cringed. "They just left."

My breath caught. They hadn't even said goodbye. Not even Mom. They did things like this on occasion, and I'd always justified it before, but I was struggling to now.

I'm sorry, baby, Bodey linked, standing behind me and wrapping his arms around my waist. He pushed his love into me, but I could tell he hated that I felt this way.

Whatever. I exhaled, forcing my body to relax. *We have things to discuss anyway.* I rubbed my hands together as the fathers took their spots against the island again and Miles went to stand at the end of the couch near Stella.

Samuel, Bodey, and I opted to stand in front of the fireplace.

"So, the bitch took poison." Jack snorted, his face twisting in disgust. "Figures."

Lucas strolled over and smacked Jack on the back of the head. "The woman just died. Have some manners."

"Hey, I carried her back here!" Jack rubbed the spot and glared over his shoulder. "If that's not gentlemanly, I don't know what is."

Stevie growled. "What?"

Someone had to bring this conversation back on track. "Our captive is dead, and we have no leads. Does anyone have any suggestions on what our next course of action should be?" I prayed that someone would speak up because I was clueless.

"What if we reach out to Queen Kel and request a parlay?" Samuel tapped a finger against his chin. "That might buy us time."

"Parlay?" I bit my bottom lip, hating that I had to ask the

question. Once again, this was further proof that Samuel was the right person for the role.

Michael bobbed his head. "It's when two warring parties meet to see if they can come to an agreement to end the fighting."

My brows furrowed. "Invite her *here*?" That didn't sound wise.

"No." Phil leaned against the island. "It would have to be neutral ground. Maybe somewhere in Nevada, near where California and Oregon meet, which isn't part of either person's territory?"

I pursed my lips. I didn't have a better idea.

Bodey exhaled. "I don't know. That sounds like a waste of time. She isn't going to settle. We need to focus on something that can give us answers, like who suppressed my mate's—our *queen's*—wolf and altered her memories. That could have been Kel's doing too, for all we know."

Answers about my past were something I could get behind wholeheartedly. I wanted them as well as any memories of my parents I could salvage. The idea of the Southwest queen having a hand in spelling me made a tremor snake down my spine. I hadn't considered it until now, but she *was* the most likely suspect. "How old is she?"

"Forties," Samuel answered immediately. "Which means she's had plenty of time to devise a plan in order to make a name for herself."

Still, that didn't add up to me. If she was the one who'd killed my parents and messed with me, why keep me alive? "Wouldn't she have made a move long before now?"

"Not if she needed to get an army ready for war." Samuel crossed his arms.

"Maybe." I wasn't going to disagree with him. He clearly knew the players and the history better than I did. But for some reason, it didn't make sense to me. "But I do think Bodey has a point. Maybe we should focus on getting my memories back and locating the witch who spelled me."

Dan pointed at Samuel. "But reaching out to her and asking to meet—that could give us some breathing room. She should theoretically hold off on any more attacks as a show of good faith. It might buy us time to find the witch and get some answers."

"And if we don't have answers by then, we could strategize, get her to stumble and reveal some answers at the meeting." Miles placed a hand on the back of the couch.

If they all thought this was the best course of action, I couldn't disagree. "Okay. How do we reach out to her?" Even as I said the words, unease crept in. Maybe it was all the horrible events of the day catching up to me.

Jack gestured to my sister. "She must have a way to communicate with the queen."

Flinching, Stevie swallowed hard. "You want my help? After almost getting me killed?"

She might as well have punched me. I was never going to get over that regret.

Blood boiling, Bodey stepped slightly in front of me, staring my sister down. He sneered, "If you hadn't worked with the queen, then the queen wouldn't have tried to have you killed. That wasn't our fault. *You're* the one who got yourself in this situation, so why don't you bite your tongue and help your sister out?"

"Hey, man." Jack jumped to his feet, blocking Stevie from Bodey's view. "You need to back off. Your *mate*—"

"That's enough." Something powerful laced my words as I commanded Jack. My wolf had asserted herself, taking me by surprise. The way that Jack was talking to my mate and was about to talk about me could not be tolerated.

Jack's mouth snapped closed, and his eyes widened. Bodey turned toward me, eyes glowing, his arousal slamming into me.

I wasn't going to stand here and accept us turning on one another. That was what the Southwest queen wanted, and we had enough issues with Zeke to contend with. "Jack, you don't get to talk to us that way. You may not agree with my decisions, but you talk to me about them respectfully. I love Stevie, and I'll admit that I screwed up. But Bodey's right—she was the one who put us in this situation, even if she had good intentions. All we can do now is forgive each other and try to right our wrongs, and throwing insults at each other isn't going to accomplish that."

The room became eerily quiet as everyone blinked at me.

"Wow." Jack's mouth dropped. "Look, I know I should be pissed right now, but fuck me. Having that power overwhelming me was both amazing and terrifying. My wolf is bowing out of fucking respect right now. No, fuck that. It did a full curtsy."

"Leave it to my son." Carl smiled while shaking his head.

I rolled my eyes, trying to ignore the heat of Bodey's arousal rushing through me. My own body was warming in response, and the last thing we needed was to leave now and have a quickie.

Damn. That thought was tempting.

Trying not to go down that rabbit hole, I moved so I could see my sister.

This time, she met my gaze.

"Look, I'm sorry. I didn't think anyone would dare attack you here, and that's why I okayed taking away your pack link. But I should have left guards with you for protection." I placed a hand over my heart. "I love you, and I never want anything bad to happen to you. I understand you were making decisions you thought would protect our family, but that doesn't make them right. So I'm asking you to help me now. We can begin repairing the damage we both did to each other by working *together*."

I laid my heart on the line in front of everyone, and I could only hope that it was enough to break through to her. This was my olive branch, and if she rejected it, we might never be okay.

CHAPTER FOURTEEN

STEVIE RAN her hands over her legs, which was her tell when she was torn on something. The warmth in her eyes was gone, making them a dark chocolate brown.

A part of me wished she was avoiding my gaze instead of going through the internal debate I knew she was having to decide if she'd reconcile with me.

I could only hope that my words had convinced her.

Babe, it'll be okay, Bodey linked and placed a hand on my arm. *I promise. You both love each other. If you didn't, you wouldn't be struggling right now.*

A part of me wanted to believe him, but I'd learned hope was one of the most dangerous emotions. The lyrics to the chorus of Lana Del Rey's "Hope is a Dangerous Thing for a Woman Like Me" drifted through my mind. Words that had taken up rent-free space in my head for the past several years.

The moment Stevie's hands stilled, I knew before she even opened her mouth, she'd come to her answer. Sweat pooled in my armpits as I waited for the gavel to bang.

She smacked her legs, the exact sound I'd been waiting for.

"You're right. I messed up." Her shoulders hunched as her

face twisted into agony. "I didn't consider the repercussions of helping the queen because I was focused on helping my family."

Those were the words I needed to hear—not that I should have expected anything else. Stevie was one of the best people I knew. She hadn't seen the big picture, but at the same time, that was still the problem. Until she could care about all the wolves in this region and not just the ones closest to her, I couldn't trust her.

She clutched her stomach. "I'm so sorry. I didn't mean to cause problems or help anyone get harmed, *especially* Callie."

Jack placed a hand on her shoulder, and she gasped, her gaze darting to him.

"We *all* make mistakes," Jack murmured.

"And most importantly, you were trying to protect my fated mate." Bodey chuckled. "Which makes me very forgiving."

Samuel cleared his throat. "You guys need to remember that she did betray us, and yes, we can be forgiving, but we can't just forget that."

Jack rumbled a warning, jumping to his feet as he turned toward Samuel. "No one's forgetting anything. We're having a conversation because she *didn't* mean to do harm."

"Everyone needs to calm down." Stella glanced over her shoulder at the people in the kitchen and continued, "We aren't enemies here, and I'll be damned if I let the stress of the situation cause our group to spiral."

Miles smiled at her adoringly. "My mate's right. This could be the very thing Queen Kel is hoping for."

At this point, I wouldn't even attempt to try to determine her motives outside of attacking us and wanting to take over the Northwest. Everything else that had happened was probably just bonus points.

"What I'm getting at is... I'll give you her number." Stevie rubbed her hands together. "That way, you can call her."

Scratching his scruff, Jack sat back down and put his head in his hands. "I don't know if I like that."

Carl's head tilted back. "Have you lost your mind? How could you *not* like that? That was what the entire conversation was about!"

"It puts Stevie at greater risk." Jack held out his hands. "The queen will be gunning for her even more."

My brows furrowed. I had to be missing something. "Why would it? They came here and left thinking they killed her."

"And they could realize they didn't succeed and come back." Jack squirmed in his seat like he couldn't get comfortable.

He's being weird, Bodey linked to me and then said out loud, "Well, we'd be on the phone, so we could lie and say Stevie gave the number to us before they killed her since Callie's her sister and all."

"Oh, yeah." Jack cleared his throat and placed his hands behind his head. "There is that."

Stevie stared at him, her cheeks flushed.

I'm pretty sure they're fated, I confided, still a little shocked by the revelation. Even though fated mates existed, they weren't common. Most people selected a chosen mate because there was no guarantee they'd ever find their fated. I'd assumed that Miles and Stella and then Bodey and I were exceptions, but maybe being fated wasn't as rare as I'd thought.

"I hate to bring this up right now." Janet bounced on her feet. "But if we want the queen to continue to believe that Stevie is dead, that means that she needs to stay here."

My breath caught as Stevie's jaw dropped.

"So, I can't go home, or I risk the queen learning that I'm alive." Stevie laughed bitterly. "This keeps getting better and better."

"The best thing we can do is make contact with her and get something in the works. Once we get her to back off, then you returning to your family and pack shouldn't be a problem." Phil smiled sadly.

Samuel snatched his cell phone from the table. "What's her number?"

"It's—" Stevie started.

However, Michael lifted a finger. "Wait. Callie needs to be the one to call her."

Lowering his phone, Samuel tensed. "Why? Kel thinks that I'm king."

"Her wolves saw Callie's mark." Bodey pinched the bridge of his nose. "The mark was visible on Callie's fur, and you know that information got back to the queen."

I blew out a breath, wondering again if I should've listened to Stevie that day and not gone to the coronation. But if no one had been marked, then we'd be in even more trouble now.

"Good point." Samuel placed the phone back on the island. He nodded toward the center where my phone sat. "Janet got these from the car for us when she pulled Bodey's car in."

"Here." Phil tossed the phone over the couch to me.

I caught it and unlocked the screen. There was no way I wanted to make this phone call alone. "I'm going to put it on speaker so everyone can hear what she has to say."

Samuel pushed off from the island and came into the den to be closer. "Sounds good to me."

As I hovered my finger over the phone, Bodey put his hand over the screen and asked, "Should we be calling her from your phone?"

"She's going to want to speak to the person in charge." Michael pursed his lips. "And be able to contact her directly if needed."

It'll be fine. It's not like I'll be going anywhere far away from you. If she calls, you'll know immediately. Despite not wanting

Queen Kel to have access to me, that was sort of the point of the entire plan. For the two of us to be able to talk.

His fingers stroked my back. *I'd better.*

Let's just get this over with. I had no clue what to say to the queen, but one thing was certain—standing here dreading it would only make the call worse. "What's her number?"

Stevie rubbed her forehead and then rattled it off.

Once I entered the number, I pressed call and put the phone on speaker. My pulse raced, and my skin grew hot.

I'm right here, Bodey linked as he grasped my hand. He stood in front of me, eyes locked with mine. *You have nothing to fear.*

Our bond jolted to life, and some of my panic eased, loosening the tightness in my chest.

As the phone rang, the thirteen of us glanced at each other. For some reason, I'd expected the queen to pick up immediately.

On the fourth ring, I expected the phone to cut over to voice mail. I was equal parts relieved and terrified since this was our only solid plan, but as I readied to press end call, someone picked up the line.

"Hello." A strong, clear female voice came over the phone.

A lump formed in my throat, and I couldn't form words.

Bodey pushed some calm toward me through our bond, finally allowing me to say *something*. "Hi."

I cringed. Okay, maybe saying nothing would've been better.

"I think you have—"

She was about to hang up on me. I inhaled, trying to keep my head on straight. "Is this Queen Kel of the Southwest Territory?" I interrupted. The one thing I knew for certain was that I didn't want to call her Your Highness or Your Majesty.

A momentary pause informed me that I'd caught her off

guard. "It is. I assume I have the pleasure of speaking to the surprise heir and new top alpha of the Northwest Territory."

My gut churned. Maybe I shouldn't have called her queen. Dammit, Samuel should've been the one to speak. Not wanting her alerted to my inner turmoil, I clutched the phone tighter. "Yes, this is *Queen* Callie."

"Ah. The ignorance of youth." She chuckled darkly. "Those are days I definitely don't miss."

Don't let her rile you, Samuel linked as he moved to my other side.

Right, because being forced to negotiate peace with a sadistic bitch during my first twenty-four hours in this role wasn't pressure enough. Now, I had to deal with the queen trying to frustrate me. Hell, I'd been frustrated before she'd even picked up the damn phone. "I'm not certain what you mean."

"Well, any new royal has a hard time during the transition. All this responsibility is thrust upon them. Even those who have been prepared for it their entire life struggle with how overwhelming it is. Trust me. I know."

My knees shook. I suspected the direction this was going.

"But for a hidden heir everyone presumed dead to be resurrected.... If everyone was as shocked as my wolves described, that offers me one very important piece of information." She paused.

Do not *say anything,* Michael linked with Bodey and me. *She wants you to ask.*

The queen *tsked*, and the corners of my vision darkened. Even if I didn't oblige her, she was still going to talk. This was a show I couldn't control, and she was *right*. I was unprepared to rule.

"Your claim is weak, and your packs will be wary of your leadership." She sighed as if she carried the burden with me. "I can only imagine what sort of weight is on your shoulders. The heir no one wants with the brother who expected to wear the crown you stole from him. It's quite a misfortune."

My wolf growled in my head, refusing to remain quiet. "While I *appreciate* your insight, forgive me if I don't give a flying fuck, seeing as your wolves attacked my *sister* and left her to die. Had she not already given me your number, we wouldn't even be having this *lovely* conversation."

Blowing out a breath, Jack rolled his shoulders as if he was relieved that I made a point of adding that to the conversation.

"Ah, maybe you do have a bit of bite in you after all. I wasn't certain since your sister came to me, begging me to save her family, which you were somehow a part of. A queen who was unable to shift and pack link. The story sounds odd. Maybe your *mate* had something to do with that? How is he doing, by the way?"

Bodey's hands clenched, and he gritted his teeth.

The bitch just threatened my mate. "Listen, I wasn't calling for you to inform me of things I already know." I laughed harshly, knowing that I was most definitely not acting regal. "I want to see if you're willing to meet to discuss a truce between our territories."

Queen Kel laughed, and Lucas and Miles flinched. "Why in the world would I agree to that?"

"Because people are dying on both sides." I couldn't hold back the bitterness in my words. "If we continue to fight, we'll both lose more people. I'm assuming you don't want that any more than I do."

"Let me give you some advice, *Callie*." The queen's tone became condescending. "I've been talking to you in hopes that we can come to a shared understanding. The *only* one. You're not in a place to fight me, so agree to submit to me."

She had some balls. I had to give her that. "I'll find it interesting to see what happens when both your people and mine learn that I requested to meet with you to try to end this conflict amicably." This time, I was the one to *tsk*. "There have been deaths on your side too, but maybe that's easily explained...you just don't care about your people. It's funny what a recording can do to public perception."

She blew out a breath. "You wouldn't dare."

"Try me." I prayed to the gods that she wouldn't call my bluff because I had *nothing*. This was just one big ol' lie in an attempt to get her to stop attacking us. "I mean, youth does have a way with technology after all."

Pride swam from Bodey into me.

"What do you want?" she spat.

"What I asked earlier." I tried to keep my voice steady and calm, but I could hear the tremors in it. "I'd like to meet and discuss a way to resolve our issues without fighting."

"It's called a parlay." Condescension crept back into each word. "Text me the time and location, and I'll think it over. Until then, don't bother calling unless you're ready to deal with the consequences." The line went dead.

Did she hang up? Lucas asked, his eyes sparkling.

I nodded, unable to link or speak. My body sagged.

You were amazing. Bodey pulled me into his arms, nuzzling my neck. *And so damn sexy.*

Amazing was a stretch, but I didn't want to reject the compliment he was trying to give me. "I antagonized her." I winced. "Which I don't think was the point."

"You did well," Michael reassured me. "You pretty much forced her to agree when she had no plan to. Not many people could do that."

I wasn't so sure. I leaned against Bodey, needing him to support my weight. The stress of everything was catching up to me.

"Now we wait." Bodey tugged me against him as he continued, "Stevie should get some rest after the ordeal that she went through, and my mate and I need a nap."

"Good idea." Phil yawned. "We can all meet here for dinner so we can talk about what happens next."

That sounded more than fine with me.

Everyone stood except for Jack, who stayed on the couch next to Stevie. Samuel stared at the two of them as Bodey started to lead me down the hall toward the stairs and our room.

Bodey detoured to Samuel and patted him on the shoulder. *Go get some rest.*

Someone needs to watch her. Samuel frowned.

I wanted to tell him that wasn't true, but to be fair, if I were him, I wouldn't trust my sister either. *Jack will stay close to her.*

"You staying here?" Samuel asked Jack directly.

"Yeah, I figure I'll make sure none of the queen's minions come back while you all are asleep." Jack shrugged. "You know, with the queen, king, and crown heir all living in one house."

See? I tugged on Samuel's arm, urging him to follow us upstairs. *It'll be fine.*

He winced, still sore from his injuries, and then relented, the three of us heading to our rooms. Inside ours, Bodey shut and locked the door.

I didn't hesitate to crawl into bed, and soon, he was sliding under the covers beside me. His hands slid under my shirt, and he spooned me.

Our bond sizzled as the heat from earlier flooded through us. I arched against him, desperate for him to touch me.

After seeing him in so much pain, followed by our argument, and then everything that just happened downstairs, I needed to connect with him again.

He growled as one of his hands inched down the boxers I was wearing while the other one cupped my breast. My breath caught as his fingers delved between my folds, causing me to arch against him again.

I love how you respond to me, he linked as his fingers slipped inside me and his mouth lowered to my neck. His other hand caressed my nipple, causing the buzzing to intensify and cloud my head.

His thumb rubbed my spot as he moved his fingers in and out. Between that, the wonderful graze of his teeth and his tongue on my neck, and how he stroked my breasts, I came unglued in minutes.

"Bodey, I need to touch you," I begged.

"Nope. This is your reward for keeping your head on straight earlier." He chuckled as he bit into my neck.

An orgasm rocked through me, and he held me tight, continuing to work my body. When I shivered, he released me, rolling me onto my back.

He stripped me slowly, taking his time, running his hands over my skin. Goose bumps followed wherever he touched. When I lay naked in front of him, his eyes glowed, taking in every inch of me. *You're so damn beautiful.*

Hmmm. I tapped my chin and smiled. *I wonder if you are. I can't tell with all that material hiding you.*

He laughed, the sound better than any song I'd ever heard, and then quickly removed his clothes. *Is that better?*

Marginally, I teased, taking in every inch of him—his six-pack, his muscular chest, and the trail of hair that led to my very happy place.

Hey, my eyes are up here. He winked.

That they are. I could easily get lost in the indigo of his eyes. They let me see his soul, and his long lashes and sculpted cheekbones were the icing on the cake. I kissed him, and he growled as he moved between my legs and pressed against my entrance.

I shifted my hips, helping him slide inside me in one quick thrust, making me whole.

He hissed. *I wish we never had to stop doing this.*

Sounds like a plan to me. My hands dug into his back, urging him faster.

Wrapping my legs around his waist, I reveled as our bodies worked in rhythm. Need clenched inside me, but I wasn't ready to be done. "On your back."

He eagerly lifted me, obeying, and when I straddled him, he somehow hit deeper. I threw my head back as he cupped my breasts, heightening the pleasure that was building in my body.

I rode him desperately, the sensations more intense than ever. His hands grabbed my hips as he tried to shove even deeper. His body shuddered, and I could feel his orgasm take hold.

My wolf howled, and I leaned forward, biting into his neck again, claiming him once more, as my pleasure flooded our connection. Our bliss melded as our love for one another swirled between us. He groaned in completion, and my body shuddered in ecstasy.

When we stilled, he pulled me against him...into his arms.

Gods, I'm so lucky that you're mine, he linked as my eyelids dropped and sleep took hold of me.

THE NEXT DAY, I found Stevie alone, sitting outside on the deck where Samuel and I liked to chat. She was sitting on one of the Adirondack chairs overlooking the neighborhood road, and for the first time in my life, my hand paused on the door instead of opening it.

I wasn't sure if she would want to speak to me...not after

how we'd left things yesterday. She normally didn't hold a grudge, but she had almost died because of my decisions.

Exhaling, I straightened my shoulders. If I was going to be queen, I should be able to talk to my own sister. So I pushed aside my nerves...and opened the door.

CHAPTER FIFTEEN

AS SOON AS the door opened, Stevie turned her head in my direction. When our eyes met, she neither smiled nor frowned, which had my breath lodging in my throat.

For a moment, we felt like strangers. Both of us were uncomfortable around each other.

I *hated* that. Stevie and Theo had been my two constants growing up, her more than him in so many ways since we'd shared a room. That was one reason we'd gotten so close—we'd had time alone without Pearl's interference.

That said, we'd had plenty of arguments growing up, but nothing remotely similar to *this*.

I moved to the chair closest to the door since she'd taken the one nearest to the room she was staying in—the same one I'd slept in when I'd first arrived here, injured.

She pulled her legs up, holding them to her chest. At least she had her own clothes now. I hoped that put her a little more at ease.

As she tugged on the sleeves of her thin, black cotton sweater, I fidgeted, trying to get comfortable in my seat. My fuchsia top caught my eye, and I smiled sadly. Normally, I'd make a comment about our completely opposite taste in colors. Stevie always said that our favorite colors spoke to our personalities. Me, the wolf who couldn't keep her mouth shut or cower, whose mix of weakness and snark was a beacon to Charles and the other bullies. Stevie, the quiet one who took things in and bottled them up. That was something we'd joked about since we were children, but the words died on my lips. I wasn't sure what I could and couldn't say now that our relationship was like this —strained.

Especially since the jokes weren't funny...not anymore. Between my heritage and the consequences of what it meant, and her actively working against our territory's packs, trying to protect our family, it was like we weren't the same people anymore—not to each other.

"Stevie," I started, knowing I needed to say *something*.

She lifted a hand. "Please don't say anything."

Hope left me in a *whoosh* of a breath.

When she turned toward me, the warmth in her eyes had returned. "I get why you did what you did." She placed her chin on her knees, the wind catching and lifting the loose strands of the dirty-blonde hair that had fallen from her braid. "And I know you didn't mean for me to get hurt."

Thank gods. "Of course not." I clutched my chest as my throat thickened. "Had I known..." I stopped, the lump so large I could barely breathe, let alone speak around it. "Gods, I wish it had been me instead of you."

"Don't say that." She frowned, her eyes glistening. "You've gone through enough shit, and you don't need to hold on to that guilt. You're new to your wolf, not to mention being *queen* and *mated*. I saw the toll it took on you yesterday with everyone's eyes on you, and I was wrong for being so cruel."

My eyebrows lifted. "That might be true, but that isn't an excuse. I still made that decision, and it was a horrible one." It would haunt me. I'd left my sister unprotected, and she'd almost died.

She rolled her eyes. "I'm not saying I'm okay with what happened. I'm not, especially since half the reason I took action was the abuse you personally received from our pack. I just don't have excess energy to waste being pissed at you when you didn't mean to cause me harm."

Her maturity somehow made it harder. I *wanted* her to yell at me, but here she was, being the good person she'd always been. Maybe she hadn't changed after all.

Since she was being honest with me, I wanted to do the same. "After a night of rest and time to think about everything, I came to my own realization." My gaze shifted to the street. I didn't want to see how she reacted. "If I hadn't been marked as queen and mated to Bodey, I wouldn't have been pissed. I would've felt disappointed that you didn't share the burden with me so we could figure it out together, but I would've felt loved. You were willing to risk so much to save us."

"But you *were* mated and marked as our queen, and that's not something we can gloss over," she said sadly. "Neither of us can because you'll think of all the shifters in our territory as a whole first, not your sister."

A part of me wanted to hang my head, but my wolf leaped forward, forcing me to lift my chin. We couldn't show weakness, not when it came to our position. "I'd like to say I can do both, but Stevie, I just don't know." I pivoted my body so I was facing her and continued, "But there are a few things I do know, and I'd like to share one of them."

She quirked a brow. "Which is?"

"That you're my sister, and I love you." I tugged at the pack link between the two of us, hoping she could feel the sincerity of my words. "And I *never* want to see you get hurt like that, ever again. I just hope we can bridge the gap that's been created between us."

"Callie." She leaned over, taking my hand. "There's no gap to bridge. I feel the same way for you, and it would take a hell of a lot more to permanently come between us. Things are different now with you and Bodey and the whole ruling over the territory thing. And if that wasn't enough, now Queen Kel wants *me* dead." She snorted and shook her head. "Who would've thought that you and I, the two lowest-ranking members of our pack, would wind up on the hit list of one queen and that one of us was a queen herself, thanks to some hidden birthright?"

"We should totally write a song about it." I chuckled. "There can't be anything out there that even exists with that theme."

"You write it; I'll sing it." She winked.

I forced my eyes to widen and my jaw to drop. "No way. We would never be able to sell it with that voice."

She stuck out her tongue at me, but she leaned over laughing. "Bitch."

Though I loved her, Stevie couldn't sing to save her life. I faced forward once more and leaned back, closing my eyes and enjoying the cool breeze on my cheeks. "We did say we wanted a different life."

"I'm quite certain neither of us meant *this*." She paused. "But hey, you're *queen*. That's amazing. You can help people who are in our situation."

That was a lofty goal. "I'm a queen who doesn't know what she's doing, *and* I don't remember a damn thing. I'm not certain that Fate isn't messing with me again."

"What did Zeke say when you went there yesterday?"

I opened my eyes and gritted my teeth. "He admitted he

knew who I was, so it's true. He didn't smell of a lie, but at the same time, he said that he wasn't the one who spelled me."

"Well, yeah. He's not a witch." She tilted her head, causing my breath to hitch.

Damn, the conniving bastard. He'd chosen the words carefully, and I hadn't caught it. "No, he can't." I banged my head on the back of the chair. "See! This is why I *need* you."

Talking to her about this was exactly what I'd needed. Not that I couldn't talk with Bodey or even Samuel, but Stevie knew Zeke the same way I did. She knew how vicious and vindictive he truly was, whereas Bodey and the others had dealt with him as equals. Not only that, but they'd grown up knowing they'd one day be in charge of their territories. Stevie and I had a completely different view than the rest of them did.

Seventeen years ago, the child version of myself had known that I'd someday be here, but the person I'd become when my memories were erased hadn't. Bodey and the other advisors had no idea what it was like to be a weak wolf, to be tormented and then thrust into the highest possible position with an advisory council trained since birth with tons of experience.

"Please." She scoffed. "I've always known there was something unique about you. You've never truly *needed* anyone. You survived so much shit, like when Pearl and the others caught you alone. You're a survivor, and you'll figure this out."

I rubbed my temples and then kissed my fingers and held them toward her. She had such good intentions, but she couldn't see things from my perspective. "That's my point. Until two days ago, all I had to worry about was making sure that *I* survived, and today, I'm worried about how I can keep over ten *thousand* wolf shifters safe. How am I supposed to figure that out?" My chest tightened, panic gripping me. "Samuel was the one who was prepared for this. Not me."

"We both know Fate's a bitch, so this shouldn't come as a surprise." She shrugged. "That's all I got."

The two of us had cursed Fate for as long as I could remember. I dropped my hands into my lap. "Maybe this is Fate's way of getting revenge, even though Bodey is definitely *not* a punishment." I cut my eyes toward her and smirked. "And I'm sure you feel the same way about Jack."

Her feet dropped, thumping against the wooden floor. "I don't know what you mean." Her voice sounded high-pitched and breathy.

I arched a brow. "When he touches you, is there a buzz or jolt? Not faint tingles but a truly physical reaction, almost like static electricity but way better?"

Her jaw dropped and her eyes widened. "I thought I was crazy. Yes, that happens. How do you know?"

Tingles flared through my body. I was so damn happy that Stevie had a fated mate and that it was Jack. "Because he's your fated mate."

"Wait. What?" Her head jerked back. "How do you know that?"

"First off, I noticed your reaction on the couch earlier when he touched you, and second, that's what happens when Bodey and I touch. Same for Stella and Miles."

Face blanching, she shook her head. "You're trying to tell me that an *alpha advisor* is my fated mate."

"That's exactly what I'm saying." I shrugged, trying to hold back my laughter at her astonishment. "Maybe Fate's not a complete witch after all. At least she chose good guys for us."

"No! That's cruel." She crossed her arms and grimaced. "He can't be with someone like me. Hell, he wouldn't want to be. I'm weak...nothing."

Heat coiled deep inside me. "First off, you're not *nothing*. Stevie, you're a sweet, funny, loyal, and beautiful woman." I hated when she talked about herself that way. "And second, if you two want to be together, then there's no problem at all. Jack's funny, loyal, and loud and likes to instigate harmless fun. You two balance each other completely."

"But—" she started, just as Bodey linked with me.

I lifted a finger to ask her to wait while he said, *I hate to interrupt you talking to your sister, but you've got a text message from the queen.*

The world stopped. *What does it say? Let's link the others in so they can hear it too.*

Stevie watched me, her hands gripping the arms of the chair. "What's wrong?"

"The queen messaged us." I didn't want to ignore her, but at the same time, this was a pressing matter. "I'm sorry, but I need to go inside."

She nodded as I got up and entered the house. Bodey linked with Samuel, Lucas, Miles, Jack, Zeke, and the dads.

I went into our bedroom, where he was sitting on the edge of the bed. He caught the others up and continued, *She wants to meet in three days in McDermitt, Nevada, at four in the afternoon. We will agree on an exact location an hour before we arrive.*

Even though this should've felt like a win, my heartbeat pounded in my ears.

This is great news, Samuel replied. *She gave in to our request.*

I snorted, causing Bodey to look up from the phone and into my eyes. "What's wrong?"

"*Is* this good news?" I tugged at the ends of my hair. "I don't know anymore."

Bodey's face softened. "Of course it is. This is what we needed to give us time to regroup, and now we have it."

Right, but...I wasn't so sure.

THE NEXT TWO days passed in a whirlwind. The first two coven leaders who came to meet me were from Montana and Washington. Their covens supported Lucas's and Jack's packs, along with the other covens in their states, but neither was very helpful. They didn't recognize the essence of the spell that had locked away my memories.

I packed a bag for the two nights we'd be away staying in McDermitt. It was about a seven-hour drive there from our place in Grangeville, and we wanted to ensure that we had time to scout out the area in case the queen tried to pull something on us.

What did your clothes ever do to you? Bodey teased, but his mood wasn't much better than mine.

Turning from the dresser, I glanced at the black duffel bag that he'd already packed. I should've tried to joke with him, but I didn't have the energy. "They didn't give me answers." I shut the dresser drawer and finished packing my own stuff, then went to the bed and flopped on my back. "I wanted to have more information before meeting the queen. Something I could use to get a reaction from her."

Bodey dropped his bag off the bed and lay down beside me, taking my hand. He murmured, "We'll figure it out."

I rolled to my side, staring at him. "How do you know that?" He radiated confidence, and I wished I just had a smidgen of it myself.

However, when he turned his head toward me, his expression might have been more strained than mine. His confident demeanor faltered. "Because there's no other option."

"That's *not* reassuring." I sighed and stared at the ceiling again.

"Well, I don't want to lie." He squeezed my hand. "Besides,

it's better if I don't because then you'd know I lied to you, and we'd have to smell the horrible stench."

Laughter slipped out, surprising me.

"There we go." He beamed. "My favorite sound in the world."

"Speaking of favorite sounds..." I stood and grabbed his guitar from the corner of the room. He'd played for me the past two nights, but I doubted we'd be bringing the instrument to Nevada. "Wanna play a song before we have to leave?"

"One song; then we have to go." He took it and strummed a chord. "The others will be ready to leave soon."

My heart hurt. I wanted to sit here and listen to him play all day, but we had a job to do...one that would protect so many others. So I nodded.

After a few chords, I recognized the song immediately—"I'll Stand By You" by The Pretenders. He launched into the lyrics, speaking right to my soul. His eyes locked with mine as he hit each note and sang in perfect rhythm as if he was vowing once again to remain by my side no matter what decision I made.

I hadn't even realized it was exactly what I needed. Every time we met someone new or had to deal with a situation, crushing fear strangled me because I didn't know the *right* decision. I felt so lost, like I was drowning, but hearing Bodey tell me he'd be there for me via song and words was the oxygen I'd desperately needed.

When he stopped playing, he laid the guitar on the bed and walked over to me, brushing his fingers under my eyes. His face twisted in concern. "Baby, why are you crying?"

I sniffled, unaware that I had been, so transfixed by the message he'd delivered to me. "I just love you so much. It hurts sometimes."

He smiled tenderly. "The good kind of hurt, right?"

I nodded. "The best."

I love you too, he linked and kissed me.

We're here, bitches, Jack linked, completely ruining the moment as the front door opened.

Bodey tensed and pulled back. "He has the worst timing."

Picking up both our bags, Bodey took my hand and led me downstairs, where Samuel, Lucas, Miles, and Jack were. The four fathers were at Michael's, loading up, and Stevie, Stella, and the three other advisors' moms were staying with Janet while we were gone. After the attack, we wanted them to stay together in case something went wrong while we were away. More shifters would also be patrolling the area.

"Follow us," Bodey said as he locked the front door and waved for us to follow him.

As we went to the vehicle, I linked to Jack, *Did you tell Stevie goodbye?*

Yeah, sure did. He smiled, but there was sadness in his eyes. *I hate leaving her, especially when she's so insistent that she and I shouldn't be together.*

Be patient with her. I patted his arm as we made our way to the garage. *We grew up in a pack where strong wolves didn't even want to talk to us.*

Fuck that shit. Jack scowled. *And don't worry. I'm never letting her go.*

I smiled, thrilled that my sister had someone willing to fight for her.

The four of them got into Jack's Navigator while Bodey and I climbed into his Mercedes-Benz. Then our group was off, heading toward the city with the dads behind us.

Though we wanted to bring a lot of strong wolves to the city with us, we couldn't risk leaving our people vulnerable again, especially if the queen somehow learned about Stevie. The plan was for the packs along the Oregon and Idaho borders to be there with us in case Queen Kel attacked.

"Turn on the music and relax." Bodey took my hand as he pulled onto the road. "We've got a long ride ahead."

My phone rang, startling me awake. I opened my eyes, my neck aching from sleeping upright in the car.

I glanced at my phone. Queen Kel's name flashed across the screen.

"Where are we?" I asked, trying to get my bearings.

"About thirty minutes away from one of my packs that's housing us," Bodey replied.

That was right; Zeke was driving down in the morning, and the rest of us were staying with Bodey's people on the Oregon side of the state line.

I answered the phone, putting it on speaker. I noted that it was close to six in the evening. "Hello?"

"Hey, Callie." The queen sounded arrogant. "I hate to do this, but we need to change the plan."

My hair stood up on the nape of my neck. "What do you mean?"

"We need to meet tonight. I can't meet tomorrow. Can you be at Split Creek, Nevada, in two hours?"

Do you know how far away we are? I swallowed nervously. We could be three hours out, for all I knew.

Tell her two and a half hours, Bodey linked, his knuckles tightening on the wheel. He then linked with the advisors, former advisors, and Samuel, informing them of what was going on.

Heart pounding, I took a deep breath.

Why is she changing locations? Samuel asked. *That sounds like she has something planned.*

Something was off, so I cleared my throat. "Why the

change? We should stick with our original agreement."

"Because, though I have no intentions of harming you or anyone you bring, your group has no reason to not arrive ahead of time to seek retribution." The queen huffed as if explaining herself was hard. "It's safer for *me* this way."

Ask her how we know that's not exactly what she's planning, Bodey linked, taking my hand.

I asked the question.

"My sole goal is to be a strong leader and be taken seriously by *all* wolf territories. No one would be willing to meet me or trust me if I did something like that. You have my word that no harm will come to any of you...at least, not at *this* meeting."

Linking with our group again, I repeated what she said for everyone in the other cars.

I believe her, Michael added. *Everything she said is true. If she wants to be seen as a strong, capable leader, she won't be if she attacks us when we've asked for the meeting. It's not ideal, but her logic isn't flawed. Does anyone disagree?*

No one countered him, so I said, *I'll make the new arrangements.*

Zeke wasn't here, which he'd hold against us, but at least we had everyone else. "We're two and a half hours out."

"Fine. Don't bring more than ten with you and make me regret the leniency," she said and then hung up.

I stared at my phone, hoping like hell we weren't making a huge-ass mistake.

"I don't like it. We'll be getting there around eight, and it'll be dark." Bodey growled. "And we won't have time to stop and coordinate with our packs here. We'll have to get them to meet us there."

That was probably her plan. "Then we do the best we can."

Bodey nodded, and he linked with his pack while I linked with the advisors and dads. I informed them of the change of plans, and no one was pleased, but no one offered a better idea. If we told Kel no, then nothing would change. She was forcing our hand.

So we drove into the mountains, and when we reached the peak where the landscape changed to dirt and trees, my phone rang. Before I could even put it to my ear, she said, "Keep going straight. You'll see a cutout coming up on your right. Get out there, and you'll find a trail that leads to the Split Creek trail-head and river access bridge. Take that path. We'll be a mile past it, waiting for you. I'll see you and everyone else in your three vehicles soon."

She was watching us. Right now.

CHAPTER SIXTEEN

I WASN'T sure what disturbed me the most, the fact that she was having us watched or that she wanted to ensure we knew it.

My head jerked toward the tree line where a flash of gray flickered between a fir and an oak tree despite the darkness. Thank gods for excellent wolf sight, or we'd be screwed.

My chest tightened. "Have you heard from the pack that's helping us?" I didn't want us waltzing into a place where we were clearly outnumbered.

"They're not far behind us." Bodey rubbed the back of his neck, his eyes trained on the curvy road in front of us. "Maybe ten minutes if that."

I linked with the other advisors, dads, and Samuel, giving them an update.

Samuel replied, *Even though I suspect what she said is true, we can't lower our guard.*

Maybe we shouldn't go? Bodey's tension swirled through the link, adding to mine.

Son, if we don't go, she'll amp up her attacks just for us not showing. We go as planned, but with caution, Michael replied calmly. *Neither side trusts the other. Based on what you said, she knows we'll have backup because she specified a number to attend the meeting.*

The plastic of my phone popped, and I loosened my grip on it. The last thing I needed was to destroy my phone and have Kel try to call me again.

Baby, it'll be all right. Bodey took my hand as the cutout Kel had referenced came into view. It was large enough for two of our cars, so someone would have to drive farther up the road and park elsewhere.

I flinched. "I'm not so sure about that." My blood turned to ice. "The queen has been targeting you. Maybe you should stay in the car."

He shook his head, his nostrils flaring as he stopped and put the car into Park. "Not happening. There's no way in hell I'm going to sit here in the car while my queen and *mate* meet with a sadistic queen. What would you say if I asked you to stay here?" His anger blazed through our connection, but I remained cold.

I couldn't help but grimace. "I'd be beyond angry." I hated to admit that because I wanted him to be safe, but if I didn't tell him the truth, he'd know anyway. Damn wolves and their sensitive noses.

He grinned, catching me off guard as his love flowed through to me. "I love how transparent your face is right now. It's like I caught you sticking your hand in the cookie jar."

I stuck my tongue out. "I don't want you to get hurt...*again*."

"Oh, I understand that sentiment." He reached over, tucking a piece of my light-blonde hair behind my ear. "You need to remember I've seen you hurt just as many times as you've seen me. And one of those times, Dina and her leaders weren't nearby to help heal you."

"True." I pouted and shrugged. "But we weren't mated then."

He arched a brow. "Babe, I fell for you the moment I saw you—which was during an attack, might I add. I just needed my head to catch up." He kissed me and linked, *Besides, what kind of king consort would I be if I stayed safe while the love of my life faced evil head-on?*

Damn him and his logic. "A live one."

"Keep it up, and I'll remember it next time that I'm desperate for you to stay behind."

I exhaled. "You win. Besides, I couldn't do this without you next to me."

"You underestimate yourself, babe." He bit his bottom lip and glanced out my window. "And Samuel, Jack, Lucas, and Miles are standing behind you."

I'd been so focused on Bodey that I hadn't even sensed them. I glanced over and yelped.

Jack's face was right against the window, and we were eye to eye. I hadn't been expecting that.

And then he beamed. *She's easy to scare. Hell yeah.* Jack nodded. *Wait until we get away from here.*

Now's not the time, Lucas replied, smacking him in the back of the head.

The shaggy top of his blond hair fell right into his eyes, and he brushed it off his face.

Miles turned toward the sparse trees, scanning the area. *We don't have time for this shit. We need to stay focused.*

Come on. Samuel nodded to the front of the car where Michael, Phil, Carl, and Dan appeared, walking back from where they'd found a spot to park their car. They stopped about twenty feet away, where I figured the trail must start.

Miles shooed the other guys away from the door and opened it for me. When I stepped out, the crisp, cool air of the mountain settled over me. Then the sound of wolves running about a half mile away sent my heart thudding.

Our wolves left their vehicles about five miles away and are shifting and running this way, Bodey linked with us. *They'll be nearby soon in case something happens.*

Even though that was great news, the knot in my stomach hardened instead of easing. *Then there's no point in delaying any longer.* I straightened my shoulders and walked toward the dads.

I glanced down at my chest, seeing the bottom of the paw print, the moon, and the clouds rolling over it. My sweater was a V-neck, so there could be no question that I was marked if this was Queen Kel's way of verifying it herself.

Bodey caught up and slid his hand into mine. The buzz of our connection made my lungs move easier, but the dread kept building with each step.

When we reached Michael and the others, he waved us forward, indicating we should be the ones to lead the way to the queen. I paused, reaching out my other hand to Samuel. I linked to him, *I'd love for you to be by my side too.*

Of course. He hurried forward, taking the spot to my right, and then the three of us stepped deeper into the woods. The musky scent of unfamiliar wolves hung in the air, indicating that the queen and her pack members had already arrived.

An owl hooted, and the sound of hooves shuffling in the distance brought me some comfort. Maybe elk. At least they weren't acting as if they sensed a threat.

We continued down the path, and I surveyed the area around me. The trees were several feet apart, and between the trunks, I spotted a light-colored wolf to the right and a dark-gray wolf to the left, trotting along beside us.

They weren't trying to stay hidden, which was why I didn't turn around and race back to the car.

Jack, Miles, and Lucas followed us with the four older men at the very back of the group.

Besides the animals, the only sounds I could hear were our breaths. Everyone's nerves were frayed.

Remember to remain calm when we get there, Samuel linked as his eyes locked with mine. *You need to chat with her and break the ice before discussing business. It'll help generate goodwill on both sides.*

Chat? My eyebrows rose, and I had to swallow my laugh. *You want me to chat with the woman who has gone out of her way to attack us and hurt you and Bodey and who tried to have my sister assassinated?* He had to be joking. I was more likely to cut the bitch than ask her how her day was.

You're a queen now. Samuel tilted his head and pressed his lips together. *You can't let your emotions get the best of you. If you do, this meeting won't be successful.*

This job wasn't the one for me. Fate should've had that ink mark Samuel. Emotions were the only freedom I'd had my whole life. I'd gotten through the pack abuse by holding on to hope and the instinct to survive. If I hadn't felt them, I would've broken a long time ago. And now, I was supposed to not react, the one thing I'd always cherished as my own. I wasn't sure I could do it, but dammit, I had to try. If Samuel said it was what I needed to do, then I'd trust him.

When we made it over a slight incline, the path dropped, revealing a breathtaking woman standing in the middle of the trail with a tall man behind her and nine others deeper in the trees.

Her dark hair was pulled on top of her head, and wisps hung in her face. The moonlight glistened on her tan skin, her haunting, gray eyes sparkling. A cream silk dress draped her body like a second skin, the low neckline showing off her own ink—a small, simple moon just under her collarbone. The most surprising part was that, despite her elegant dress, she had bare feet. Her toes dug into the dirt as her crimson-painted lips broke into a smile. "Right on time."

I stiffened, wanting to stop in my tracks, but I forced my legs to keep moving forward. Bodey moved closer to me, our arms now brushing. We stopped several feet in front of Kel's group.

"Sorry I didn't dress for the occasion." I lifted my chin, trying to pretend I wasn't uncomfortable. "You gave us such short notice. Fortunately, we were driving down the night before, or we wouldn't have made it."

She chuckled. "All is forgiven. Not every queen can balance duty and keeping up appearances."

Two seconds in, and she was already insulting me. This was already going so well. My wolf snarled in my head, but I forced my face into a mask of indifference, repeating Samuel's words about not becoming emotional.

That woman really is a bitch, Jack scoffed.

Miles replied, *What did you expect? Someone nice, kind, and amicable? She's been attacking us nonstop.*

At least she's hot, Lucas added.

"But, while we were on our way here, a matter came to our attention that we needed to handle." She clasped her hands, putting them in front of her stomach. "So...that was why there was a last-minute change."

She's being careful with her words and paused so you'd ask, Michael linked. *Don't push it.*

Silence stretched until Kel laughed. "I see the spare, the advisors, and their fathers didn't find you adequate to handle this alone. However, there appears to be one advisor missing." She arched a brow. "Which intrigues me. Is he aware of this meeting?"

We informed him, Phil linked. *So he knows.*

She was fishing for information, but luckily, we had a good response. "He was planning to drive down in the morning since the meeting was scheduled for tomorrow. After the time was changed, he couldn't be here."

"Very well." She gestured, and the tallest and hairiest man stepped forward to stand beside her. "This is my right hand, Herald."

Herald held out his hand to me.

Be careful, Dan connected. *He's known to be vicious.*

The thought of touching him made my skin crawl, but I didn't want to be rude, especially in front of the queen. Against instinct, I reached out, and he clasped my hand hard. He watched my face, most likely anticipating a reaction.

This prick was just like Zeke, so I knew the best way to piss him off. I schooled my face into an expression of indifference. My wolf snarled as my gaze met his, and I smiled. "Nice to meet you."

The corners of his mouth tipped downward as he tightened his hold on me. He must not know that I hadn't been raised with privilege and kindness. I'd been hurt and beaten, and I'd refused to submit to those pricks, so I definitely wouldn't start cowering now. I pretended I didn't notice.

Bodey clearly felt my pain because he growled beside me. "You can quit touching my *mate* now." Then he bared his teeth at Herald.

"You must be the king consort." Herald chuckled and dropped my hand.

"Oh, yes," the queen said as she ogled Bodey. "It's so good to see you here."

I couldn't help reacting to that. I stepped in front of my mate. I wasn't sure if she was flirting with him or threatening him, but either way, that shit ended now.

The queen smiled.

Callie, you're letting your emotions control you. Samuel

cleared his throat and said, "It's nice to meet you after all this time, Queen Kel."

Her gaze landed on my brother, and a mischievous glint entered her eyes. "Ah, the spare and his manners. It must have been a blow when you weren't marked."

"All my life, I wished I could've gotten to know my family before they died." Samuel placed a hand on my shoulder and continued, "Nothing could ever compare to finding out I have a sister."

Kel sniffed as if searching for the lie, and her smile flattened. "Well, isn't that nice?"

Her irises glowed, and she turned back to me. "How many wolves did you bring? One of mine saw a group cross their path."

"Does it matter?" I lifted a brow. Giving her a number wouldn't be smart. If she had more, then she might attack us. If she had fewer, she might feel threatened. Either way, I wasn't going to play that game. "As long as you don't attack us, it won't be a problem. Will you reveal how many you have?"

She pursed her lips. "Fair point. I don't mean harm to any of you, including the new arrivals, as long as you don't threaten me."

Jack snorted. "Yeah, okay."

"This one is an advisor?" Herald wrinkled his nose, running his hand along his dark beard. "He speaks as if he has more authority."

Now is not *the time.* Carl linked with Jack, Bodey, and me but spoke to Jack.

"Callie, why don't you and I take a walk together so we can discuss things more privately?" The queen gestured behind her. "They'll still be able to hear our conversation, but they might not feel as free to contribute." Her attention flicked over my shoulder to Jack.

Bodey tensed while Samuel said, "Maybe I should join you two."

Tsking, Kel shook her head and placed a hand on her chest. "Oh, Callie. This is unfortunate. Neither your mate nor your brother believe that you can handle talking to me alone."

The insinuation rang clear. They didn't think I was a strong leader. We were helping her campaign.

"That's not true at all," Bodey snapped, his body quivering. "I don't trust *you* not to hurt her."

"As I said on the phone, I won't hurt anyone here tonight." Kel tapped a long, crimson fingernail to her lips. "So that's the only explanation I can come up with."

"Do you smell a lie?" Bodey countered, moving up beside me again. "Callie's more than capable of ruling our territory."

Huffing, Kel straightened her shoulders. "And did you smell a lie when I said I had no intention of harming any of you?"

"Let's go talk." If we began arguing, this whole meeting would become pointless. If we were going to work out an agreement, then I needed to be accommodating...to a point. After all, Kel hadn't given me a hard time about not telling her how many wolves we'd brought.

"Perfect."

She looped her arm through mine, and a warning sensation raced down my spine. However, I didn't pull away, and we walked past Herald, whose eyes stayed locked on me.

The moon was high in the sky, which was mostly clear, with the stars shining above us. This place would be beautiful if I weren't here with her.

We walked about half a mile toward a river, and the trees thickened slightly as we got closer to the water.

Kel paused. "I think we're good here." Releasing my arm, she turned toward me. "Let's talk."

I wanted to get straight to the point, but Samuel's words

came back to me—build goodwill. I tried to find something neutral to begin with. Despite the nausea churning in my stomach, I said, "Yes, I thought it might be nice to meet since we rule territories that share borders. I'd like to find a way to live harmoniously with one another." My wolf whimpered, as disgusted with me as I was myself.

Kel rolled her eyes. "*This* is what you want to discuss? An *introduction*? We could've done that over the phone instead of wasting each other's time with the drive."

It wasn't what I wanted, but clearly, I hadn't lowered her guard like Samuel had suggested. "It's just—"

She lifted a hand. "Is this how you plan to lead your people?" Her nose wrinkled. "Being passive and not getting to the point? My people have attacked yours... Hell, I had your sister killed, and you're trying to be my *friend*? If you aren't going to address anything important, then we're done here."

My wolf leapt, and there was no pretending any longer. "Fine. You want honesty? I can't stand you, and I want you to stop attacking my mate, my brother, my family, and my people —*now*."

Throwing her head back, Kel laughed hard before her mouth twisted into an eerie grin. "There's only one way that will happen, and it's the *only* reason I agreed to meet with you."

My heart dropped. "And what is that?"

"Submit to me."

Lungs seizing, I blinked. "You've got to be kidding."

"I'm not." She shrugged. "Submit to me, and the attacks are over. You'll be with your mate, the Northwest packs will be safe, and I'll let you live out your life in peace."

She had to be drunk. "There has to be another solution."

"None that I'll accept." She pointed to the ground. "Bow, acknowledge me as your alpha, and all this will be over."

My wolf howled so loudly she made my head pound. "Never." Even if I wanted to, my wolf wouldn't allow it.

"You need to realize that, by coming here, you've acknowledged I'm a threat to you." She gestured in the direction we'd come from. "I know that you care for all of them dearly. Submit now before I have to rip away everything you love in order to break you. Spare yourself the pain and heartache. Keep those you love safe."

That was the thing with people like her and Zeke. I'd never be safe. She'd still see me as a threat, and even if she believed she wouldn't hurt me now, she would eventually. Or I'd do something to piss her off, and she'd need to teach me a so-called *lesson*. I'd grown up with a person just like her, and I wasn't foolish enough to believe in some far-fetched promises. "We're strong. We don't need protection from you. You're better off killing me."

"Is that what you believe?" She chuckled. "Oh, no, dear. Your death is the last thing I want."

I stared into her eyes. "Why?"

"That question proves you're not fit to rule." Her eyes glowed, and then she snickered. "Just remember, I gave you a chance, and you didn't take it." She turned and started walking back toward the others. Then she tossed over her shoulder, "Oh, and when you do change your mind, you know how to get a hold of me." With that, she left me behind.

It didn't work, I linked to the others. My eyes burned with unshed tears. I didn't want anyone to know that I was close to crying. *She wanted me to submit to her. She claims that's the only way the attacks will end.*

I knew I didn't trust the bitch, Jack roared. *Let's kick their asses now.*

We can't, Samuel replied. *A parlay happens on neutral ground, and we promised not to attack one another. If we attack her, we'll look bad to everyone, including our own packs. We'll become untrustworthy.*

The queen darted off the path in the opposite direction as I headed back toward the cars. *She's going east.*

They must have parked on a different road, Bodey replied. *I'm heading to you now.*

I should have told him no, that he'd only wind up retracing his steps, but dammit, I needed him. I picked up my pace, ready to get the hell out of there. Meeting Kel had been pointless, but at least I had a sense of who we were up against. She was evil, vindictive, and out for blood. There wouldn't be any negotiating with her.

A shiver ran down my spine, and I began jogging back toward the others. Something in the air didn't feel right.

When Bodey and I met up, he pulled me into his arms. I nestled into his chest, taking a moment in his strong embrace to help me move past the confrontation.

You did everything you could, he linked as he pulled away to cup my cheeks.

The problem was, I didn't believe him.

He frowned and took my hand, and together, we met up with the others.

On our way back to the vehicles, Zeke popped into Bodey's and my heads.

We need your help now, he linked. *An Ontario pack is under attack. They're pretty sure that it's Queen Kel's shifters.*

CHAPTER SEVENTEEN

I FROZE as my wolf came forward. *The queen?* She'd just left our meeting. That shouldn't be possible.

Yes, the very person you were supposed to parlay with, he scoffed via our pack link. *You know...the one who hurt my son.*

Bodey's blood boiled. *She knows who the fuck the queen is, asshole.*

Well, it didn't sound like it, Zeke snapped back.

We just met with her. I shook my head, trying not to get caught up in my hatred for Zeke. It would be so easy to focus on that, but right now, lives were at stake. *Which pack?*

The Ontario pack—the one you and Theo visited together. A little bit of smugness pulsed through the link.

Snarling, Bodey tensed, which no doubt had been Zeke's plan. He clearly wanted to taunt Bodey with the time Theo and I had spent together. And it was partly Bodey's fault. If he hadn't pushed me away, saying he wanted to wait for his fated mate—who so happened to be *me*—I wouldn't have been there with Theo. I was quite certain that was one reason it angered Bodey so damn much.

What did you say to her to make her attack so quickly? Zeke added, his annoyance flaring through between us. *Clearly, you pissed her off.*

"Callie, what's wrong?" Samuel asked from behind Bodey and me.

"The queen is attacking a pack in Oregon." The words chaffed my throat, causing it to burn.

Lucas gasped while Michael groaned.

"We underestimated her viciousness again," Phil growled. "She had wolves in fucking place, suspecting that Callie wouldn't submit to her. This attack is to show us that she's a step ahead of us in all ways."

Her earlier threat hung over my head. She'd made it clear that the wolves here were safe to come and go. She'd been oddly specific, but I'd thought she was trying to reassure me. Now I knew better. She was making sure she didn't say everyone in my *territory*.

Gods, I hated politics.

I didn't submit to her. I couldn't ignore Zeke; he was the one who had information I needed right now. I snatched my phone from my back pocket, tapping in the address. I had no clue how far away we were from Ontario, but I was certain that we wouldn't be able to reach them in time to fight alongside them. Thankfully, I'd met the alpha before and knew he was strong and competent. His pack had a coven that lived near them. One of the witches had been in his house while Theo and I were there discussing the coronation dinner.

I grimaced at the map. As I'd suspected, there was no way we'd get there in time to help. "We're six hours away, so we need to hurry and get there as quickly as possible." Even if we weren't there to fight, we could help pick up the pieces of what remained, bury the dead, and offer our support.

I took off running toward the cars as a chill tracked down my spine. It felt as if we were still being watched. The queen might still be close by, enjoying our panic. *Do you feel that?* I linked with just Bodey.

Yeah, I suspect it's the queen herself, wanting a view of her handiwork. Bodey wrinkled his nose and removed the keys from his pocket.

I hated that the hair on the nape of my neck was standing on end.

The dads headed to their car as Bodey hollered, "Follow us. We'll pull out in front of you in a second."

We broke into a faster pace as we raced to our own vehicles. Bodey had already started our car when Lucas, Miles, Jack, and Samuel climbed into the Navigator behind us.

He zoomed out of the spot, and Jack wasn't more than a few seconds behind as we took the curve to where the dads waited, Carl in the driver's seat. The three vehicles drove seventy miles per hour around the turns and bends despite the speed limit being twenty-five.

I held on to the door handle and the center console, clenching my teeth. "Is it safe to drive like this?" We wouldn't be much good if we died before we even reached the other pack.

Bodey chuckled but kept both hands on the wheel and his eyes on the road. "Yes. I'm used to driving on winding mountain roads."

Not only that, but wolf shifters had quicker reflexes than humans, so I was being silly and paranoid. He wouldn't put me in danger.

Maybe you should've just submitted, Zeke's voice intruded into both Bodey's and my minds.

Bodey growled. *Why the hell would you say that?*

Because a second pack is being attacked, Zeke snapped. *They're near Lakeview, which is close to where you are now.*

Bile churned in my stomach, and a salty taste filled my mouth. *What's the address?*

He rattled it off, and I added a stop to the GPS, wanting to see if we could reach this one in time. It was only thirty minutes away. *Yes, they're a lot closer.*

Then I'd recommend getting your asses there, considering it's one of the weakest packs in Oregon. I'm heading to Ontario now and have a pack closer to them en route as well.

I swallowed past a lump lodged in my throat and linked with everyone in both vehicles. *We're heading to Lakeview instead. She's attacking there too, and it's only thirty minutes away.*

Less, if I have anything to do with it, Bodey interjected, his jaw twitching from his clenching.

Jack replied, *This is seriously fucked up.*

All because you refused to submit to her, Michael linked. *She must have known you wouldn't, or these two attacks wouldn't be happening. Ontario is one of the strongest packs in Oregon, and Lakeview's one of the weakest.* He confirmed Zeke's assessment.

Kel's words repeated in my head. *She told me I'd wind up coming to her, but if she's this type of monster, submitting to her would be foolish.* If she could do this to people she wanted to lead, then all she would ever do was instill fear. *Did you all hear that part?* Wolves could hear for miles, and we'd been maybe a half mile away.

We heard bits and pieces of your conversation, but the guards were purposely talking, so we couldn't hear everything, Samuel replied, his frustration churning through our connection. *She set this up to teach you a lesson.*

What would submitting to her accomplish? That was the part I truly didn't understand. *Wouldn't she rather I be dead?* If I were alive, then I would continue to be a threat to her rule.

If you submit to her, then all of us do as well because we recognize you as our alpha, Michael explained. *So, instead of having to force each advisor and each pack to submit one by one, she just has to get you—the ultimate alpha—to do it. It's smart, but she's underestimating you.*

Bodey's disgust surged through our bond. *But she wouldn't hesitate to kill you after you submit to her.*

I glanced out the window, staring at the trees and dirt that flashed by as Bodey navigated the road. I rubbed my temples. *Then why go after Bodey and Samuel? You'd think she'd know that if she killed them, I wouldn't ever forgive her.*

That's probably the point. She doesn't care about you forgiving her. Samuel paused. *She wants to break you. If you lose your mate and your brother—the only other royal who could replace you—you'd be left with nothing. She intends to take everything from you so you can't function.*

She'd mentioned that I couldn't see the bigger picture, and I hadn't. But Samuel had.

Pack links began to disappear from my chest, and pain cracked through me, causing me to double over. Five warm spots vanished almost at once.

"Callie, what's wrong?" Bodey glanced at me from the corner of his eye, slowing down the vehicle.

"People in our territory are dying." I rubbed my chest as the warmth of another two faded slowly. My vision blurred as I took a shaky breath. Coldness began engulfing my chest as if I were soaking in ice water.

Bodey's face strained as his wolf fought forward. "I feel it now that you mention it, but I'm not as connected with them as you are. You'll be impacted more than me."

A tear trailed down my cheek, another one falling right after. I hated sitting here in a car and being unable to do anything. I felt extremely helpless. I'd made the wrong call. I should've known she had something up her sleeve, but once again, I was reminded how unprepared I was to rule.

Placing a hand on my arm, Bodey drove faster. "We're going to get there, and we'll help them."

I leaned my head back as the chill seemed to drag me under. I hoped that we would get there in time to save our people.

THE GPS's automated voice told us to turn on a back road, and I noticed we were five minutes away from the pack neighborhood. Bodey had gotten us here in twenty-three minutes.

Bodey and I talked with Zeke, keeping him informed of our progress while we kept the advisors, Samuel, and the dads updated on the pack links. Zeke was still two hours away from Lynerd, but he'd been checking in, and they were holding their own. The other pack Zeke had sent to aid them was thirty minutes out, so they'd arrive before him.

During the drive here, at least twenty more wolves had passed, and though my skin was warm, everything inside me froze as I tried to acclimate to the continued changes to the number of links in my chest.

I dropped the phone in my lap and rubbed my legs. I was eager to get there and fight, but I also didn't want to because of Bodey and the risk Queen Kel posed to him and my brother.

"Hey, it's gonna be okay." Bodey squeezed my upper thigh. "We'll get there and help the pack. Then we'll figure out the next step together."

Gods, I loved the sound of that. Hope flared in my chest, warming it temporarily. I had to temper that emotion fast. "I don't know if we can," I whispered, knowing that he'd hear me.

I turned toward him, taking in his sharp cheekbones and full lips. His shirt clung to his muscles, and I took a moment to really look at him. Who knew if this was the last time we would be together like this? If the queen was intent on killing him, and she'd already planned these attacks, who was to say that she wouldn't make his death a reality?

If I'd thought my chest was cold before, the mere thought of Bodey dying shattered my heart. The pain was overwhelming. Gasping, I sucked in air, filling my lungs.

His head snapped my way. *Babe, what's wrong? Did something happen?*

A sob broke through. *I can't imagine my life without you. She wants you dead. I don't know if racing to help them is the right answer with you and Samuel in tow.*

Warmth spread through our bond as he pushed the sensation toward me. "I need you to hear me, so I'm saying this out loud. I have no intention of dying or leaving you behind. She wants you dead too, and I plan to be here to make sure that *never* happens. If you want me to stay on the sidelines, then that goes for you as well."

My wolf snarled. These were my people. Even if I wasn't the most competent leader, I sure as hell wasn't going to stay safe and let them all get hurt. I had to protect them...it was my duty. "I can't—" I flinched, knowing that had been his point all along.

"And neither can I, especially if you're in danger," he said, taking my hand and interlacing our fingers. "We're in this together. Always and forever."

He pushed his love toward me, the sensation eddying through my chest, relieving some of the coldness. It didn't take away the pain of the people we'd lost, but there was a promise of the future in it. I nodded. "Always and forever."

I would go anywhere with him, even into death if necessary, as long as the two of us were together.

"We're here," he said, forcing my eyes away from his face and forward once more.

We were blowing past thicker firs, which meant we were at

a lower elevation, and several small one-story homes came into view. They appeared to have been built many years ago, and just like all the other pack neighborhoods I'd seen, each house had a backyard that connected to the woods.

At first glance, it didn't appear as if anything was happening. It was close to ten, and most houses had lights on inside.

But when Bodey pulled to the side of the road and turned the car off, I could hear the growls of battle.

We're here, I linked with Zeke. *And they're still fighting the queen's wolves.*

A flicker of trepidation came through from Zeke before he replied, *Keep me informed of the status.*

The only silver lining about that was that I hadn't felt as many deaths from Lynerd's pack as I had down here.

The other two vehicles pulled in behind us as Bodey and I shed our clothes and called our wolves. Seconds later, I was running on four legs.

As we darted between a blue house the shade of a robin's egg and one painted a pastel green, the doors of the other vehicles slammed shut behind us. Bones cracked, informing me that they were already shifting as well, and paws soon padded in our direction.

All of us wanted to protect the wolf shifters here.

As we passed through the backyard, the stench of blood filled my nose and throat. The scent was so thick I didn't want to see what lay ahead, but at the same time, I knew that if I didn't, things would only get worse from here.

We ran into the woods, the sounds of battle now not even a quarter mile away. I dug my paws into the ground, pushing myself to reach them. Bodey ran beside me at the same pace.

As we breezed past a tree, I faltered.

Ten dead wolves lay in front of us, each one about twenty

feet from the next. Each lay in a tangled mess on the ground with their throat ripped out.

A yelp drew my attention from the carnage, and I shook my head, trying to clear it. I needed to focus on the living, not the dead.

We need to stick together, Bodey linked, knowing exactly what my thoughts were. *If they managed to do this to a whole pack, we can't run in blind. They're almost done here anyway.*

I huffed, pawing at the ground. My wolf wanted to rush forward, but he was right. The queen was counting on me not thinking strategically.

The advisors, Samuel, and the dads caught up. We'd slowed for only a few seconds, but it had felt like a lifetime, knowing my people were in trouble.

I began darting through the trees again, Bodey beside me and our wolves right on my heels. We ran into a clearing.

Bodey's hackles rose, and my heart stopped. There were at least fifty wolves attacking about thirty of my pack members in this area alone.

My wolf took over, lunging for a dark-gray wolf that had already slashed a smaller tan wolf in the shoulder. The gray wolf lunged, aiming for the tan wolf's throat.

I leapt, soaring over the brush that blocked me from reaching them, and slammed into the dark-gray wolf just as his teeth broke the skin of the tan wolf's neck. The tan wolf's blood splattered my face as I knocked the rival wolf to the ground. I could feel the flicker of a bond in my chest, cooling once more.

I hadn't been able to save her.

Anger like I'd never felt before boiled inside me, sizzling through my blood. This asshole was going to pay for what he'd done.

CHAPTER EIGHTEEN

THE DARK-GRAY WOLF rolled over on his back, trying to get all four paws underneath me to injure and throw me off. Before he could manage to succeed, I struck, sinking my teeth into his throat.

Blood poured into my mouth, the copper taste invading my senses. I tightened my jaws, using my bottom teeth to sever his artery. I snarled, wanting the last thing the asshole heard to be me.

When the wolf gurgled, I wrenched my head back, finishing the job. He wheezed and flopped to the ground as I took a step back, surveying the area. There were plenty of enemy wolves still here and people I needed to protect.

Every one of us was now engaged in battle, and my eyes were drawn to Bodey, needing to make sure he was all right.

He was about twenty feet away, protecting one of our pack members who lay helpless on the ground. Bite marks covered his body, and he whimpered as he struggled to breathe. Bodey crouched in front of the injured wolf as a dark-beige wolf attacked.

I was moving to help him when my eyes caught on a hazelnut-colored wolf cowering in front of a tree while two foes approached her. She whined, not even pretending to want to fight, and my heart squeezed.

Her submissive nature seemed to encourage the auburn and slate wolves to descend on her, taking pleasure in her fear. For a moment, Charles's and Pearl's wolves replaced them in my mind, their demeanor so similar to that of my sister and her boyfriend.

Resentment spiraled inside me, making my legs move before I'd completely thought it through. If these were the type of wolves the queen encouraged, then she was no better than Zeke. The hazelnut wolf needed my help, whereas Bodey didn't.

I growled, drawing their attention away from their prey to the incoming threat.

The auburn wolf spun in my direction, taking eager steps toward my left side while the slate wolf charged at my right. Timing it so that she was a few steps behind the slate, the auburn wolf picked up speed to attack a few seconds later.

I hunkered down, ready for them. The slate wolf lunged, mouth open wide as he aimed for my neck, while the auburn one locked her gaze on my left leg.

I forced myself to wait a second more, not wanting to alert them to my next move, then stood on my hind legs. Without my body to stop its forward motion, the slate wolf fell in front of me. I sank my teeth into his shoulder, pushing him back as the auburn wolf crashed below me. I dug my claws into her back, leveraging her body to help slam the slate wolf's head to the ground.

With a loud *thwack,* the slate wolf hit his side, and I jerked his body, so he then landed on his back. My right paw dug into his stomach while my left one dug into the dirt.

Keening, the slate wolf frantically thrashed, trying to throw me off as sounds behind me hinted that the auburn wolf was back on her feet.

Before I could react, the auburn wolf landed on my back, digging her claws into my side. I released my hold on the slate wolf and threw myself backward so that all my body weight landed on the auburn wolf.

As she rolled, I lunged forward and sank my teeth into her throat. She shoved her paws into my chest, drawing blood, but she didn't manage to get too deep before I ripped out her throat.

The slate wolf slammed into my side, causing me to roll over the dying auburn wolf. When my feet were underneath me, I rose just as the slate wolf bit into my right shoulder.

Pain blinded me as I swiped his left leg, making sure to hit him hard enough that his leg gave out. He jerked, his hold loosening, but still maintained a strong enough grip for his teeth to slash through my skin.

Callie, Bodey linked, his fear tightening the thread of our bond. *I'm coming. Hold on.*

Putting all my weight on my back legs, I clawed the slate wolf's shoulder, giving him an injury matching my own.

He snarled and jumped back to his feet, my blood dripping from his teeth and staining the dirt. He inched toward me, wanting me to cower like the wolf I was protecting.

I lifted my head, doing the exact opposite. I refused to give him even the illusion of being stronger than me. Wanting him to attack me, I pawed at the ground and bared my teeth, meeting his gaze. Challenging him to fight me.

That was enough to make him snap. He lowered his head, clearly planning to steamroll me by aiming for my injured shoulder. I spun left, barely avoiding him. I heard him stumble as my gaze landed on a dark-blond wolf sneaking up on one of my pack members from behind.

No.

I surged forward as I pulled on the tether that attached to my unsuspecting pack member and linked, *Watch out.*

Before she could react, I slammed into the dark-blond wolf, knocking him into a fir tree that was maybe five feet away.

The targeted wolf pack member glanced over her shoulder as the other wolf she was fighting bit into her side. She yelped, turning her attention back to the more immediate threat, just as slate fur flashed in the corner of my vision and something sharp pierced my back left paw.

A cry bubbled in my throat, but I swallowed the noise and moved to the right. I kicked the slate wolf in its face with my back right leg, the impact straining my injured shoulder.

I stumbled back to face both my attackers. The dark-blond wolf swiftly faced me, and the slate wolf growled as blood poured down its split ear.

My back left leg wobbled, struggling to support my weight, and my right shoulder throbbed from the bite. The magic inside me, trying to repair my injuries, wasn't anywhere close to witch magic.

The slate wolf smiled, his teeth tinged pink from my blood. My chest tightened, fear that I might not make it out of this without getting seriously hurt taking root.

Their eyes glowed as they no doubt talked strategy, and I forced myself to take deep, steady breaths to keep my mind as clear as possible. They moved in tandem, each focused on one side of my body, and lunged, going for my shoulders, knowing that my back paw was severely injured.

Gritting my teeth, I rose on my hind legs and jumped, certain they wouldn't expect that. I put as much weight as possible on my back right leg, but the jarring was horrific. I forced myself to remain standing, and both wolves corrected, ready to lunge at me once more.

Callie! Bodey linked, his worry so thick that it added to the terror strangling my heart.

I dropped one front paw on each of their backs and ignored the agony surging through my shoulder. My muscles felt like they were separating as I shoved both wolves to the ground, their faces hitting the dirt.

Dust kicked up around us from the impact, burning my eyes, but I blinked through it, focused on my end goal.

Survival.

Both wolves recoiled, and I dug my claws in and ripped from midback to the tops of their heads. Unfortunately, I wasn't able to dig as deep into the slate wolf since he was on the side of my injured paw, but at least I got in another swipe.

Blood, fur, and skin clumped in my nails, and my back leg gave out under the pressure.

My back end hit the dirt, causing a sharp pain that caught my breath.

The slate wolf choked out a laugh. The prick knew I was injured, and he was enjoying every minute of my suffering. He prowled toward me, treating me as prey.

Bodey bounded in front of me, snarling as he bit into the wolf's neck. The slate wolf whimpered and twisted, trying to shake him loose.

The dark-blond wolf lunged at me, going for the attack.

Adrenaline pumped through my body. If I didn't take out this wolf, they'd gang up on my mate. I couldn't allow that.

I dropped to my belly, and the wolf landed on my back. His nails dug into my sides, and he bit the back of my neck. With a deep growl, I forced myself to stand on all four legs and then rolled so I lay on top of him.

My back and neck burned from his bite, but I slammed my head back into his with a *thwack*. His hold slackened.

I turned and got back onto four legs and then bit through

the dark-blond wolf's neck. He huffed, his eyes widening as life slowly left him.

Leg spasming, I forced myself to remain on my feet as I spun around to check on my mate, only to find Bodey on his back with the slate wolf on top. Bodey raked the wolf's belly so deep that blood gushed out, coating my mate's fur.

His adversary jerked, trying to get away from Bodey. It was futile. Using all four legs, Bodey tossed him several feet away. When the wolf hit the ground, he yelped as Bodey got back on all four paws and raced to him. He bent down and ripped out the wolf's throat.

At least those two assholes were done. My leg was shaking so hard that it would give out any minute, but I tried to ignore the inevitable. I'd fight until I couldn't stand anymore, and then I'd do what I could from the ground.

Callie, Bodey linked, running to me. *Here, let me help you.*

We've got to fight. I glanced around to see who needed help next but found the remaining thirty or so opponents racing away.

I started to chase after them, but I was limping badly. There was no way I'd be able to catch up, but we couldn't risk them returning with backup.

They're retreating, Samuel linked as Bodey reached me, nuzzling his head against mine.

What if they're getting a witch or reinforcements? I didn't want to be unprepared again. The queen had blindsided us already, and I was sick and tired of playing defense.

Miles linked, *Lucas, Jack, and I will follow them to see where they're headed.*

I blew out a breath. *No, let's all stay close. We don't need to separate with the possibility of more of us getting injured. We just need to make sure we have enough people watching the area in case they return so we aren't caught off guard.* I almost added *again* but bit the bitterness back. That would only make me look even less competent. Granted, I wasn't sure that was even possible at this point.

She's right, Bodey added, backing me up immediately. He nuzzled me again before pulling away to examine my injuries. *We need to stay together and help the survivors.*

As Bodey inspected me, I did the same to him. Other than the slate wolf's blood covering him, I noticed only a few nicks and scratches. He'd weathered the battle better than I had.

Knowing he was okay, I scanned the area.

There was overwhelming death, mostly on our side. My heart constricted under the pressure.

I swear. Jack's light-blond wolf trotted over to us. He had blood splatters across his coat but not a scratch on him. *Every damn time, it's one of you two getting your asses kicked. I'm thinking I need to give you two fighting lessons.*

Bodey growled. *Callie went after the strongest wolves here.*

I did? I hadn't meant to; I was merely looking for people to protect.

Your wolf probably did it without you realizing. Michael hurried toward us. Unlike Jack and Bodey, the older man had fared a bit worse. He had a bite mark on his side, but he seemed to take it in stride.

I focused on my connections, counting links to this pack. I linked to Zeke, *The enemy retreated. It looks like there are about sixty remaining pack members here.*

So about thirty died in the attack. Zeke paused, and I didn't sense any emotion from him, which I found odd. *Heather just linked—she's on her way to you to discuss the situation. She's very upset. Her father and brother died, making her the new alpha of this pack.*

Stomach knotting, I tried to ease the tension from my body so that I could heal and my pain might recede.

I'm so sorry it took me so long to get to you, Bodey said, his eyes almost black. *They kept attacking me when I tried.*

You have nothing to apologize for, I reassured him. *We were in a battle.*

Miles's voice popped into my head. *We need to reassure these people.*

Yeah? Lucas responded. *And exactly how do we do that?*

That was an excellent question. It wasn't like I could vow that this wouldn't happen again. With the queen involved, they might very well attack at any time.

I examined the area, noting that several of the wolves here had injuries. We'd lost five more even after we'd arrived to help. My eyes went back to the first wolf I'd tried to save and failed. One of them was directly my fault.

Hell, *all* of them were my fault. *Maybe I should've just submitted to the queen.*

No, you shouldn't have, Bodey linked, his determination flowing through me. *She's no better than Zeke.*

I'd had the same thought earlier, but it was nice to hear that Bodey felt the same way.

We have to get my memories back. I wasn't sure if that would give us answers about the queen, but it might guide us in the right direction. My parents' death had benefited Queen Kel, and I wanted to learn why she'd had Zeke wipe my memory instead of killing me. Maybe, as the others were discussing, she'd wanted to wait until I could submit to her...but then, why not make me right then and there instead of leaving me for Zeke?

We will, Bodey vowed. *We'll figure it out together.*

Ten wolves trotted toward us, and I focused on their links. They were my pack members. A russet-brown wolf trotted directly up to me while the other nine spread out to tend to the injured.

I take it you're the queen, the wolf I assumed to be Heather said as she stopped before me. Her topaz irises were dark and stared at me with distrust.

I swallowed. This was the first time I'd met someone outside of the people I already knew as queen, and it was most definitely under less-than-stellar circumstances. *I am. And this is my mate, Bodey.* I nodded toward him as Samuel trotted up and sat on my other side. *And my brother, Samuel.* I quickly introduced the other men as Lucas, Miles, and Jack split off to watch the perimeter and the dads went to shift to help bury the dead. Only Bodey and I could link directly with this pack.

Heather and I stayed in wolf form. I noticed she had a deep scratch in her stomach, which probably prevented her from shifting.

Do you know why she attacked us? Heather asked, her eyes staying on mine. *I just lost my father—our alpha—and my brother, who was meant to be the next alpha of our pack, in one night.*

Queen Kel wants to take over the territory, I answered simply. I didn't want to lie to her, but at the same time, I didn't want to tell her everything. I noticed that about fifteen of her remaining pack members weren't with us. *Where is everyone else?*

Watching the borders. She huffed, shaking her head. *You aren't the only one to consider that they might circle back.* Her words dripped with contempt.

My head jerked back. *I never said—*

You didn't have to.

Bodey stiffened beside me and linked, *Don't talk to her that way. She's your queen, and I won't tolerate the disrespect.*

I stepped closer to him, ignoring the way my left back foot and chest ached. *She just lost a ton of pack members and family.*

Doesn't matter. Bodey snarled. *She can't treat you that way.*

How were you so close by when you live over eight hours away? Heather's nostrils flared. *That seems a little convenient.*

My lungs seized. That was a valid question. *Pack business.* I didn't have to tell her everything.

She nodded. *I guess we were lucky.*

And we'll help to bury the dead, I added, not wanting her to think we were going to rush away and leave them to pick up the pieces alone. *We won't leave you like this.*

Some of her anger ebbed, and she nodded. *I'm sorry. It's just—*

You lost people you love. I remembered my fear when I thought I'd lost Stevie. Sometimes, empathy wasn't appreciated enough. *Let's get to work and bury the dead and tend to the injured.* Standing out here with the stark reminders of the hell that had come wasn't good for anyone. *We all need time to grieve and rest.*

A FEW WITCHES helped heal us, but even so, it'd taken us all night to bury the dead. Heather had allowed us to rest in her house, sleeping on the floor for a couple of hours until Bodey's pack members arrived.

Now that they were here, we were heading to the Ontario pack to check on them. According to Zeke, five of them had died, and they hadn't suffered nearly as much as Heather's pack. Nonetheless, lost pack members hit the same, no matter the quantity.

Bodey opened my car door just as Heather jogged down the sidewalk of her robin's-egg blue house. "Queen Callie," she called out. "May I talk to you for a minute?"

My mate's hand stilled on my back, and I noticed Samuel

pause where he'd been about to climb into the back seat of Jack's Navigator.

"Yes." I remained outside the door and smiled. "What's up?"

She cleared her throat. "I was hoping to talk to you alone."

My head tilted. "Sure."

Let me know if you need me, Bodey linked, his eyes glowing.

Though Heather had been amicable after our initial conversation, she'd remained a little standoffish, which Bodey hadn't liked. But she'd lost her dad and brother last night, and I couldn't imagine what that felt like.

I went to meet her as the guys all climbed into our vehicles, though they kept their gazes on me.

Heather stopped in her yard. Her face was strained.

Is everything all right? I linked. *Do you need something else?*

She nodded. *I need to know how you're planning to fix this.*

My brows lifted. *Well, Bodey's pack members will stay with you for a week or so.*

How are you going to fix this permanently? She bit her bottom lip. *Look, I appreciate you coming and fighting with us. And not many people would've stayed and helped bury our dead like you did. But Bodey's pack members can't stay with us forever; even if they could, there are only five of them. And there are twenty other packs that live along the Oregon border. Something has to be done about Queen Kel to make us safe again.*

That was the equivalent to a kick in the gut. I exhaled, trying to figure out how to give her an honest answer when the truth was that I didn't have an answer to provide. Bodey's pack didn't have enough land for them to move there. And I suspected they wouldn't want to, not after losing so many wolves and needing the time to mourn and heal. Not only that, but other packs were at risk, and moving all twenty that lived near the Oregon border wasn't an option.

I'm not trying to be disrespectful, but we need you to step up. Heather lifted her hands. *You're the one person who can keep us safe, and you can't be everywhere at once.*

You're right. I nodded. I wanted to yank my hair out because I couldn't yet promise she'd be safe. She'd already lost so much. *And we're working on a solution.* I had to get my memories back. There was no other way.

I hope so. Heather frowned. *Otherwise, a lot more of us might die soon.* She turned and headed into the woods toward where we'd buried the dead.

My feet moved back toward the vehicles, but my mind was reeling.

What happened? Bodey linked, his concern pulsing between us.

I repeated the conversation, feeling like such a damn failure. All these people were counting on me, and I was letting them all down.

Babe, we'll figure it out, Bodey replied yet again. *I promise.*

When I slid into the passenger seat, he reached over and took my hand. *If anyone can help these people, it's you.*

I wasn't so sure, but I clung to his comfort.

He pulled onto the road, driving in the direction of Ontario. I leaned my head against the window, concentrating on the electricity from Bodey's hand on my leg when my cell phone rang.

Dina's name flashed across the screen, and my stomach tightened. She'd never called me before, and I hurriedly picked it up. "Hello?"

"Hey, are you on your way home?" Dina asked, her voice tight.

"No, we're going to check on the other pack that was attacked." Acid burned in my throat. "Is something wrong?"

"I need you to come back home," she answered. "There's someone here who wants to see you."

CHAPTER NINETEEN

MY HEART THUNDERED in my chest. That sounded ominous. "Is the queen there?" At this point, I wouldn't be surprised if she was, though that would mean more than a battle. That would be a declaration of war.

The pack would've alerted us, Bodey linked, squeezing my leg. *It can't be her.*

"No, she's not," Dina bit out. "Everyone here is okay."

I took in a shaky breath. The queen had rattled me, and I wasn't thinking clearly. Another way I was failing at this entire thing. "Right. Of course not." I groaned, leaning back against the headrest.

Dina sighed. "You sound tired. Janet told me you helped to bury the dead. Did you get any rest last night?"

"A few hours." I yawned, which caused my eyes to water.

And it wasn't good rest. Bodey glanced at me. *You need sleep.*

So did he, but I didn't want to argue with him. "So, if it's not the queen, and you aren't under duress, is another witch coming to visit?" If I'd had enough energy, I would've crossed my fingers.

"Yes. Priestess River from the coven that lives with Miles's pack contacted me. She didn't want to visit until Miles and Stella got back. But under the circumstances, she's willing to come for a day and offered to be here tomorrow. She needs to know if that will work because she'll drive down tonight. Since the queen has been attacking mainly in Oregon and Idaho, she wants to meet with us sooner rather than later so she can return before Queen Kel decides to attack their area."

I bit my lip and took a deep breath, filling my lungs. I wanted to think this through, especially since we could put it off and go check on the Ontario pack. But I wasn't sure that would be wise. We needed answers.

"Could she come in two days?" That wouldn't be too much of a stretch and would give us time to stop and check on Lynerd and his pack.

"She could," Dina agreed. "But more attacks could happen before we learn anything."

And then more people would be asking questions...the very ones Heather had asked that I didn't have answers for.

And the queen had made it clear last night that she meant to teach me a lesson, shortly followed by two attacks happening within ten minutes across Oregon. I doubted that she would slow down now. Meeting the witch as quickly as possible was as much of a priority, if not more. "Give me a moment."

I connected with Samuel, informing him of what was going on. Then I linked Bodey into the discussion and said, *If we drive to Ontario, we'll get there around eight this evening, and then it would be another six hours before we would reach home.*

Babe, I know you want to check on the pack. I do too, but if we go there, it won't be a quick trip. We'll need to stay and reassure them before we leave for home. We won't get back until early tomorrow morning. Bodey exhaled. *And if Heather was asking those questions, demanding answers...*

He didn't need to finish that sentence. Lynerd would want to know the same thing, and he wouldn't be as tolerant as Heather. When we did visit them, we needed to be able to tell him *something*.

Samuel interjected, *We need to meet with the witch.*

Since Samuel agreed, there was no doubt in my mind it was the right choice. "Tell Priestess River to come, that we'll be ready to meet with her in the morning." I pinched the bridge of my nose. "We're heading home now."

Ask if we need to prepare a house for the coven. There are two vacant wolf houses near our coven if she needs them, Bodey linked.

I repeated the question, and Dina replied, "No. We have a house she can stay in, but thank you for asking. We'll come to your house in the morning around nine. I just need you to make sure you rest well so she won't have a hard time connecting with your magic to feel the spell."

I'd take her word for it. She'd never lead me astray. "Okay. We'll see you then."

I hung up and rubbed my sweaty hand on my pants leg. I wasn't sure if this was the right call to make, but I was beginning to believe that there was never a *right* call, just a bunch of shitty ones. There was no guarantee that meeting this priestess would give us any answers. We might be blowing off a strong pack to chase a dream.

Samuel's voice popped into my head. *You need to inform Zeke. He'll need to make Lynerd aware that we aren't coming today.*

There was no getting out of it—Bodey and I were the only ones that could pack link with Zeke. A fact that I tried not to think about. I needed to check on them anyway.

I tugged on the connection, opening up the communication between Bodey, Zeke, and me. *Are you still with Lynerd's pack?*

Yes, I'm in the Ontario pack's neighborhood. They've buried their dead, but the pack is on high alert. They want to know how Queen Kel's wolves managed to attack the coronation, the crowning ceremony, and now their lands. I'm hoping you'll arrive with answers, otherwise, I'm not sure what's going to happen.

My shoulders slumped, and I hung my head. *We might have a lead, so we're heading back home.* Though I hadn't spoken the words, my throat ached as if I had. *But if you need us to come there—*

No, I'm fine, Zeke interrupted. *I've been an advisor for over twenty years. I know what I'm doing.*

She wasn't implying you didn't. Bodey's jaw clenched. *She was saying that if the people need us, they are our priority.*

Do you truly think that you two showing up here and fumbling over your words with nothing of substance to offer is going to ease their minds? Zeke's disgust oozed through our connection. *It won't. What's your lead?*

I flinched. I'd hoped he wouldn't ask. If I held back the information, even though I was tempted, it would only cause further issues between all of us and put Oregon at more risk. *A witch is coming to see if she can determine who altered my memories.*

For a moment, he didn't respond. *Well, keep me informed if you learn anything.*

Will do. I wished fervently that Theo was in charge. It would be easier for me to deal with him instead of the man who'd tormented me and hidden me for all those years. *And let them know they're in our thoughts.*

I'll make sure to reassure them of that. I'm sure it will keep them warm at night. Zeke's sarcasm dripped from every word. *Talk soon.*

Bodey snarled. "I really hate him. When things settle, his ass is gone, right?"

"I'd love for it to be one of the first official things I do. Lynerd should be in charge of Oregon. It was technically his right, and he's stronger than Zeke. I don't know what my parents were thinking." I shivered. Calling the king and queen my parents for the very first time overwhelmed me, but I needed to accept my heritage. The mark on my body told the story even if the words felt strange.

"The way Dad explains it, Mila and Zeke were close, and she felt bad that she left Zeke's pack behind to be with King Richard." Bodey shrugged. "Maybe that was her way of making it up to him."

There were way better ways to accomplish that than handing over power to a narcissistic abuser. "I don't think that makes it any better."

Bodey shrugged, taking my hand and holding it on the center console. He linked, *At least, she had good intentions even if they were misguided. And Dad said Zeke didn't start out that bad. He became worse over the years, and when Mila died, something inside him died along with her.*

That sounded sad, but Zeke wasn't the victim. He'd become an abuser, which terminated any sympathy I might have had for him. Only someone who had meanness in their heart would mistreat others the way he did daily. I didn't believe that was something that would've grown over time. It must have always been lurking in the shadows.

I was done with this conversation. I'd spent too much of my life thinking and talking about Zeke. *Do you think we should send the advisors to Ontario since we aren't going?*

I'm pretty sure that will just upset Lynerd and Zeke more and set them against one another. Zeke is the advisor for that region, so having Miles, Jack, Lucas, or even Samuel go there would make him feel threatened and would also make him appear weak in front of Lynerd. He shrugged. *Besides, River will want to talk with Miles to touch base on things with his pack and territory. It'd be best if we all go home.*

This crap was hard. The power dynamics seemed almost petty, like if someone farted a little too loud, too soft, or too stinky, someone would be offended.

Bodey turned onto a new road to take us back toward Idaho instead of central Oregon.

Michael linked, *Hey, what's going on?*

I realized that we hadn't informed the dads, so I gave them a quick update.

Michael didn't say anything until I was done. *That was the best call to make.*

Hearing another person say that was exactly what I needed. *I wish there were an easier answer.*

I think we all do. I'll inform Dan, Phil, and Carl about what's going on. Let us know if anything else happens.

I closed my eyes and leaned over the center console, placing my head on Bodey's shoulder. I needed the thrumming of our bond to be as strong as possible right now. His touch and smell made me feel whole.

He kissed the top of my head and wrapped his arm around my shoulders, embracing me as much as he could while driving. "We're going to figure this out," he promised.

I nodded, knowing that both of us needed to believe it... especially right now.

"Get some rest." He used the controls on the steering wheel to turn on the radio, and he stopped when Wilson Phillips's "Hold On" started playing. The lyrics spoke to my soul, and I focused on being with my mate and what the future might hold.

Even though I tried to sleep, it evaded me. My neck hurt from having lain on Bodey's arm for so long, and my back was stiffer than ever. The one nice thing that sitting for hours had accomplished was that my wounds were now mere scabs, and I wasn't tempted to ask Dina to heal anything.

When we pulled into our neighborhood, the moon was hidden behind thick clouds, and rain drizzled the windshield. I glanced at the clock. It was almost seven thirty at night, and I felt like I hadn't slept in ages.

Soon, we drove up to our white house. Lights were on inside as Bodey pulled into the garage.

Is Janet here? Bodey's family and friends liked congregating in Bodey's house, which I didn't mind. I enjoyed having everyone there.

Mom wanted to surprise you with dinner. He parked the car, his eyes shining.

My stomach grumbled in response. We hadn't eaten anything but snacks since we'd left Heather's, and we'd stopped once only for gas and a pee break.

The advisors and the dads pulled into the driveway behind us, and we all climbed out.

Bodey and I entered the house first, the smell of steak and potatoes filling my nose. Janet had to be cooking on the grill on the lower deck. The others shuffled in behind us, everyone removing their shoes and heading into the house.

We found Stella, Stevie, and Destiny sitting on the couch with Taylor and Alicia standing at the island holding glasses of red wine.

My mouth watered in response to the beverage and the delicious scent of food.

The three women on the couch jumped to their feet and rushed to greet their mates.

Stevie patted my arm as she brushed by, headed straight for

Jack. He wrapped his arms around her, lifting her up and twirling her around despite Lucas and Miles standing close to him.

"What the hell, man?" Lucas complained, taking four large steps toward the hallway. "We're right here."

"Not in my mind," Jack said, pulling Stevie into his chest. "All I see is my girl here, standing in front of me."

Her cheeks turned crimson, and I swallowed my laughter, not wanting to embarrass her.

The four former advisors headed inside, each of them making his way to his mate. Michael didn't pause as he practically jogged across the den to reach Janet on the back porch.

I rubbed my chest, feeling so warm. Even chosen mates who'd been together for a long time were still excited to see one another. My eyes turned to Bodey, who winked at me as he snatched the bottle of wine from the center of the island, where it stood next to a huge container of baked potatoes in aluminum foil. He filled a glass and handed it to me.

"Thank you." I took a large sip and walked around the island as Jack, Miles, and Carl followed their mates back to their places on the couch. The guys took their spots behind their women, probably wanting to stand after being cooped up in the car.

"Always." Bodey came behind me and wrapped his arms around my waist.

I nestled into his chest, taking another sip of wine. The warmth coated my throat and settled into my stomach like an internal hug. Being home felt so damn nice, especially after the hell we'd just gone through.

Stella glanced over her shoulder, moving so she could see around Miles's huge form. "Are you still injured?" She scanned me from head to toe.

"I've pretty much healed." I lowered the neckline of my fuchsia shirt, showing her the scratches by my mark.

"We're glad you're all back." Stevie pressed her lips together, staring at me.

"Please." Jack nuzzled her neck and said, "Don't lie. You were only worried about me."

She snorted. "I was, but I care about my sister and everyone else as well." She thumped him on the back of the head, and he stilled.

"Man." Jack straightened and pointed at Lucas. "You've even got her doing that now."

Lucas shrugged. "Don't be an ass, and you won't have a problem."

"You wanna see an ass?" Jack reached for the belt of his jeans.

"Dude!" Lucas shook his head. "Don't. I've seen you on the toilet enough times while you're pooping. I don't need additional visuals. The image is too damn vivid already."

"Jack Landry, if you drop your pants, I will spank your ass." Destiny pointed at him. "Right here in front of everyone. I don't care if you're an advisor or not."

Bodey's shoulders shook with stifled laughter against my back.

"And when *she's* done with you..." Stella lifted her chin. "I'll make sure your balls itch for a month like I did when I learned that you tried to hire a stripper to come to the house while Miles was there."

"What?" Stevie asked loudly. "You did *what?*"

"Whoa." He lifted both hands. "First off, I hadn't met you yet." He pointed at Stevie. "I would *never* do that now." Then he lifted two fingers. "And second, it was a joke."

Miles crossed his arms. "That no one found funny."

"Oh, believe me." Jack shuddered. "My balls were so itchy

that I couldn't stop scratching, and they bled for a whole night. You got your revenge."

I told you Stella was scary, Bodey linked. *She goes for blood.*

"And we handed over our states to them." Dan shook his head. "What were we thinking?"

Michael opened the door for Janet, who carried in the steaks. All of a sudden, the conversation was over. Taylor rushed to the refrigerator and started rummaging around, pulling out condiments for the potatoes.

Everyone was quiet as we loaded up our plates. Stevie, Jack, Miles, and Stella stayed at the island while the rest of us headed to the rectangular dining table and took seats.

Samuel launched into filling in the women about everything that had happened while we were gone, which I appreciated. I couldn't focus on anything but what the hell we were supposed to do next. What if the witch didn't recognize the magic in me? I wasn't sure how many more options there were, and even worse, we were running out of time for answers.

When everyone was done, Bodey stood, taking my hand. "You all stay as long as you want, but Dina wanted to make sure that Callie got rest for tomorrow." He helped me out of my seat.

I shook my head. "I need to help clean up. Janet cooked all this for us."

"Nonsense." Destiny wagged her finger. "There are plenty of us here to do that. Stella, Stevie, Taylor, Alicia, and I haven't done much all day except for worry. We can handle this."

My chest expanded like it might explode. This was what having a family must feel like. "Thank you."

Come on, Bodey tugged on my hand, easing me toward the hall. "Good night, everyone."

When we made it to our room, he shut the door and locked it. My body warmed in response, and he chuckled.

"Not tonight, my love." He guided me into the bathroom.

"You're achy, hurting, and need rest. Tonight, I will take care of you, and tomorrow, I promise I'll ravish you."

He turned on the shower, and we bathed together. But every time I tried to touch him, he'd growl and swat my hand despite his body's clear response.

When we were both clean, I crawled into bed while Bodey grabbed his guitar. He played "Make You Feel My Love" by Bob Dylan and then "When a Man Loves a Woman" by Percy Sledge. His voice and the lyrics eased a part of me that only he could connect with, the cadence taking me to a safe place that I never wanted to leave.

When he was done, he slid into the spot beside me and kissed away the tears I'd cried while listening to him play before wrapping his arms around me in a gentle cocoon of warmth and falling asleep.

THE ALARM on my phone dinged, pulling me from my deep slumber. Bodey's arms were still around me, holding me tight against him, and I didn't want to leave them.

His hardness pressed into my back, creating a deep need that seemed to knot in my stomach. Ever since our shower, I'd wanted his body, but I hadn't pushed it last night since he'd been desperate to take care of me.

I couldn't help but wonder if he'd softened at all since our shower.

I snuck out a hand, turned off the alarm, and then rolled toward him. I slipped my hand into his pajama bottoms and began to stroke him. His body shuddered as his eyes flew open.

He smirked, his irises almost cobalt underneath his long, dark lashes. "I said we weren't supposed to do anything."

"Last night." I leaned forward and sucked gently on his bottom lip. "It's morning."

Snarling, he flipped me onto my back and slid between my legs. *Waking me up like that makes me damn desperate.* He thrust against me despite us both being clothed.

I'm not complaining. I lifted up, capturing his lips.

Oh, you will be, he vowed, holding me against his chest as my hands tangled into his hair. He moved, clutching my ass cheeks and standing. I wrapped my legs around his waist as he walked me to the wall.

He pulled away from my mouth and kissed his way down my neck as my hands caressed his bare chest. The heavy thrum of our mate bond left me dizzy.

Pressing me against the wall, Bodey leaned away and tugged my shirt over my head, then tossed it over his shoulder. My breathing hitched as he kissed down my chest and took my nipple into his mouth. His finger slipped under my boxer shorts and slid between my lips, rubbing circles and causing flames to course through me.

His tongue flicked my breast, and I arched against him, searching for the friction I needed.

I've needed you since last night, he linked, his tongue rolling over me again. *But the witch is going to be here soon, so we need to be quick.*

"Yes, please," I moaned, not caring that I begged. I needed this connection with him. I moved my hands to his pajamas and pushed them down. He sprang out, hard and ready, and desire soared inside me.

He chuckled as he set my feet down and removed my boxers. Within seconds, he had me back in his arms, his tip at my entrance. I pressed against him, making him groan.

I need to make you ready. He guided his tip into my folds

and circled it like he did with his hands, and soon, the friction had me writhing with need.

Both of us were so damn frantic for each other; my body was ready to explode. *Now, please.*

He thrust into me, our bond opening for one another. After all the deaths, the threats, and my injuries, we needed our souls to connect more than ever before. We normally didn't do hard and fast, but today we were desperate. We both needed the release.

Each time he entered me, he hit deeper, and I rolled my hips against him. His mouth found mine as we kissed, not separating even when we got sloppy and fast.

Soon, we were both slick with sweat, our bodies in sync. His pleasure built, combining with mine, and orgasms ripped through us both. The ecstasy kept cresting as our bodies continued to move as one.

His body convulsed at the end of his own release, and soon, our frenzy ebbed away. He peppered kisses all over my face and remained inside me for a little longer.

I love you so much, he linked, pressing his forehead to mine.

I cupped his cheek and pushed my love for him through our bond. *I love you too.*

The sound of the front door opening reached me, and I glanced at the time. *Bodey, it's nine.*

"Callie?" Dina called out.

"We'll be down in a second," I answered, my heart pounding.

Below, Jack said, "Come into the kitchen with Stevie and me. Those two have been busy this morning."

Oh my gods. We'd been loud, and I hadn't even considered Samuel and Stevie might hear us. I wanted to die, but the longer we took to get down there, the worse it would be.

Bodey and I rushed into our clothes and hurried downstairs.

I was ready to hide, but Bodey was grinning like he'd won the lottery.

When we entered the kitchen, someone gasped. And when I saw the woman standing next to Dina by the Keurig, she dropped her mug.

CERAMIC SHATTERED, hitting the floor and scattering around her. However, her dark eyes didn't move from mine as her tan complexion paled. From what I could tell, she was older, around the same age as the former advisors, with faint crow's-feet at the corners of her dark-brown eyes.

Bodey edged in front of me, blocking me from her intense stare.

"Good thing I have shoes on." Dina sighed and started picking up the pieces of the mug.

My attention darted to her feet, which were encased in brown leather boots. Her sky-blue dress hung down to the tops of them.

"Sorry." The other woman, who I assumed was River, shook her head, her dark-brown hair swaying from side to side. "She looks *just* like him. It caught me off guard." Her attention remained on me.

Stevie slid off the barstool. "I'll get the broom and dustpan if someone will tell me where they are."

"Mudroom," Bodey answered, his voice a little tight. His worry swirled between us as he watched the witch with unease.

Running a hand over her dark-gray dress, Priestess River tilted her head. "It really is uncanny. Samuel looks nothing like him, but her...she's the spitting image of Richard at that age."

My breath caught. "You knew him?"

"His mother was from our pack's coven, so he visited regularly when he was young." She smiled sadly. "It was a terrible day when she died and he had to take the crown at thirty."

Stevie hurried from the mudroom with the cleaning tools, and River and Dina moved out of the way, heading toward the den.

I followed them, wanting to learn more about my parents. That River knew my father as a kid tugged at me. The former advisors had known them, but since we'd been constantly addressing threats, I hadn't asked more questions about them. I hadn't even thought about asking who they'd been as people. "What was he like?"

Samuel and Bodey joined me. Samuel bit his bottom lip and wiped his hands on his pants legs nervously.

"Strong. Loyal." She went to the fireplace and faced the room. "He cared deeply for his people, including the witches."

"That's how Michael described him too." Samuel lifted his chin. "I would've loved to have gotten to know him and had his guidance."

River laughed. "Oh, sweet boy." She placed a hand on her chest. "Your father is still with you. His and Mila's magic is part of both you and your sister. They created you, after all. A part of them will continue to live through every generation if you have children of your own."

Those words struck something deep within me. I rubbed my own chest as Bodey stepped behind me, placing his hands on my hips. Even through my jeans, the buzz of his proximity caused a hitch in my breath.

"You have a very strong fated-mate bond." River sucked in a

breath, staring at us. "I can feel the magic rolling off you from here. A royal hasn't had a fated mate for some time now."

Dina nodded. "I believe that it's a sign that things are about to change." She gestured to Stevie, who was finishing cleaning up the mug. "This one is the fated mate to Jack and Miles and Stella are fated mates as well."

"Interesting." River pursed her lips. "I wonder if Lucas will find his fated mate too."

"Does that matter?" Samuel asked, his brows furrowing. "I was under the impression that chosen mates were equally worthy."

Sitting on the couch, Dina crossed her legs. "It's not that chosen mates aren't fine. Michael and Janet are chosen, and they love each other dearly. You were raised around them; you've seen that through the years. But a wolf being with their fated mate strengthens both of their magic once they fully settle into the bond."

Bodey's hands gripped me harder. "What do you mean?"

"A soul divided in half is stronger when made whole again." River ran her hand along the mantel. "You and Callie are amazingly strong wolves in your own right—that's why I can see the magic between you without searching hard. You two are still settling and learning your place with each other and your roles within the packs, but once you figure things out, you can share magic with one another through your bond. A chosen mate can't do that."

"My place is beside Callie—that and taking care of Idaho," Bodey said confidently. "I'm unsure what you mean by 'still settling.'"

I swallowed, hearing the contradiction in his words. Leading Idaho was the future he'd expected. I couldn't ask him to give up his position just because Fate chose him to be with me. That would be selfish, and he'd grown up knowing all these people and caring for them as a packmate and a leader.

Samuel came to my other side and placed a hand on my shoulder. "I'll be there to help her with all the royal duties if she wants me. We won't let my sister flounder."

"Of course I do." I couldn't do this alone, and having Samuel's help to make decisions alongside me was something I would never take for granted. "I need all the help I can get." He was able to make hard decisions quickly, whereas I couldn't tell which option was the least wrong. Each felt like I was picking between a hole in the head or a hole in the chest.

"And I'll be here for you in any way I can," Stevie said softly, uncertainly—like I might not want her help.

My heart ached. I hated that she felt like I might shun her help. But what else was she supposed to think when we'd grown up with the idea that we were worthless and didn't matter to our own pack?

River mashed her lips together and straightened. "As much as I would love to stay and discuss your magic and future, we will need to do that another time when there isn't an imminent threat. Being away from Miles's pack and my coven members is detrimental to our people, especially while Miles and Stella can't be there."

I should've thought of that. Here I was, wanting to pepper her with questions when she'd come here to help me get answers about what had happened the night of my parents' death. "You're right. I wasn't thinking."

"It's not your fault." She smiled and gestured to the couch. "I was the one who mentioned Bodey's and your bond."

A knot formed in my stomach as I moved to the couch. I'd learned from the last two witches that this would not be comfortable, but I'd deal with it for a chance to get some answers.

I'll sit next to you, Bodey linked, taking my hand. *Maybe if we touch while she examines you, it won't be as bad.*

You don't have to. I squeezed back lovingly. *It's not painful, just...not comfortable.*

Bodey sat next to me. In other words, he still wanted to try to help ease some of my discomfort, and I adored him for it.

Dina sat on my other side as River walked toward me.

When Samuel didn't move, I cleared my throat and linked, *Do you mind joining Stevie at the bar? I feel as if I'm on display.* Two weeks ago, if people had stared at me like this, it usually ended with me being punished or getting hurt. I wasn't sure I'd ever get comfortable with being the center of attention.

Yeah, sure. He quickly moved into the kitchen.

As River kneeled in front of me, I took a deep breath. I didn't understand why, but I hated how witch magic felt when they were probing inside me. It felt dirty. As if I'd been violated.

I shivered, and Bodey let go of my hand and slid his arm around my shoulders.

River frowned. "I'm sorry. I know it's not pleasant."

"So I'm not being paranoid?" A part of me thought that my mind was playing tricks on me. "When Dina heals me, it doesn't feel the same."

She shook her head. "The purpose of the magic is different. When we heal, we're mending a person's magic and body. What I'm doing now is peeling back layers, trying to find the spell that binds you. My magic isn't trying to soothe yours, but find what's different."

That was exactly what it felt like—probing, like when Tina had given me shots or taken my blood.

"Just focus on your mate's touch," she urged as she placed her hands on my forehead.

Her magic seeped into my skin, causing a chill to rack my body. Bodey leaned into my side, and I focused on the jolt of energy soaring between us. Everywhere he touched warmed me, like lying in the sun on a summer day, and helped push away the coldness of the witch digging inside me.

I closed my eyes, remembering Bodey's and my time upstairs this morning, but then my body slowly heated in a very inappropriate way.

Uh...should I be jealous of River? Bodey chuckled. *Or are you thinking about when I had you pressed up against the wall and sank into you over and over again?*

Need built even stronger, and Stevie groaned, "I don't know what's happening, but I think Bodey needs to remove his hands from her. I love my sister, but I don't want to smell whatever's going on over there."

"Same," Samuel huffed.

Bodey growled. "Leave my mate alone. If she wants to remember our time together this morning..."

My eyes flew open to find River smiling, but the mirth was missing from her eyes. Her look was like a winter breeze blowing through my body.

From the corner of my eye, I noticed Dina had clenched her hands. She asked, "Do you recognize the magic?"

Time seemed to stop, but then River nodded and dropped her hands.

Oh, thank gods. Relief flooded through me like water through a dam.

The lightheartedness vanished from Bodey as he leaned forward and placed his other hand on my leg. He asked, "Who?"

"Salem." River took a few steps back. "She was part of my coven."

That I hadn't expected. "Was?" That didn't sound good. A lump formed in my throat. What if I wasn't able to get my memories back?

"She fell in love with a man who lived with a wolf pack in Oregon." She clasped her hands together. "She moved there, but she died. Seventeen years ago."

I flinched. "That's when my memories were blocked." My eyes burned as devastation took hold of me. I couldn't believe that I'd hinged all my hope on this.

Damn hope. I knew better than to feel that emotion. It was such an evil bastard. I'd learned that while living with Zeke's pack, and the first time I'd dared to feel it again, Fate smacked me around like I was her bitch.

We will figure this out. Bodey's breathing quickened. *I promise.*

"Which Oregon pack?" Samuel asked.

"The one located south of Ontario." River rubbed her temples. "But I can't believe that she would have done *this*." She shook her head. "This isn't like her."

My voice cracked. "Is there no way to get my memories back?"

"Oh, child." River's face softened. "Her daughter can undo it, and I met her at the coronation dinner. She was there with the pack's alpha, Lynerd. She can undo the spell."

Ontario. Lynerd. My parents had given Oregon to Zeke instead of him. Nausea roiled in my stomach. Had Lynerd been involved in my parents' deaths? My mind flashed to Sybil, the witch I'd met that day when I visited with Theo.

I wanted to curl up in a ball. Lynerd had seemed kind, but was that because he'd had a hand in my parents' deaths and in erasing my memories? And I'd gone there feeling sorry for him and trying to diminish Theo's aggression instead of letting Theo make a stand.

"It's a damn good thing we didn't go there before learning this." Bodey's anger pulsed through our connection, mixing with my devastation.

The little bit I thought I'd known crumbled away. How were you supposed to fight your enemies when they lived among you and you didn't even know their faces?

"I'm telling you, she wouldn't have done that without a reason." River placed a hand over her heart. "Her husband died that same day, leaving behind their ten-year-old daughter."

Spiraling wouldn't accomplish anything. I needed to focus. We had a lead, and she was alive, which meant there was still a chance for answers. This time, I'd be a little more wary. If Lynerd was involved, then he'd make sure we didn't get any.

"Please don't share this information with anyone else," I pleaded, glancing from Dina to River. "I don't want anyone to warn Sybil and have something happen."

"Of course, My Queen." Dina bowed her head.

River cupped her hands. "I won't betray you. You're our ruler just as much as you are the shifters' queen. But please keep in mind that Sybil is innocent."

I had no qualms about Sybil, but at least now I understood why she'd been so curious about me when I'd met her at Lynerd's house. She must have sensed her mother's magic. If anything, Lynerd was the person who'd had Salem work against my parents. "I promise to keep an open mind."

"Thank you." River sighed. "Well, if that's what you needed, I should get back to the coven immediately."

"If there is ever anything I can do for you, please let me know." The fact that she'd come here when things were so turbulent meant a lot. "I appreciate you being here to help me."

"It was an honor, my child." She grinned and headed to the front door. "And I hope that one day soon, we can visit so I can tell you all the stories I remember about your father."

My cheeks hurt from the grin I couldn't hold back, surprising me. I couldn't believe I was smiling at a moment like this, but I really liked that thought. "I'd love that."

"Great."

Dina followed River while I turned to look at Bodey, Samuel, and Stevie. Our body language mirrored one another. Tense, strained, and unyielding.

"We need to get Jack, Lucas, Miles, and the former advisors here." Samuel lifted a brow.

He was right. I linked, requesting their presence, and began to pace in front of the couch, unable to stay still. There were countless burning questions, and we needed to wait for the others to get here before we discussed strategy.

But I did have some questions that the others would know the answers to. "Every time we deal with witches, they're always women. I hadn't thought about them being married and having children, but clearly, they do. Are there male witches too?" Zeke had kept us away from witches my entire life, and I had no clue how their lives worked.

"Like shifters, witches have male and female children, but the males don't typically harness magic." Bodey bit his lip. "Since we shield humans from our existence, witches typically marry men from other covens—or sometimes from the same coven if it's large enough. Some witches have fallen in love with shifters or humans because of how closely they interact, but a child never results from the union. The witch's magic dies with her and isn't passed on, which is detrimental to the coven. They have annual gatherings where the women meet the men, and that's when a lot of them find their lovers. That's probably what happened with Salem. The couple decides which coven they'll join once they're united."

I hadn't ventured far into Bodey's neighborhood, so I hadn't been to the witches' homes. I'd seen none of the men. I realized I needed to get to know all of them better, not just those who had magic. If I was supposed to protect the witches, that extended to the men.

The front door opened, and Miles, Jack, Lucas, Phil, Dan, and Carl hurried in. They stood in the hallway, looking on edge.

"Hey, what's going on?" Jack hurried over to my sister. "Did you learn anything?"

"We learned where we need to go." I didn't want to explain until Michael got here.

Even as I thought it, Bodey hurried to the sliding back door where Michael stood, waiting to come in.

Thank gods, we were all here.

When Michael entered, he brought the scent of the spring air and rain from the drizzle outside. "Sorry, I was out running."

"No worries." I smiled even though it was forced.

Then we filled them all in.

The seven of them wore varying expressions of concern. Michael ran a hand down his face. "Lynerd. Gods. He was so young and angry. But they said your parents died in an explosion. A freak accident."

"People can make things appear like an accident." Miles scowled. "Especially with a witch who can alter people's minds."

"We can sit here and talk about it all day." Samuel crossed his arms. "But it would be better if we went there and got answers."

He was right.

A spot in my chest grew warmer as if a new pack member was getting closer. One I hadn't met before. I hadn't noticed the feeling until now.

Bodey tensed and growled. "I thought you told her to stay at the university."

My breath caught. *Is your sister here?* I rubbed my chest as the spot, which was close to Bodey's, settled in me similar to the way Samuel's, Janet's, and Michael's felt—as if my wolf recognized them as family.

"She linked yesterday about coming home, and I told her no." Michael grimaced. "She didn't argue. I should've known better."

My mate went still as a statue as his fury swept into me. It reminded me of the anger he'd directed at me after I'd jumped in front of the death spell to protect him.

Footsteps pounded up the front porch, and the door flew open, revealing a slightly older version of the girl in the family picture in the den. Her strawberry-blonde hair curled around her heart-shaped face, and her jade eyes narrowed at all of us.

"Jazzy." Jack shook his head and smirked. "What have you done?"

CHAPTER TWENTY-ONE

MY MUSCLES BUNCHED as Bodey broke through the advisors to reach his sister. She shut the door and planted her fists on her hips. Her fluffy teal sweater bunched around her hands, and she stomped her furry black boots on the hardwood floor.

"You need to go back to Chicago," Bodey growled. "We told you not to come here."

Bodey, I linked, easing between the advisors. *This is the first time I'm meeting your sister, so maybe we could at least try to be cordial. Introduce me, please.*

Michael trailed behind me, his own concern snaking from him, but I could also sense his joy.

"*That's* the welcome I get?" Jasmine lifted her chin, staring Bodey in the eye. "I missed you too, brother."

I looped my arm through his, his muscles relaxing at my touch. I cleared my throat and said, "He's missed you. I promise."

Laying my other hand on my mate's arm, I pushed my love and calm toward him. That was one of the qualities I loved best about Bodey. He was loyal and protective.

"Well, I, for one, have missed my daughter." Michael swept her into a hug. "Though I wish you'd stayed away for your own safety."

She laughed. "Now *that's* the greeting I wanted."

When Michael placed her back on her feet, Jasmine's gaze landed on me then slid down to my neck and chest. There was no doubt what she was looking at—my tattoo. She gasped, "No way!"

Bodey rumbled, stepping in front of me.

Jack *tsk*ed. "Come on, Jazzy. You know her eyes are higher than that."

Now *my* sister snarled. "Don't flirt with her!"

"Oh, love." He booped Stevie's nose. "You're my fated. You don't have shit to be worried about, babe."

The corners of Jasmine's mouth twitched. She looked at Stevie and snorted. "Don't worry, Jack and I aren't like that. He's like another annoying big brother. He used to shove my face into his armpits when they stank. Believe me, there's nothing beyond tolerance of each other's presence between us."

"Yeah, he tried to do that same shit to Miles, Bodey, and me, but we were older and stronger." Lucas gagged. "Still, we didn't need our noses in there to smell his reek."

"Can I just say... I'm glad I wasn't around Jack when he was younger." Stella shivered. "He's horrible enough in his twenties."

"Oh, girl." Jasmine rolled her eyes. "You have no clue." She focused back on Bodey. "And what do you think I'm going to do to not only the new addition to our family but to my queen?" She pivoted around him and hugged me.

I froze, her affection catching me off guard, especially after how she'd been scrutinizing my mark. Before I could manage to hug her back, Bodey gently pulled his sister away.

"You're making her uncomfortable." He frowned.

"No, it's fine." I waved off the awkwardness again. "I'm just not normally a hugger, that's all."

"And that is *not* the proper way to greet your queen." Michael arched a brow.

Jasmine lifted both hands. "She's my sister. What the hell do you mean?"

"She's right." I smiled. She accepted me. Which shouldn't have surprised me—she'd been raised by the same people as my mate. "We're family, and honestly, I prefer that you not be formal with me at all." I pointed to Stevie. "And this is my sister, Stevie."

"Yeah, the growly one." Jack waggled his brows as he placed his arm around my sister's waist. "So be careful not to get too close 'cause she's my fated mate."

"I'll try." Jasmine snorted.

Samuel squeezed through the rest of the group and opened his arms. "Do I not get a hug? Or has my sister already replaced me in your eyes?"

"Never." She embraced him for a long moment before pulling back. "So what's going on? Everyone looks tense."

Bodey's irritation was palpable, so I went to him and laid my head on his shoulder. Our connection hummed, and he pulled me against his chest. "Nothing you need to worry about."

"That's not fair." She leaned to one side. "I'm part of this pack and family too, and I want to help. It's spring break, and I missed my family and home, so here I am. Deal with it. I'm not going back, and I want to help our new *royals*—the king consort is my brother!"

My heart ached. I understood not feeling included. Granted, Bodey and Michael were acting out of love and not because they didn't think she was competent. Still, that didn't make a difference when you were the one feeling slighted.

I think we should let her help, I linked with Bodey. *She clearly wants to, and we need all the allies we can get. Besides, I'd like to get to know her. She is my sister now too. And if you don't let her, she might do something foolish to prove herself.*

His resolve softened. *Nothing is going to happen to you, so you have the rest of your life to get to know her. But you are right about the latter part. She has a knack for getting herself into trouble, trying to keep up with the rest of us.*

Tomorrow is never guaranteed. And she's determined to be here, so it would be easier to oblige her and keep a close eye on her instead of having her trying to sneak around to help.

You're right. Bodey kissed the top of my head and said, "Fine. But you don't go off on your own. Got it?"

Her mouth dropped open before she snapped it closed again. "Really?"

He released me and moved to her, pulling her into a hug. "If Dad's okay with it." Bodey turned to his father.

"It's probably safer this way." Michael laughed. "I'll never forget the time she was determined to race with all of you when we told her no. She snuck out of the house and wound up breaking her ankle, and I'd rather not have a repeat of that while we're fighting Queen Kel."

"And that's not even the worst of the stories," Lucas interjected and rolled his eyes.

Dan, Phil, and Carl glanced at each other and nodded.

We were all in agreement, so that was one thing settled.

"Come on," Samuel said, leading Jasmine into the den. He sat with her on the couch, putting her in the middle. The rest of us filed in as Samuel quickly caught her up.

Jasmine's eyes got wider and wider with every word. "Wow. I had no clue things were that bad here. I should've guessed, though, when you told me not to come home for the coronation."

"You had exams." Michael patted her arm. "It was better that way."

"So...what's the plan?" She rubbed her hands together, glancing around the room as if expecting solid answers.

Everyone's eyes turned to me.

I didn't know what to do. I guessed that Bodey, Janet, and Michael would want to spend some time with Jasmine as a family. Even though we needed to act fast, family was important. "We should leave tomorrow morning. Give everyone another good night's rest. If Lynerd is part of all this, we need to be sharp and ready to handle anything. It'll be a little over three hours' drive to his pack lands, and it's already lunchtime."

"Agreed." Miles leaned back on the island between his mate and father. "I'd like to stay here until River confirms she's back with our pack."

I understood the sentiment. The closer, the better in times of uncertainty; we all needed to stay together to resolve the current threat. Splitting up would make deciding things much harder.

"Then we leave first thing in the morning." Bodey rubbed his chin. "Let's say nine, so we get there around lunchtime."

"We should ask Dina to join us." Samuel steepled his hands. "She and Sybil are friendly, and we could use a witch to help ease any tensions with Lynerd's coven."

Dan paced in front of the couch. "Let's also get Zeke to coordinate having some local packs ready in case backup is needed. If Lynerd is part of this like we fear, then he's not going to willingly allow Sybil to unblock Callie. We need allies on standby for aid if needed."

Groaning, Lucas tugged the ends of his dark hair. "Which means we're going to need to talk to Zeke since it's his territory."

My stomach dropped. I didn't like the sound of that either. Even if Lynerd was behind my condition, I still didn't trust

Zeke. However, Oregon *was* his territory, and tensions were already high. We didn't need him trying to separate Oregon from the rest of the Northwest. "I say we let him know in the morning." I didn't want to give him too much notice.

"Sounds good to me." Jack clapped his hands and then led my sister to the door. "So, if I have the rest of the afternoon off, my girl and I are going to go running." He waggled his brows. "While I try to persuade her to finally give in to the mate bond."

I flinched. "I'm happy she has a fated mate, but I don't want to know about you trying to get into her pants. Can you leave that out, and I'll just see and smell the change when you two come back?"

Stevie giggled, her face turning crimson. However, her smile was full of happiness.

My heart sank. I hadn't thought about it, but when she and Jack did complete their bond, she'd be moving to Washington with him. Though he didn't live too far away, the idea I wouldn't see her every day anymore clogged my throat. She was my one constant, and I didn't want to lose her.

I watched the two of them walk out the door while Lucas, Miles, Phil, Carl, and Dan headed off to be with their families and check in with their packs.

Hey, what's wrong? Bodey linked, tucking a piece of hair behind my ear. *Did your sister say something?*

I forced my gaze away from the door and toward my mate. *No, but I just realized she'll be moving to Washington. It's sort of silly that it took me a few days to think of that.*

Not at all. He leaned his forehead against mine, cupping my face. *There's been a lot of shit going on, and it's hard to process the everyday things when we're facing threat after threat.*

Somehow, I suspected that it shouldn't be that hard for me. I was the queen after all.

"And I thought you and Mom were bad," Jasmine remarked. "Are those two always like that?"

Michael and Samuel laughed, which had me turning back toward the couch.

"Oh, yes." Samuel placed his hands behind his head. "Even before they figured out they were fated mates, they would stare at each other like that."

"Damn straight." Bodey pulled me so I stood in front of him. He continued, "I fell in love with her without Fate even needing to tell me that she was my other half. Being fated was just the icing on the cake."

Jasmine's face twisted in mock horror. "Who is this guy, and what happened to my broody brother?"

"Don't worry." Michael patted her leg. "He still broods just fine. Just give him a little time."

Janet appeared on the back deck, flinging open the door and running straight to Jasmine, who met her mom halfway. They threw their arms around each other.

Janet placed her head on top of her daughter's, a tear running down her face. "Silly girl. You shouldn't be here. You're supposed to stay at school where it's safe." But even as she chastised Jasmine, there was joy in her voice.

"Sorry, you're all stuck with me all the time. Not just when it's safe." She fiercely returned the embrace.

If I didn't know they were mother and daughter, I'd have thought they were sisters. The two of them were almost identical.

"Well, I shouldn't be glad that you're here, but I'm thrilled." Janet released Jasmine and wiped the moisture from her cheeks. "This calls for a celebration. My entire family is home and complete for the first time in months. I'll make something special for dinner tonight—triple meat lasagna."

"That's my favorite." Jasmine beamed.

Janet winked. "I know, dear."

Even though a part of me was envious of their easy relationship, a smile stretched across my face. This was the family my mate had grown up with. The kind that loved and supported each other unconditionally. He'd never had to experience an indifferent parent, a sister who hated his guts, or a pack that didn't deem him worthy. He'd flourished, and I was so damn lucky that he was mine.

Wanting to give them some time together, I eased out of his grasp.

His brows furrowed. *Where are you going?*

I'm going to talk to Dina and inform her of the plans.

He pushed off the wall. *Okay, let's go.*

I shook my head. *Stay here with your family.* I turned to head out the door.

A hand caught mine, turning me back toward him. He smirked. "Mom."

"Yeah, honey?" She faced us, taking her attention off Jasmine. "What's wrong?"

I blinked. *You're telling on me? Why?*

He chuckled. *You'll see.* Then he said out loud, "Callie just informed me that she's going to go talk to Dina so the rest of us can spend time together as a family."

"*What*?" Janet screeched and placed her hands on her hips.

Rolling my eyes, I lifted my hands. "I don't know what he's doing, but you just said—"

"That my family hasn't been together in months." Janet marched over to me, pointing a finger in my face. "Which means if you traipse off to see Dina, I won't get to enjoy this moment anymore."

My back flattened against the wall. "But you said months."

"Because *you* only officially became family a week ago, so the time before now was before Jasmine left for the University of Chicago." She crossed her arms. "Don't test me, Callie. You're just as much my daughter now as she is. You and Bodey can call Dina from here. If you need to talk to her in person, she can come see you. I won't have all of you here tomorrow, so today is family day. Got it?"

Chest expanding, I nodded. My eyes burned as my vision blurred. I'd never expected to have anyone care about or talk to me that way...and I fucking loved it.

Samuel snorted. "You do realize she's your queen?"

"Not right now." Janet softly patted my face. "Right now, she's my daughter, and she needs to know that she belongs. And we all feel that way, so don't try sneaking off again when I want you here with me. I just need a moment to feel complete."

A tear escaped, and I nodded. "I promise."

And Bodey wrapped his arms around me and linked, *I'm not the only one that feels this way about you. I needed you to see it for yourself.*

Thank you. And for the first time, I felt like I had a complete family.

Later that night, Bodey played guitar for me out on our lower deck while Janet and Jasmine cleaned up in the kitchen and Samuel and Michael watched some game on television.

We sat at the edge of the deck as he played "I'll Be" by Edwin McCain. His voice was smooth as his fingers strummed the notes. I hung on every word and drank it all in as his full lips sang promises to me and his arm muscles bulged with each chord change. His gorgeous blue eyes stayed on me the entire time, ensuring that I knew the song he sang was from his heart to mine.

When he finished, the back door opened, and Janet, Michael, and Jasmine strolled out.

"We're off to our house for the night." Janet yawned. "Everything is cleaned up, so you two can get some rest. I'm a little surprised that Stevie hasn't made it back."

I grimaced. "She's staying with Jack." I was pretty certain that they would be mated by morning, and I reminded myself to be happy for them.

"Right." Michael chuckled. "Well, good night, you two. See you in the morning."

Janet and Michael hurried off across the yard while Jasmine squatted beside me. She bumped her shoulder into mine and linked, *I liked hanging out with you tonight. We're going to be besties before Bodey knows what hit him.*

I laughed. *I'd like that.*

Bodey wrinkled his nose. "Why do I feel like you two are talking about me?"

"Because we are." She stuck out her tongue and linked, *And I like how he is with you. He's almost a different person...more relaxed. So I'll need your help in the morning.* She jumped to her feet and headed off while calling out, "Night."

Wait. What do you mean? I asked.

You'll see. She glanced over her shoulder, her strawberry-blonde hair hiding half her face as she winked.

I snorted. I already suspected what it might be.

Bodey stood and helped me up. "Finally, they're gone."

"What?" My eyebrow rose as he led me inside and set his guitar in the corner. "I'm surprised you feel that way."

"I'm ready to make love to my mate." He bent down and lifted me over his shoulder.

I yelped while Samuel groaned, "Dude, I'm right here, and she's my sister."

"Then plug your ears," he shot back as he jogged up the stairs to our room.

When he reached our room and he tossed me on the bed, I laughed. But once he'd shut the door and removed his shirt, the sound cut off as I took in his bare chest and the curves of his muscles. It was time to connect with my mate.

And we did...multiple times.

My hands shook as we pulled into the Ontario pack neighborhood, especially since Dina didn't want to leave the pack and her coven with all the strongest wolves gone. Meaning Bodey, Michael, Samuel, and me. Zeke hadn't been thrilled about us coming, but we'd already taken too much time to get what little information we had. We'd informed him this morning that we'd gotten a lead and that we were coming to not only reassure Lynerd but to talk to Sybil.

Despite Bodey's resistance, Jasmine managed to talk her way into coming with us. She'd threatened to take her car and follow us there if we left her behind, so, in fairness, he'd been forced to bring her if he wanted to keep watch over her.

Samuel and Jasmine rode with Bodey and me, but we'd been silent most of the way here. I hadn't even wanted to play music, lost as I was in my thoughts. I didn't understand how killing my parents would have benefited Lynerd since Zeke had already been named the Oregon advisor. And if Lynerd was working with Queen Kel, then why would his pack be attacked...unless they were trying to make it appear that he wasn't working with her? There were so many possibilities churning in my head, and I couldn't land on anything but more doubt.

Your thoughts have been running the entire time. Bodey rubbed his thumb against my arm.

There's a lot to consider. I leaned back. The closer we got to Lynerd's, the more the hair on my neck stood on end.

Bodey kept glancing at me, taking me in. *I can't wait until this is all done. You can redo our bedroom, and we can devour each other multiple times a day.*

That sounded so nice. *Kinda hard to do with my brother and sister in the same house and Jack sleeping on the couch, trying to convince her to complete their mate bond.* My sister still didn't think she was worthy of Jack, but I suspected he had her coming around after witnessing the long kiss they shared this morning.

He arched a brow. *I call bullshit. You were screaming my name in our room this morning. You didn't give a flying fuck that they were somewhere nearby.*

My lips pressed together. *Hey, you weren't quiet either.*

Hell no. I want everyone to know you're mine. He arched a brow. *Even your brother and sister.*

I snorted, feeling a moment's relief thanks to my mate. I shouldn't have been surprised. *I love you.*

I love you more. He winked.

Then, the neighborhood came into view, and my chest constricted. Blocking the entrance was Lynerd and twenty of his packmates.

CHAPTER TWENTY-TWO

MY WOLF GROWLED, wanting to assert dominance, and a part of me agreed with her assessment. But something could've happened to cause them to act like this, so I didn't want to assume anything...I didn't want to be like Zeke.

Uh...they don't seem welcoming, Jasmine linked to the three of us in the vehicle with her and Michael.

That was one way of putting it. Lynerd's massive frame towered in front of us. But Bodey seemed unfazed. He was taller and just as large as the leader staring us down, and my mate's wolf was stronger...though Lynerd wasn't far behind.

Lynerd's wavy dark-blond hair was mussed as if he hadn't slept, and there were dark circles under his cognac eyes. He wore jeans and, despite the cool weather, a blue short-sleeve shirt that cut off at his biceps, emphasizing his muscles.

No, they are most definitely not, Samuel replied. *If that doesn't suggest that they're guilty—*

We can't be sure of that, Michael interjected. *They were just attacked. My more pressing concern is why Zeke didn't alert us to how bad it was.*

That was an even better point.

Jack linked with Lucas, Miles, Bodey, and me, *Please tell me you're about to step on the gas and smack down those assholes blocking us from their pack.*

Leave it to Jack to hope for us to run over a group of my own people. I rolled my eyes as Bodey replied, *They're only five feet away. How much damage could I do?*

Fine, he capitulated. *I'll back up to give you more room so you can get some oomph behind you. Just...when you do, swerve right, and I'll swerve left. We can take them down all at once.*

The twenty shifters behind Lynerd stepped forward, looking uncomfortable with us sitting in our vehicles. I needed to decide how to proceed, and fast, before they became even more agitated.

I linked with everyone in our group. *Stay put.* Then I looked for the string of magic that tied to Lynerd and tugged so I could link with him. *Why are you preventing us from entering the neighborhood?* If I wanted to be a jackass and prove a point, we could get out of the cars and walk in, but I didn't think that would be wise.

I'm sure there's a reason that you're asking from the car, Lynerd shot back, scowling. *Don't want to risk me smelling any of your lies?*

My head snapped back. *What do you mean? I have nothing to lie about.*

Then, please. He gestured to the pavement. *Come out and join us if you have nothing to hide.*

There was a dare in his words, and I was torn. Part of me didn't want to step out if he was demanding it, but the other part didn't want another person in Oregon to find me inadequate.

I linked with Samuel and Bodey, *Will you two join me?*

I'll follow you anywhere, Bodey replied, pushing his love and pride into me.

Uh, ditto, but not for the same reasons. Samuel chuckled from the back seat.

I smiled at Samuel's joke. He'd been so serious ever since the coronation, and I'd missed the playful side of him. Hopefully, we could get through this shit and get to know each other...the real versions of ourselves, not the ones who came out under pressure.

I opened my door and climbed out as Bodey and Samuel did the same.

Jasmine's displeasure wafted through our connection, but to her credit, she remained in the vehicle.

As I lifted my chin, Lynerd sneered.

"What's the problem?" I asked, making sure my voice was loud and clear.

Lynerd shook his head. "Is that how you're going to address this?" He laughed bitterly. "I hoped for better from you. When I first met you, you held firm and put Theo in his place. Now you're pretending to be ignorant." His nose wrinkled. "I should've known better, especially since you were with Theo and now knowing who your parents were."

"This isn't an act." Oh, how I wished I could've said anything besides that hard truth. But I needed him to tell me what the problem was. "If you're upset we didn't come here sooner after the attack, there were—"

He scoffed. "Please. We're strong enough to fight Queen Kel's wolves, and I was fine when I learned that you were going somewhere to get answers. You coming here with no solution would've been a waste of time for the both of us. This has *nothing* to do with that."

Then I crossed my arms as Bodey and Samuel flanked me. I held out a hand. "Then what *is* the concern?" I gestured to the twenty strong shifters behind him. "I'm here to find answers now and to check on you all."

Lynerd bared his teeth. "After the stunt you pulled this morning, we don't want your help. You've made it clear where your priorities lie."

I stared at him, holding his gaze. Every damn time, he spoke in riddles.

Bodey's hand clenched. "You will not continue to talk to your *queen* and my *mate* like that."

"She may be the queen, but I don't respect her." Lynerd straightened, his gaze mocking me. "Not anymore."

A lump formed in my throat, but I tried to ignore it. "Please enlighten me as to what I've done wrong. All I want to do is talk to you and Sybil."

He laughed darkly. "That will be hard to do after the shit you pulled this morning."

I froze, hoping like hell I'd misunderstood him.

Samuel cleared his throat. "What do you mean? We're going to need you to be clear."

Eyebrows rising, Lynerd's gaze flickered between Samuel, Bodey, and me. His tone held disbelief. "You truly don't know?"

"Unfortunately, we don't." Bodey's jaw clenched. "So please, enlighten us."

"Zeke left with Sybil two hours ago." Lynerd crossed his arms. "Saying that you wanted him to protect her."

My blood boiled, and I blinked, trying to take a moment to gather my thoughts. "Where did they go?"

Lynerd snorted. "Like you don't know. Stop playing games. You're no better than he is."

Growling, Bodey walked past me and shoved Lynerd back. My mate rasped, "Talk to her like that one more time, and I *will* teach you some manners. You're about to push me too damn far."

Lynerd stumbled back a step and caught his balance. "And

here I thought we were friends. But I guess that's what happens when you're mated to someone like *her*."

In a flash, Bodey punched Lynerd in the jaw, causing the twenty pack members behind him to take several steps forward.

We didn't have time for this shit, but Bodey'd given Lynerd what he was asking for. Alpha will infused my voice as I commanded, *"Stand down."*

The pack members halted their progress, though their faces contorted, trying to break through my command.

Lifting his fist as if to punch Lynerd again, my mate snarled. "We are friends, but that will change if you don't get your ass in line when it comes to my mate. I will not stand back and let some entitled douchebag talk to her that way."

Fucking punch him again, Jack cheered through the link.

Things were escalating, which was the opposite of what I'd hoped.

Lucas replied, *Don't encourage him. This isn't what we need right now.*

"What did he say when he came for her?" I needed the full picture before I linked with Zeke. He had a way of bending the truth to skirt around telling a lie, so I wanted to be as prepared as possible to know what to ask him.

Tilting his head, Lynerd focused on me. "You didn't tell him to take her?" He pointed at me. "I want to hear *you* answer."

He wanted to see if I would lie. No matter what, I'd look bad—either I didn't have control over Zeke, or I was trying to hide my involvement. "No. I linked with him three hours ago to tell him we were on our way to check in with you and to talk to one of the witches here. That we might finally get some answers. That's it. I didn't instruct him to do anything other than make sure everyone remained safe."

"So that's how he got around the lie." Lynerd's hands fisted. "He played on what you said to him as if Sybil being here with us made her unsafe." His breathing turned rapid. "Maybe that was his plan because, without Sybil here, our pack is greatly weakened."

"Is Sybil your strongest witch?" Samuel rubbed a hand over his mouth.

He nodded and winced. "If we're attacked right now with the force we were two days ago, a lot more than five of us would probably be killed."

The information hung heavy around us. "Did Salem join the coven here to increase its power?" River hadn't filled in that information.

Some of the anger in Lynerd's eyes ebbed. "You've been catching up on our pack history, haven't you?"

"Yes, and you aren't answering the question." If he was going to call my ass out, then I'd give him the same courtesy.

He chuckled, catching me off guard. "Yes, that *is* why she joined the coven here. And Sybil's the priestess today, which means we need her back. Now."

"What do you know about Salem's death?" I wanted to hear his version of the story to see if it clicked in some missing pieces.

Any leeway I'd gained with him in the last few minutes vanished. His neck corded. "Both she and her husband died, leaving Sybil an orphan."

His response made me even more wary of him. "How?"

"Don't you think our time should be focused on the *living*?" Lynerd growled.

"Refusing to answer is defying *your queen*," Samuel said, standing even taller beside me.

"Sure, let's focus on that instead of Zeke taking off with Sybil, which she supposedly didn't authorize." Lynerd glared at him.

When I saw Zeke again, I was going to strangle him. Just enough pressure to slowly dwindle his oxygen, so it was slow and painful. He was causing issues, and it felt like he was doing it on purpose. "Don't worry. I'll address that with him."

"I need more than that," Lynerd snapped. "I need her back here *now*. Once you get her home safely, we can talk about strategy."

For a moment, my suspicion wavered. He wanted me to find Sybil and bring her back, which meant that my memories could be restored. If he was behind taking them away, I would think that he'd want to be the one to get her, not the other way around.

Don't agree to that, Samuel linked to Bodey and me. *You need to show dominance and make your way inside. He's disrespecting you.*

I understood his point, but I wasn't sure I wanted to waste energy on this battle. *Isn't it better if we find Sybil instead of prolonging our time here? Not playing some stupid alpha game that doesn't truly matter if Queen Kel overtakes us?*

Bodey looked over his shoulder at us. *She's right. Pushing our way inside will waste more time and create more tension between us and Lynerd. We have enough problems with Zeke without adding another pack to the list.*

"Fine." I nodded. "We'll go find her."

"What?" Lynerd's face creased. "Just tell Zeke to bring her back. That's all we need."

Maybe he didn't want me to find her after all. He expected me to make Zeke bring her back, but if Zeke didn't want her here, he'd find a way around the alpha will. That was how he operated. "I don't trust Zeke. I'll find her and bring her back myself."

Something passed across Lynerd's expression, but I couldn't home in on what it was.

I turned to the car, already regretting how much time we'd spent here. I wanted to get in touch with Zeke and hear how the hell he'd try to get himself out of this one. "We'll inform you when we're with her." I opened the door and slid into the vehicle.

Samuel was right behind me, but Bodey stayed in front of Lynerd for a few minutes longer. Neither his nor Lynerd's mouth moved, which made me certain they were using the pack link. I suspected they were finishing their altercation since Bodey had been brimming with anger the entire time...either that, or they were professing their undying love for one another.

Probably not the latter.

The two of them sneered, but when Lynerd's forehead and upper lip beaded with sweat, Bodey laughed and marched to the car. The two vehicles behind us pulled out as Bodey put our car in reverse.

I lifted a brow. "What was that all about?"

"He and I needed to come to an understanding." Bodey placed his right hand on the back of my seat as he looked out the back window and pulled out. "If he talks to you like that again, I won't be so nice next time."

I laughed. "That was nice?"

"You haven't seen my brother when he truly throws down." Jasmine laughed. "He protects the people he loves ferociously—I can only imagine what he'll do for you."

Bodey cut his eyes to his sister, giving her a look of warning as he glanced forward again. "She's seen me in battle. She knows. Besides, it won't come to that. Lynerd is aware of his place. He won't be so stupid again."

I could only hope not. I had no doubt that no one in our group would put up with it. This was a one-time exception because Lynerd's pack had been through hell. But so had we.

Not wanting to waste more time, I linked with Zeke and Bodey. *We just reached Lynerd's, only to find that you and Sybil are gone. What are you doing? You knew we were on our way.*

In my haste, I forgot to link with you. Zeke's pack connection was cooler and smaller, indicating he wasn't close by. *But I felt the need to take her away from there, especially with all the uncertainty, if you thought she might have answers to some of your questions.*

Some of my worry eased, and Bodey glanced at me. I could feel his own doubt mixing with mine. I wasn't sure if I believed Zeke or not, but it sounded as if he was trying to do the right thing by us even if it was misguided.

Where are you? Bodey asked as his fingers intertwined with mine, the buzz of our bond springing between us.

I swallowed, unsure if Zeke would actually tell us.

I'm at Trevor's real estate office in Halfway.

I leaned against the headrest. The fact that he'd answered lifted some of the strain from my shoulders.

"Where's Halfway?" Bodey squeezed my hand comfortingly.

I snatched up my phone and plugged in the address. "It's where I was working for a day when the scouts attacked me. Thirty minutes west of Oxbow." Most people in Zeke's pack worked in Halfway since Oxbow was so small. We all went grocery shopping in Halfway too, since there weren't any local food stores.

"Is that where Zeke is?" Samuel asked.

"Yeah. Will you let the others know where we're going? We'll have an update soon." I nodded and linked back with Zeke and Bodey. *What if the queen is watching that area?* I'd hate for her to see Zeke and decide to attack because he was an advisor.

Don't worry. The Halfway alpha and his pack are keeping an eye out for strange wolves. Also, I asked Theo to meet us here since he's pretty much healed. We'll be fine.

And you're going to stay there until we reach you? I had to ask after the shit he'd pulled this morning.

Yes. We'll stay here until you arrive.

Let us know if anything happens. I stared at the tan ceiling, wishing we were closer than we were. I was so damn close to getting answers that I wanted to cry. However, if Zeke truly thought she was at risk, then taking her had been the right thing to do. He should've just let us know so we could've driven straight there.

Bodey added, *I don't care what it is—if something seems even slightly wrong, you let us know immediately. I don't care if it's that Sybil farted weird and could be getting sick.*

I arched a brow. "That was a Jack-type comment."

Bodey exhaled and hung his head. "We need to figure this out and eliminate the threat so his sorry ass can go home."

Laughter bubbled out, and I relished the moment of normalcy. "It has nothing to do with spending quality time with me?"

"Fuck yeah. Getting rid of Jack is just a bonus." He winked.

"Maybe I shouldn't have come back from college," Jasmine grumbled. "All I do here is listen to my brother flirt, smell his arousal, and watch him eye-fuck his mate every few minutes."

"You've been home for only twenty hours," Samuel retorted. "You can't complain until you've been around them as long as I have."

I turned around and stuck my tongue out at them. "I can't help it that we're happy we found one another. Besides, if it weren't for Bodey, *we* wouldn't have found each other." I pointed my finger at Samuel and then myself.

Samuel chuckled. "That's true."

What would've happened if they hadn't stumbled upon me that night I was attacked in Hells Canyon? Would I even be alive? Would Samuel be king right now?

Let's inform the others what's going on, Bodey linked, tightening his grip on my hand. He must have realized that my thoughts had taken a dark turn.

What-ifs wouldn't accomplish anything beyond wasting precious energy. So I linked with the others and filled them in.

It's like Zeke wanted you to look bad, Miles linked, his disapproval heavy.

That thought had merit. Zeke did have a way of skewing things in his favor. *Well, Theo is with him, so hopefully, we'll get some real answers.*

We should declare Theo the new advisor, Carl added. *Zeke agreed to it already. Now that he's healed, we should make the transition happen.*

I trusted Theo more than Zeke any day. Theo hadn't known who I was or that my memory was blocked. Zeke had kept too many secrets that didn't sit right...even if he'd done so for my protection. *I'm good with that, but we need answers from Sybil first and then to return her to calm Lynerd down. The last thing we need is for Zeke to tell the Oregon packs that we forced him to step down.*

We fell silent. I didn't even have the desire to turn the radio on.

Jasmine gasped, and I turned around to see where she was looking.

"What's wrong?" Bodey asked. His own gaze darted to the sides of the road, searching for the threat.

"Maybe my friend's pack could help us." She stuck her head between our seats. "Her dad is an alpha advisor—like you, Bodey—in the Midwest territory, and maybe they'd be willing to help us fight the queen."

Bodey exhaled. "Next time, don't almost give me a heart attack. I thought we were under attack."

She blushed. "Sorry. I just got excited."

"You think they'd help us?" I raised my brows. The thought had merit. "They'd be our allies?"

Samuel scoffed. "Callie, you can't possibly be considering this. If they learn that we're under attack and weak, they could begin attacking us on top of Queen Kel. We could be worse off than we are now. It's too much of a risk. Besides, we're about to see Sybil and get answers."

"Her father and pack aren't like that." Jasmine pouted.

"You don't know the others. Just the one girl. You can't be serious." Samuel then linked to just me, *It's too dangerous.*

I nodded. Samuel was trained for this. He'd know better than me. "Let's see what we find out from Sybil."

"But—"

"You heard my mate." Bodey arched a brow at his sister. "And I agree with everything she said."

Jasmine crossed her arms and slumped back in her seat.

I hated to upset her, but we had to be smart.

We all fell into silence again until, finally, we pulled up by Trevor's building.

As I stepped out of the car, a chill ran down my spine like we were being watched. I turned my gaze to the woods and stilled.

CHAPTER TWENTY-THREE

BODEY'S HEAD snapped in my direction, his gaze following mine. "What's wrong? Do you sense something?"

I blinked several times, but nothing out of sorts caught my eye. "No." However, that chill lingered, seeping down my spine and causing goose bumps to sprout all over. I tried to brush off the odd sensation. Sybil was close, and I didn't need to get distracted. *I just hate being here.* This was where Kel's scouts had attacked me after Zeke had forced me to work for Trevor, the father of Charles, a pack member who'd tormented me for my entire life in the pack.

Tugging at the connections that were larger and warmer than the others, I noted at least twenty of Halfway's pack were out in the woods.

My chest tightened. Only twenty. If Queen Kel attacked, they wouldn't be able to stand up to her.

Samuel stepped out of the car behind me and placed his hands on my shoulders. "Do you want to stay out here? We can go in—"

I snarled, turning toward him. My wolf was furious that he was treating me like I was weak and couldn't handle going inside. "I was attacked outside, not in there, and not only that, I've survived attacks like that one since I was five. I'm perfectly okay going inside."

Jack got out of the other car, chuckling. "Put him in his place, Callie."

"Shut it," Lucas scowled and then turned forward, watching Samuel and me.

Lifting his hands, Samuel sighed. "Sorry, I didn't mean to imply you're weak. I can only imagine the attack that happened here. From what I heard, it was bad."

The hot tendrils of anger flowed through my connection with Bodey, adding to mine. He growled, "Nothing like that will ever happen to her again. I'll make sure of it. I'll kill anyone who tries."

"See?" Jasmine snorted. "Don't mess with people Bodey loves."

We all need to calm down, Michael linked as he and the other three former advisors reached Jack's Navigator. *We're tired and stressed, but we can't turn on one another.*

I blew out a breath and hung my head. I felt as if I'd been scolded. "You're right. It's just that something feels off here, and I can't put my finger on what."

I'd count on it being Zeke and his friends, Miles linked. His lips flattened as if he didn't like being here either.

"Let's get some answers." I linked my arm through Samuel's. I then linked to just him, *I'm sorry for snapping. I'm letting my nerves get the best of me, and my wolf took control for a second.*

Bodey gave me a nod as he walked in front of us to the door. He was giving me time to talk to Samuel, and I loved him for it.

It's fine. Samuel patted my arm. *If your wolf is likely to feel threatened by anyone, it would be me.*

I lifted a brow. *Even though we're family?*

He nodded. *We weren't raised together. Even though I didn't mean to make it sound as if I thought you were weak, your wolf took it that way. She knows that, out of everyone here, my wolf is the only one that can potentially rival yours. But don't worry.* He patted my hand. *I know you're stronger than me.*

I wasn't sure if that was the real reason I'd reacted that way or if my wolf was in agreement with me that she and I shouldn't be in charge and thought Samuel should be. But none of that mattered right now.

We walked up the concrete steps to the front door of the house that had been converted into an office at the edge of town. They'd chosen this location due to its proximity to downtown while still having woods beyond the backyard, in case they wanted to shift.

I don't want us to feel like each other's competition. You mean more to me than that.

He bumped his arm into mine and replied, *I know. No offense taken.*

We're here, I linked to Bodey and Zeke as we reached the door. I didn't want to walk in on them without alerting them, though I suspected Zeke already knew.

A tense moment passed before he replied, *We're in the front room. Come on in.*

Bodey didn't hesitate to open the door.

As the eleven of us crammed in, I scanned the room. The two sizable wooden desks were still there, the one that was supposed to have been mine across from the identical desk where the receptionist usually sat. Right then, it was occupied by Theo.

Zeke sat at the other desk, his chair scooted back so he could lay his head against the light-blue wall. He stopped pressing the buttons on his phone and placed it on the desk.

One person was missing.

I tensed. "Where's Sybil?"

"In the bathroom." Zeke shrugged, and I didn't miss his scowl.

"Is she okay?" Bodey asked, placing a hand on my lower back as he glared at Theo.

Zeke blew out a breath. "She's fine."

Behind me, Jasmine inhaled sharply, and I spun around to see her gawking at Theo. Theo frowned, and then his eyes widened as he returned her stare. Something was going on, but I couldn't focus on that now.

"Who else is here?" Lucas asked as he flanked Bodey, and Miles and Jack took the other side of Samuel, keeping Samuel and me in the center.

The former advisors stood behind us, protecting our backs.

"I already told you." Zeke straightened and then smiled cruelly. "Unless Callie didn't share that information with you. It's sort of nice knowing that I'm not the only one she withholds information from."

"She informed us of everything." Jack lifted his chin, staring down his nose at the older man. "We were just wondering who you hid from us."

Bodey nodded. "Callie's not the one who enjoys playing games."

Standing, Zeke puffed his chest. "I'm the one who took Sybil away from Lynerd's pack. You should be *thanking* me."

I laughed, surprising myself. "You made us look foolish. Don't try to switch things around. I'm not like the others you've manipulated all these years. I know *exactly* who you are."

A toilet flushed, and wariness crept over me.

Until I remembered the numbers outside. "Why are there only twenty wolves out there?" I gestured toward the woods. "You know better than any of us that Kel has been sending more wolves than that to attack our packs."

Zeke's neck corded. "That's all the Halfway alpha sent. Be thankful for them."

"Why didn't you bring Trevor and some others from Oxbow?" When he'd told me he was here, I'd assumed he'd have people from his pack and the Halfway pack protecting Sybil.

"Did you forget that the scout we took hostage escaped from there?" Zeke spat, his nostrils flaring.

I crossed my arms. "Did you forget that I was attacked in these woods? Kel knows about both locations and how close these two packs are."

"She's right." Theo cleared his throat. "Maybe we should—"

"I didn't ask *you*," Zeke thundered, glaring at his son.

A soft warning growl came from Jasmine behind me, giving me pause.

Light footsteps tapped down the hall, and soon, Sybil stepped into the room.

Her expression was strained when her emerald gaze landed on me. Even with her dark-tan skin, the circles under her eyes were pronounced. Her long blue hair hung over her shoulders, contrasting with her pale-green dress.

It was shocking. "Are you okay?"

She wrapped her arms around her waist. "Just wishing I was back home."

"We'll take you there," I promised, stepping toward her. "I didn't mean for Zeke to take you away, but I'm glad that you're safe."

Her irises lost their warmth as she glanced at Zeke.

Something definitely wasn't right.

I hated to jump right to the point, but Queen Kel's wolves had a tendency to show up and turn things to shit without warning. "Do you mind if I ask you a few questions? I learned some information, and I was hoping that you'd have some answers for me."

She started. "Um... Maybe. If I know anything."

Bodey tilted his head, watching her every move.

"Why did you look at me so oddly the day Theo and I visited Lynerd?" Even though I could smell a lie, I focused on my hearing, wanting to see if I heard even a slight elevation of her heartbeat.

"Oh." She wrung her hands, and her heart did beat slightly faster. "That."

I linked to the group who'd come with me, excluding Zeke and Theo. *Is it me, or does she seem to be under duress?*

Bodey stepped toward me, readying to protect me.

"I sensed something strange about your magic." She laughed a little too loudly. "Dina noticed the same thing."

"Yes, but Dina's mom wasn't the one who repressed my mate's memories." Bodey clasped his hands. "So I'm thinking you realized there was more than just a strong wolf being suppressed. The magic resembles your own."

She flinched but didn't say another word.

"Is that true? Did you recognize who'd spelled me that day when you met me?" I wanted to make sure there wasn't a way that she could get around the truth.

Zeke stood. "Do you know how crazy that sounds? Her parents were from Lynerd's pack, hours away." He waved a hand. "If this was the information you thought she'd be able to help you with, you're more delusional than I realized."

"Maybe." Samuel narrowed his eyes at Zeke. "Or *you're* not smart enough to realize the brilliance in having a witch from far away cast the spell for that exact reason—especially if Lynerd wanted to punish the royals for naming you the Oregon alpha advisor."

"The police confirmed a gas leak set off the fireplace explosion." Zeke rolled his eyes. "There was no evidence of foul play."

"And a witch can alter a person's mind," Phil said from behind Samuel. "If someone killed Mila, I would think you'd be the first person who'd want to know."

We were wasting time on Zeke and not focusing on the person who could hopefully provide us with answers.

"If you're worried about retaliation for what your mother did, you don't need to worry." I placed a hand over my heart and hoped to the gods that she could sense my sincerity. "You were a *child*. You did nothing wrong."

Sybil's bottom lip trembled.

I hoped I was getting through to her. "If someone has threatened you, forcing you to remain quiet, I give you my vow that I will protect you. This answer isn't just for me—it might give us insight into what's going on with Queen Kel, or at least who to talk to for more answers. You could help save so many lives."

"I'm sure no one—" Zeke started.

But Sybil nodded. "I'll help you. I'll remove the spell my mother placed on you and allow you to access your memories. But it'll take a little time. If I peel back the layers too quickly, it will be extremely painful."

The relief hit me so abruptly that I sagged into Bodey. He wrapped an arm around my waist, the electricity arcing between us. I'd never believed I'd have someone to stand beside me, and once again, I was thankful that I had a strong, loyal mate by my side.

"Well, *wonderful,*" Zeke said, the last word strained. "But we should probably wait until we're somewhere safe before we allow that to happen."

Bodey arched a brow. "I thought you said this place was safe."

"It is, but Callie's right. Maybe we should head back to my pack neighborhood, where more wolves can guard us." His voice rose a little.

"Or..." Theo stood from his desk, coming to stand next to Jasmine. "We could ask for some of our pack to come here. There are several working in town who could come immediately."

"Now that," Michael said, snapping his fingers, "is a smart idea. The more, the merrier, especially since we're so close to town. This would be a harder location to breach if we have enough wolves outside."

Zeke glared daggers at his son.

Conflicting emotions came from my mate. *I'm not sure if I'm pissed or happy about Theo having a good idea. I really hate that guy.*

I somehow managed to swallow my laugh before the noise escaped. *Theo's a good guy.*

Bodey's eyes darkened as they met mine, and he linked, *There. You solved the problem. I am definitely pissed.*

Rubbing his hands together, Jack's blue eyes sparkled. "So how does this work? Do you chant? Do we need candles? Does Callie need to take her shoes off so she can channel the earth better?"

"Son." Carl sighed. "Sometimes I wonder about you."

"We all do, sir." Lucas nodded.

Sybil grinned. "It does have merit, but Callie's bare feet touching dead wood wouldn't help. And no candles are required. It's actually a relatively easy spell. However, the return of memories repressed that long will likely be painful."

I laughed bitterly. "All magic comes with a cost."

She nodded. "That's true."

"Is there a way to dull the pain?" Bodey bit his bottom lip. "Like herbs or something? The witches used something like that for Samuel when we all thought he'd be the one to get marked."

"Yes, but we don't have the supplies here." She turned her

back toward Zeke. "And it would take some time to gather them. It depends on your priorities."

I know you don't want me to be in pain, but who knows what could happen? I straightened, pulling away from his comforting embrace. *I need to do this now.*

Bodey scowled but didn't try to stop me.

"It's fine." I took a step toward her. "I handled being marked —I can handle this."

"We all saw you in pain." Zeke's face had gone pale. "Maybe we should gather the items first." He snatched his phone from the desk and started typing frantically.

Samuel's brows furrowed. "Who the hell are you texting? You can link with everyone you should be communicating with now."

He rolled his shoulders. "I'm ordering food. I thought we'd all be hungry."

"Uh...I think that can wait." Jasmine snorted. "Especially if a witch is going to be practicing magic."

I couldn't help but notice that Sybil kept her back toward Zeke as she made her way to me. She gestured toward the wooden floor. "You might want to sit down."

"Yeah." If it was going to hurt, I probably shouldn't stand.

"Here." Theo gestured to the desk he'd just vacated. "Take this chair."

That would be more comfortable than the floor. I made my way to the chair as Zeke kept frantically looking at his phone. Bodey followed me, making sure that when I passed Theo, he blocked me from my friend.

Once I sat, he stood next to me, taking my hand.

Everyone turned to watch.

Sybil stood in front of me, her hair hanging like a curtain between her and the others. She gently touched both hands to my forehead. She whispered, "I'm going to search for the root of the spell first. It won't be pleasant."

"It's fine," I gritted. "I'm ready." And those words were so true. I wanted to remember everything, even the bad stuff.

Her magic entered me, doing that horrible probing, and unlike Dina, she seemed to speed through to the source.

"Found it," she breathed, her herbal scent hitting my face. "Now, I'm going to undo the spell. It'll take a few minutes, and I need you to not move and be patient." Her voice hardened, and she turned to Bodey. "And you can't interfere even if she whimpers. Got it?"

He clenched his teeth but nodded.

"Good."

Something like a needle stabbed my brain, stealing my breath. It was sharp and intense, worse than the burning sensation of the ink marking my chest.

I moaned, almost regretting that I'd agreed to this. Agony swirled through me as my brain seemed to be hit repeatedly by a hammer.

A loud howl rang in my ears—my wolf suffering as well.

My head hurt so much that even the buzzing from Bodey's touch didn't ease the pain churning within.

A voice popped into my head. *Unfamiliar wolves are here, and we need help!*

CHAPTER TWENTY-FOUR

FOR A SECOND, I wasn't sure if that was a memory returning or something happening in the present. Then Bodey stiffened, answering my question. He'd heard whatever it was as well.

"We're under attack," Zeke spat, and all of a sudden, Sybil's hands vanished from me.

The pain receded just as quickly as it had come, and I opened my eyes to find Zeke holding Sybil's wrists. His forehead was creased as he breathed raggedly.

I tried to pull up my earliest memories, hoping that something new would be there. But I couldn't remember anything earlier than the night Zeke had dragged me through the door of my parents' house, informing them that I was the newest addition to their family. I remembered the sneer Pearl had on her face as she observed me and the hesitant smile on Stevie's.

Of course, we hadn't gotten enough time for Sybil's magic to work. Somehow, Kel always knew when to interfere.

Standing, I gritted my teeth. A part of me wanted to tell Sybil to keep going, but protecting her, Bodey, and Samuel was my priority.

We need help now, the Halfway alpha, Blake, linked again. *There are forty of them.*

And there were only twenty of our wolves outside. I wanted to scream at Zeke, but that wouldn't accomplish anything.

Call for backup from anyone close by, Bodey linked to everyone as he moved in front of me. His eyes locked with mine as he connected solely with me, *Stay here with Sybil.*

Before he could turn, I grabbed his arm and replied, *No way. Not happening. Yes, we need to protect Sybil, but Queen Kel made it clear that she's coming after everyone I love. Well, there's no one in this world I love more than you, so if you're going out there, so am I.*

I glanced around at the others. "We're going to help defend this place. Kel is putting on a show of force because we're here." I couldn't fathom any other reason for her to attack Halfway.

"If she's here because we are, then we should leave." Samuel lifted both hands. "Taking ourselves out of the equation is the best way to mitigate deaths."

My heart stopped. "How can you be so certain? She attacked Lynerd's and Heather's packs at random. If we leave and Kel continues to attack, there'll be even fewer people to protect the Halfway pack." I hated this. Samuel could be right. There was a chance the fighting would halt if we left, but what if it *wasn't* about us being here and she just wanted to make the point that she was willing to kill to get what she wanted?

"Let's try this." Samuel glanced at the back door. "You, Bodey, Sybil, and I leave. We won't go far, and we'll come back if the fighting doesn't cease."

That was still iffy, but at least it was workable. We could take Sybil somewhere safe and then come back to help if the scouts didn't retreat. I bit my bottom lip and glanced at Bodey.

"Whatever you think." Bodey squeezed my hand and continued, "There's a risk, whichever strategy you go with."

I decide. The words rang in my head and caused my heart to race. All the damn pressure was making me feel like I'd implode. And we were wasting too much time. I just needed to make a decision, and if Samuel thought that was the right way to go, who was I to disagree? Even though a part of me screamed it was the wrong call, I went with Samuel's advice. "Let's get Sybil, Bodey, Samuel, and me out of here and see if Kel's wolves retreat."

That was all it took for everyone to swing into action. Another reminder that I was taking too long to make decisions, and I needed to do better.

"The rest of us will go fight with the others." Lucas hurried toward the hallway that butted against the kitchen that contained a back door. "We'll keep you updated."

I grabbed Sybil's wrist and tried to pull her toward the front door. She hesitated until I said, "Come on. Let's get you out of here and back home."

She nodded eagerly, any hesitancy gone.

The former advisors and Lucas, Jack, and Miles hurried to the door, but Theo hesitated, looking at Jasmine.

"Don't *even* tell me goodbye." Jasmine placed her hands on her hips and then gestured toward the back door. "I'm going out there to fight with the rest of you."

Bodey raced in front of me, grabbing her. He snapped, "No, you aren't."

"She said only the four of you were leaving." Jasmine lifted her chin, her bottom lip quivering as she fought Bodey's strong grip. "So, I'm going out there with Theo and our allies to help protect everyone."

"You're coming with us," Bodey emphasized, making it clear that there was no room for argument. A hint of alpha will rose to the surface. "You aren't trained for fighting."

Her chest heaved, but Theo came over and placed a hand

on her arm. He murmured, "He's right. You need to go with them. We'll be fine."

When Jasmine opened her mouth, Bodey snarled, "Get your hands off my sister, and Jasmine, I *will* alpha will you if I have to."

She *hmph*ed, but there wasn't much she could do with the threat hovering in the air. "I'm still a wolf, and we need numbers. But whatever. I'll go with you."

Theo dropped his arm and brushed Jasmine's cheek before turning and rushing after the others.

Jasmine's face twisted into agony, and I couldn't help but wonder if she and Theo might be fated mates. Just how many fated pairs had been waiting to meet?

"Let's go." Samuel hurried toward the front door. "We've already taken too much time."

His words were like a kick in the gut, but I deserved them. If he'd been in my position, he would've made the decision several minutes ago.

As we left, I heard an extra pair of footsteps coming from behind. I glanced over my shoulder to see Zeke coming after us.

I didn't slow down as I focused forward once more, but I linked to him and Bodey, *You need to help Blake and his pack.*

I took Sybil, so I need to make sure she gets to the car safely first. He had his phone in his hands, typing once again.

"Then get off your fucking phone and actually help." I didn't understand what could be so important that he had to be on that damn thing during an emergency.

He nodded guiltily, putting the phone into his pocket. "You're right. I'm sorry."

His agreement caught me off guard, and the mistrust within me brewed even more. "Give me your phone."

Brows rising, he shook his head, which had Bodey growling.

"Listen here, you pompous prick—" Bodey started, but I

lifted my hand and laced my words with alpha will. "Give me your phone now. I will not risk you being distracted by whatever you consider more important than protecting wolves in your territory."

Jasmine snickered as Samuel linked, *Good call. He's up to something.*

Zeke's eyes flared as he reached into his pocket and then handed me the cell phone. I'd alpha will him to allow me to look through it later to figure out what was going on. Right now, we had to get everyone out of here.

Samuel was the first out the door, followed by Bodey. I held on to Sybil for dear life, worried if I let her go, she'd somehow slip away. With the way Fate kept kicking me in the teeth, I didn't want to chance losing Sybil, my only hope of getting my memories restored.

As we went down the steps, I searched the yard. There were no wolves around, just a few humans driving by.

The knot in my stomach loosened. It would be too risky for Kel's wolves to attack us with humans around, so we should be able to get away without issue.

Jasmine followed us. Though I couldn't see her, I could feel anger through our connection. She was pissed at Bodey, but I couldn't blame him for making her come with us, especially after what the Southwest queen had done to my own sister.

The scent of unfamiliar wolves hit my nose.

Stomach hardening, I looked toward the woods just as two wolves bounded out of the fir trees.

I faltered as the magnitude of the situation washed over me. Kel didn't give a shit about causing a stir among humans as long as she got what she wanted. My blood turned to ice.

How much was she willing to sacrifice to make me submit?

When we were halfway to the vehicles, eight more wolves

appeared behind them. All ten were sprinting, rushing to reach us before we could get to the car.

I linked to all the wolves close by. *If anyone is free, we need help. Ten wolves are out front, and we're struggling to get to our car.*

Bodey pressed the unlock button as the wolves ran full speed, their attention locked on Sybil. My heart thundered as I realized that she couldn't run as fast as the rest of us.

The car was now closer than the front door to the office. We wouldn't make it to either before the wolves reached us. We should've stayed inside.

I'm on my way, Theo linked back. *I'll be there soon.*

And so will we, Miles replied.

I hated to take them away from the fight, but we needed help to get Sybil into the car.

The rival wolves barreled toward us as Bodey and Samuel opened the car doors and waved us in as if we weren't trying to get there as quickly as we could.

As I tugged on her arm, Sybil lost her footing and stumbled. I reached down to catch her as the two wolves leading the ten reached us. The dark-brown wolf lunged at Sybil as the off-white wolf went for my arm.

Desperate to keep Sybil safe, I pivoted toward her just as she lifted her hands and yelled, "Push them away." A wind picked up, pushing the dark-brown wolf and causing him to fall on his back, but the off-white wolf pivoted around the wind and struck.

He smashed into the side of my body, his teeth sinking into my left arm. Instinct kicked in, and I punched the mutt in the face with my right hand. The wolf released my arm and landed on all four legs as Sybil focused on the other wolf, which kept trying to push through the wind barrier.

Fuck, Bodey linked as his fear and anger wound together.

Bodey and Samuel ran toward the eight other oncoming wolves as Jasmine and Zeke placed themselves as a barrier between the enemies and Sybil and me.

Linking to just me, Bodey said, *Get Sybil in the car and guard her. Don't shift. We don't have the time or luxury.*

The bite on my arm throbbed, and the stench of copper hung heavy in the air. The sleeve of my shirt was shredded, and blood poured from the wound onto the grass. I tried to push through the pain, reminding myself that I'd been through worse.

The off-white wolf shook his head and bared his teeth at me. He snarled and then lowered his head like he planned to knock my feet out from under me. I jerked to the right, barely getting out of the way as the wolf ran past where I'd been standing a mere moment ago.

I wanted to shift, but I didn't have time for that, and I noticed that Sybil's hands were shaking as she shot spell after spell at the dark-brown wolf.

I glanced at the other wolves descending upon us as two of them peeled off to fight Bodey and Samuel, and the other six barreled toward Sybil.

Zeke removed two knives from his sides, ready to fight.

Give Jasmine one of the knives, I commanded, wanting Jasmine to have a way to protect herself. I'd been foolish not to bring anything with me. I would never again be so unprepared if I survived this.

Zeke's nostrils flared, but he tossed a knife at Jasmine's feet and then struck the first wolf running past him. When Jasmine picked up the weapon, a little bit of my concern eased, and I focused back on Sybil.

Getting her to the car wasn't going to be easy, thanks to their determination to reach her. I'd expected more to target Bodey and Samuel, but today, Sybil seemed to be their goal. I didn't care about her the same way I did the others, so why would they be focused on her? Unless Queen Kel thought that Sybil could provide answers the queen didn't want me to have.

"Run," I wheezed as the off-white wolf pivoted to attack Sybil while she was distracted.

Sybil's forehead beaded with sweat as she kept her focus on the dark-brown wolf. She didn't see the off-white one charge toward her.

"Watch out," I shouted, moving but unsure if I could reach her in time. The wolf was faster than I was in my human form.

Sybil turned, and her wind hit me and blasted me back several feet before she turned her magic onto the off-white wolf, leaving the other wolf open to attack.

The six wolves circled us as the wind she was controlling faltered.

Sybil croaked, "I can't use any more magic. I'm out."

A part of me hoped it was a ploy, but there was no scent of a lie. Between the attack at Lynerd's and whatever magic she'd used on me, she must have been running low already.

We're here, Jack linked, and I saw a flash of blond fur racing toward us.

Help had arrived, but we had to survive until they reached us.

Using as much leg strength as I could muster, I jumped, tackling the dark-brown wolf with my body. She hit the ground first, protecting me from the brunt of the landing, but then she rolled over and pinned me to the ground. Her light-yellow eyes flashed with hatred, but she didn't go for the kill.

Queen Kel wanted me alive.

She still expected me to submit to her.

As five wolves attacked Sybil, I slid my feet underneath the dark-brown wolf and pushed her off my body. Her eyes widened as she flew several feet and crashed to the ground.

I rolled over and got up then lurched toward Sybil. Without

thinking, I leapt into the pile of wolves, ignoring my throbbing arm, knowing I would wind up with more injuries. I grabbed the back of a light-brown wolf and yanked her off Sybil then moved into her spot and clutched a black wolf's neck, snapping it.

The black wolf went down as Zeke appeared beside me, helping me break Sybil free by stabbing a white wolf in the neck and yanking at a golden wolf with his other hand.

I kicked the golden wolf in the side, forcing him to fall, but his claws left deep scratch marks down Sybil's arm.

Zeke and I flanked Sybil's sides as the dark-brown, light-brown, golden, and tan wolves got back up and headed toward us. I ground out, "Are you okay?"

"I'll be fine," she rasped. "They got a few bites in, but nothing that can't be healed if we get the hell out of here."

I nodded, and the wolves descended again. I glanced around to find that Lucas, Jack, and Miles had reached Bodey and Samuel. Jasmine was fighting a merle-colored wolf who wasn't interested in her, just trying to get to Sybil. Still, Jasmine had a bite mark on her leg that seemed pretty deep. Blood pooled over her sock.

Lucas and Miles helped take down the two wolves Bodey and Samuel were fighting as Jack kept dashing toward us.

I wanted to cry with relief. I had become certain Sybil was going to die, but for once, Fate might be on my side.

The wolves circled us, and Zeke and I fought them once again. I didn't know what to do. I had no weapon, and I didn't have the time to shift, but I'd be damned if I'd let them kill the witch.

The dark-brown wolf smirked as if she knew this was the strike that would bring us to our knees. When the four of them lunged, I moved in front of Sybil, knowing Kel had told them not to kill me.

They must not have expected me to risk myself for the

witch. The dark-brown wolf had been aiming for my neck, but she snapped her mouth closed at the last second. All four of them landed on me, causing me to fall back onto Sybil. It turned out that Sybil being underneath me was the best outcome because they couldn't get to her easily.

Suddenly, Bodey was at my side, kicking the dark-brown wolf off me so hard that she hit the car, shutting the door.

Jack, Lucas, and Miles fought the other three as Bodey went to help his sister.

I stretched out my arms, protecting Sybil, and Zeke fought alongside Bodey to protect us all.

Then Theo linked to us, *I'm surrounded by five wolves just past the tree line by you.*

My lungs seized.

I linked to everyone, including Blake's pack, *Theo needs help. He's surrounded near the tree line by the house.*

No! Jasmine took off toward the woods.

And that was when Bodey froze just as the light-brown wolf leapt for his throat.

CHAPTER TWENTY-FIVE

MY WOLF HOWLED and launched me toward them with a burst of speed, and I caught the tan wolf by its neck just inches before it would have struck Bodey. I squeezed, cutting off the wolf's airflow as my blood boiled.

This wolf had tried to take my mate's life, and now I would teach her a lesson.

Bodey's head snapped toward me, and his face twisted. Horror and concern shot through our connection.

Go after Jasmine, I linked. The tan wolf thrashed in my hands, trying to get away.

But... Bodey punched the wolf in the head, and her eyes rolled back.

I released my hold, allowing the tan wolf to crash to the ground. *You're distracted. Jack and Miles can go with you. I've got this.* I glanced at the tan wolf, hoping like hell she woke up with a sore throat and a horrible headache.

Callie... he hedged as I turned and went for the dark-brown wolf before she could swipe Sybil's leg.

When I kicked her in the side, she sailed several feet through the air and slammed into Jack's vehicle.

Really? Jack linked, but there wasn't any anger in it. If anything, humor flitted to me from him.

You can get it fixed. I knew the royal advisors weren't struggling for money. I refocused on Bodey. *Babe, go after your sister. You know the queen wants me alive. Get Jasmine and come back to me.* I understood what it was like to want to protect your family. The sight of Stevie after the queen tried to have her killed would haunt me for eternity, and I didn't want anything like that to happen to Bodey.

I ran in front of Sybil and faced down the remaining wolves. There were only four left standing. *We'll be fine with Samuel, Lucas, Zeke, and me here.* We were finally on more equal ground.

A calm settled over him. *I'll be right back.* He called his wolf, the magic flowing through our connection as his clothes ripped off and fur covered his body. When he landed on four legs, he took off in the direction of his sister, Miles and Jack at his side.

The other two wolves were locked in battle with Lucas and Samuel. The golden wolf and the light-brown wolf charged at Sybil.

Zeke appeared at my side, and the two of us faced down the wolves together. He swiped his knife at the golden wolf as I jumped onto the back of the light-brown one. I wrapped my arms around its neck as it tried to lunge at Sybil, making it miss its intended mark.

My left arm throbbed from the bite, but I ignored the pain and tightened my grip. The wolf began to buck, trying to get me off its back, but I held on tight. This had to be similar to riding a bull while drunk.

I tried to cut off the wolf's air supply, but it didn't seem to be working. The wolf panted but continued to writhe and twist with all its strength.

Shit. Maybe I wasn't putting pressure in the right place.

My head jerked with each buck, and my ears rang. I needed to weaken him, but instead, he dropped and rolled onto his back, pinning me beneath him.

The weight crushed my lungs, and I tried to squirm out from under him, but his body was too heavy. I could barely breathe.

Callie, Bodey linked, his fear rushing into me. *I'm on my way. I never should've left you.*

I'm fine, I lied, thankful that he wasn't here to smell the stench.

I turned my head just as Zeke lurched toward Sybil. I stared in disbelief as the golden wolf trotted past Zeke, reaching the witch with a snarl.

Get to Sybil! I linked to Samuel and Lucas.

I couldn't see them, but I heard a yelp as someone's fight ended. The whimper of death was undeniable.

The golden wolf was now on top of Sybil. It opened his mouth wide, bit into her neck...and then ripped out her throat.

Sybil's hands clutched her neck, her eyes wide, as blood gushed between her fingers and poured down her body to the ground.

"No," Zeke screamed. "What are you doing?" And then he swung his knife down into the back of the golden wolf's head.

Samuel's crisp scent filled my nose as the light-brown wolf's body jerked, and then he rolled off my chest. I blinked up at Samuel, who stood over me with a hand outstretched to help me up.

Instead, I rolled onto my stomach and ignored the pain in my chest and arms as I army crawled to Sybil.

Zeke dropped to his knees beside her, yanking the dead golden wolf off her and tossing it to the ground. He wrapped his own hands around her wound, trying to stem the bleeding.

Are you hurt? Bodey linked, his panic mixing with mine.

A wolf ripped out Sybil's throat. I continued to crawl toward her, ignoring the grass rubbing my elbows raw. "Get away from her," I barked at Zeke, the words like sandpaper in my throat. "You allowed her to be killed." I couldn't process why he'd given the wolf the go-ahead and then pretended to care that Sybil was dying.

"Now isn't the time for your drama," Zeke snarled, his eyes locked on Sybil's neck as he kept trying to put pressure on the wound.

Sybil's skin was already waxy. Death was imminent.

Samuel bent down beside me as Sybil's eyes locked with mine. Her gaze softened into kindness, shocking me to my core. She'd been hurt on my watch—if anything, she should hate me. I'd failed her. I wasn't fit to be queen. The mark shouldn't have chosen me. It was wrong.

Something wet hit my face as I reached out to touch her arm, wanting her to know I was there.

"I'm sorry I let you down," I murmured, a sob building in my chest and almost taking control.

"Don't." Samuel squatted beside me, his jaw tense as Lucas trotted up to Zeke.

Blood splattered Lucas's dark fur and dripped from his mouth, but the fact that he didn't appear to be injured eased my mind. The blood must belong to our enemies.

They're all dead or knocked out. Lucas glanced at Sybil and Zeke. *What do you want me to do with him?*

Nothing yet. I didn't want Sybil's last seconds of life to be her watching us kill someone. I wanted her to have peace. *But when she dies, he won't be a royal advisor any longer.* His time in power was over. Hell, I should've removed him as soon as I was marked, but I hadn't wanted to cause more unrest. Now Sybil was dead, and that was my responsibility.

Her eyes glazed over, and my heart shattered. What good was being queen if you couldn't save someone? White-hot rage pumped through my veins as I watched the witch who'd held the key to my memories take her last struggling breath. Her heart sputtered.

Snarls still sounded in the woods, and a truck skidded to a stop in front of the house.

Fucking fantastic.

The truck door opened, and a human man climbed out. "You all get back. There's a rabid wolf beside you."

My throat closed as I took in the human's wild look. His eyes flicked from Sybil to the wolf. Lucas.

Shit.

Bodey's fear rolled into me, causing the world to tilt underneath me.

What's going on? I scrambled to my feet, ignoring the pain in my ribs. I had to get to my mate *now*. He was supposed to be returning here to me.

I love you, he replied. *Just remember that.*

"Ma'am," the human called, but I turned my back to him and took off running toward the woods. Lucas's paws sounded right on my heels.

That better not be a fucking goodbye, I threatened, then linked to everyone, *Bodey's in trouble!*

"The wolf," the man yelled. "It's chasing you!"

I'll stay here and handle the human and Zeke, Samuel linked. *We need to get a witch here to alter his memory.*

Good. I didn't have time to deal with that. I had to get to Bodey.

Don't come. Bodey's desperation soared through me. *I'm surrounded. I'll find a way out of this without risking you.*

Not alone. If he thought I wouldn't come to him when he was in trouble, he'd soon be learning otherwise.

My wolf was more than ready, but I couldn't shift in front of the human. I had to wait until I got past the tree line. I pushed myself toward the fir trees as Lucas soared past me, faster than me in animal form.

I was nearly there when agony flashed through the bond and our connection went lukewarm, like he'd gone to sleep...or been knocked out.

Lucas, hurry. I connected to everyone, *Bodey's connection cooled off!*

Fuck the human. I had to get to my mate. *Now.*

I let my wolf go. She brushed my mind, taking control, but then froze. She moaned, and my legs faltered, forcing me to the ground. A strange pulse surged through me, causing me to fall.

A scream lodged in my throat, making it hard to swallow. I didn't know what was going on, but I needed to get to my mate.

Unable to sit up, I lay on my back, staring at the cloudy afternoon sky. Dark rain clouds were forming, and the sounds of battle still rang out.

Help Bodey, I linked to everyone. I focused on our bond, trying to make it flame once more. I needed him safe and beside me.

But the clouds began to morph and change, darkening.

Callie! Lucas linked, his trepidation tangible even through our pack link. *Bodey's gone.*

Fear strangled me as my surroundings changed, taking me somewhere far away.

The sound of howls and the stench of blood rushed me as I succumbed to the darkness.

ABOUT THE AUTHOR

Jen L. Grey is a *USA Today* Bestselling Author who writes Paranormal Romance, Urban Fantasy, and Fantasy genres.

Jen lives in Tennessee with her husband, two daughters, and two miniature Australian Shepherds. Before she began writing, she was an avid reader and enjoyed being involved in the indie community. Her love for books eventually led her to writing. For more information, please visit her website and sign up for her newsletter.

Check out her future projects and book signing events at her website.
www.jenlgrey.com

ALSO BY JEN L. GREY

Twisted Fate Trilogy

Destined Mate

Eclipsed Heart

Chosen Fate

The Marked Dragon Prince Trilogy

Ruthless Mate

Marked Dragon

Hidden Fate

Shadow City: Silver Wolf Trilogy

Broken Mate

Rising Darkness

Silver Moon

Shadow City: Royal Vampire Trilogy

Cursed Mate

Shadow Bitten

Demon Blood

Shadow City: Demon Wolf Trilogy

Ruined Mate

Shattered Curse

Fated Souls

Shadow City: Dark Angel Trilogy

Fallen Mate

Demon Marked

Dark Prince

Fatal Secrets

Shadow City: Silver Mate

Shattered Wolf

Fated Hearts

Ruthless Moon

The Wolf Born Trilogy

Hidden Mate

Blood Secrets

Awakened Magic

The Hidden King Trilogy

Dragon Mate

Dragon Heir

Dragon Queen

The Marked Wolf Trilogy

Moon Kissed

Chosen Wolf

Broken Curse

Wolf Moon Academy Trilogy

Shadow Mate

Blood Legacy

Rising Fate

The Royal Heir Trilogy

Wolves' Queen

Wolf Unleashed

Wolf's Claim

Bloodshed Academy Trilogy

Year One

Year Two

Year Three

The Half-Breed Prison Duology (Same World As Bloodshed Academy)

Hunted

Cursed

The Artifact Reaper Series

Reaper: The Beginning

Reaper of Earth

Reaper of Wings

Reaper of Flames

Reaper of Water

Stones of Amaria (Shared World)

Kingdom of Storms

Kingdom of Shadows

Kingdom of Ruins

Kingdom of Fire

The Pearson Prophecy

Dawning Ascent

Enlightened Ascent

Reigning Ascent

Stand Alones

Death's Angel

Rising Alpha

Printed in Great Britain
by Amazon